THE DEAD CHIP SYNDICATE

Andrew W. Pearson

Library of Congress Control Number: 2023934593

Cover Design by: Alexios Saskalidis
www.facebook.com/187designz

For information please contact:
Brother Mockingbird, LLC
www.brothermockingbird.org
ISBN: 979-8-9863305-7-0 Paperback
ISBN: 979-8-9863305-8-7 EBook

To Vicky, as the Chinese proverb says, "有緣千里來相會",
"Though born a thousand miles apart, souls which are one shall
meet." You fill this spark of light between two voids with more
laughter, love, and bliss than one man deserves.

To my parents, from the outside, I'm sure getting here looked like
chaos, but, as Nietzsche once said, "One must still have chaos in
oneself to be able to give birth to a dancing star."

To Judy Grano, thanks for reading those early drafts, supporting
the vision, and keeping the faith for what probably felt like forever.

To Ira Hammons-Glass, a partner in crime in this larceny we call
life. A one-of-a-kind man, synonymous with style, substance, and
class.

And to Macau, for being so extraordinary, wondrous, and bizarre it
was impossible not to write a book about you.

 # CHAPTER ONE

唔熟唔食
"You always cheat the ones closest to you."

– Chinese proverb

March 24ᵗʰ, 2019

THROUGH A DARK bank of swirling grey clouds, the flickering lights of Manila's Ninoy Aquino Airport came into view, but the sight gave Anthony Wilson little relief because he knew it was the one airport in the world named after someone murdered on its tarmac and he feared a similar fate awaited him there, too.

Crackling bolts of lightning flash-whitened the cabin, revealing the wide eyes, raised eyebrows, and flared nostrils of the two flight attendants strapped into their jump seats by the emergency exit. These were classic signs of fear. The body and mind identifying outside threats, preparing for a "fight or flight" response, which was, Anthony recognized, useless on an actual flight. In any other situation, he would laugh at his wit, but the panic etched on the flight attendant's faces along with the trembling fingers covering their mouths meant this flight could be in real trouble. These women were too scared to remember their most important professional obligation – show no fear.

Plus, he had bigger problems. With his hand shaking from the pitching and shuddering of the plane, Anthony tried to focus on the email that had just pinged in with the plane's descent into mobile range. *"Mr. Wilson, wherever you are, you need to get to a police station immediately. Several men hired to kill you have been arrested in Zhuhai."*

Anthony glanced out the window. The haloed neon lights of Resorts World Manila across from the airport seemed to be growing rather large. Raindrops pelting the plexiglass felt as powerful as bullets being fired from a gun, as if to remind him just how precarious his current situation was. Suddenly, the plane shook as the lights flickered off.

Mumbled prayers and breathless *Our Fathers* broke out around the cabin, increasing in volume and intensity as the plane pitched forward on its final approach. Being irreligious, Anthony didn't fear judgment from above but rather a mortal threat from below. He struggled to make sense of the email. Although his situation had nothing to do with morality or religion, it echoed the story of the Bible's first slaying, fratricide driven by rage and ending in coldhearted betrayal.

As Anthony sat through the white-knuckle ride, he tried to figure out who could be responsible for these hitmen, but nothing about the conspiracy made any sense.

The plane's nose eased up. When its wheels skidded along the wet runway, the cabin broke into raucous applause as well as relieved and congratulatory laughter. Anthony smiled in relief for a split second, but then fear gripped him, tightening his chest in a way the tear gas he'd run from in Hong Kong a few days before had. He needed a plan to ensure not only his safety but perhaps his very survival. It was one thing to sacrifice one's life to become a martyr forever etched in a nation's lore as Ninoy Aquino had done decades before; it was something entirely different to be lured into a trap by a greedy and sociopathic business partner, a man who also happened to be his twin brother.

CHAPTER TWO

ONCE HE CLEARED customs, Anthony called Detective Fonseca, who answered in his usual laconic tone, "You're a very lucky man, Mr. Wilson. Someone hired a hitman to kill you. That hitman hired a second hitman at half his price, who hired a third hitman at half his price, who then hired a fourth hitman. That guy felt so slighted by the lowball offer, he reported the conspiracy to the Zhuhai police, who contacted me since you're a resident of Macau."

Anthony felt his cheeks flush as sweat dotted his brow. "But who ordered the hit?"

"You tell me."

"I have no idea."

"Maybe a business partner you pissed off? Say, Cash?"

Anthony shook his head. Of all the people he knew, Cash Cheang, the man whose biography he was writing and whose cryptocoin was dropping in a few days, was the least likely to do something as deranged as this. "You're suffering from confirmation bias, detective."

"In law enforcement, we call that 'incarceration bias.'"

Anthony shook his head at the attempted joke. "Look, I have to go."

"We can offer protection."

"That won't be necessary." The last thing Anthony needed was a pushy cop peering over his shoulder at a time when most of what he was doing was anything but legal.

"Where are you?"

"Not in Macau."

"Obviously. You just stepped off a plane in Manila."

"If you knew where I was, why'd you ask?"

"A moral man doesn't lie to the police."

"It's called being protective, detective. Not sure who I can trust at this point. Many view that badge you carry around with you as a license to steal, not something to respect."

"If that's so, I've been doing something wrong my entire career."

"Look at that, I just gave you a brilliant idea for a side hustle."

"When do you plan on returning to Macau, Mr. Wilson?" Detective Fonseca asked, his tone turning deadly serious.

"Maybe never. Having a few contracts taken out on your life tends to take the fun out of that black sand beach place."

"Wouldn't blame you if you never came back. Actually, I'd advise it. Make my life a whole lot easier."

"I'll keep that in mind while I'm trying to stay alive, detective."

"Be careful, Mr. Wilson. The tentacles of these triad operators reach all over the world. Manila's like a second home to them, especially with all the casinos opening up there catering to the flush Chinese gambler."

"It's more frightening in the Philippines," Anthony said, riffing off the Philippine Tourism Board's spritely tagline, 'It's more fun in the Philippines.' He'd seen it plastered all over the airport on his previous trips. Maybe a return to America was in order? Back to sanity. Although America had seemingly gone off the political deep end since Trump's election, so maybe nowhere was safe these days?

"We can never outrun our destiny, Mr. Wilson. Don't forget that."

Anthony shook his head at the detective's trite and clichéd words.

"I can put a notice out on you. Have you picked up for questioning," Detective Fonseca said.

"Please don't. You know I'd be free within an hour, but with my wallet considerably lighter. And you know how we Americans hate having our freedom infringed upon."

"As do we Macanites, but, trust me, you get used to it."

"Never. Look, I'm as much in the dark about all of this as you are, but trust me, I'll fly under the radar. Call me if the Zhuhai police beat a confession out of any of these men."

"China's got cameras all over the place, so maybe somewhere in those facial recognition databases, they've captured a meeting between the hit-man and this person who wants you dead."

"Maybe the panoptic surveillance state is good for something, after all."

"If you can think of anyone who might want you dead, please let me know."

"You'll be the first to know."

"You just better hope there's not a fifth, hitman that is."

Anthony hung up. He had put on a brave face for the detective, but now the reality hit him hard. Someone wanted him dead. Wiped off the face of the earth. It was a horrific realization, about as painful as they come, especially since the clues pointed to only one person. This turn of events probably had a lot to do with the millions of dollars sailing towards a Cebu rendezvous on a boat aptly named *The Gambler*.

Anthony pulled out the ArgoTrack GPS tracker, connected it to his phone's mobile hotspot, then checked the location of *The Gambler*. Latitude 11.3244° N, Longitude 123.8941° E: a few miles off Kinatarkan Island. But that was odd. The boat hadn't moved in eight hours. Were Cyrus and Jada sheltering from a storm? That made no sense as Typhoon Deria was still 18 hours away and heading much farther north, towards Taiwan. The weather forecast was clear in *The Gambler's* area as well. Had they been attacked by pirates? That made no sense either as the waters around Cebu were pretty safe. Maybe someone along the way had gotten wind of the millions in loot sailing towards Cebu in a small yacht with two lightly armed Americans?

Anthony put away the ArgoTrack and headed to the gate for his domestic flight to Cebu. He had a few hours to kill, so he jumped on his laptop to check emails. However, he had trouble focusing. Instead of work, he ruminated on buying a gun. Guns were legal and plentiful in the Philippines but could only be purchased by locals. Foreigners couldn't acquire them legally, but for the right price, anything could be bought in the Philippines. Murder went for $20 a pop in Manila these days thanks to Duterte's extra-judicial dragnet against drug dealers and the addicts who needed a fix to blur out their squalor-filled lives. Cheap murders meant cheap guns. What luck his attempted murderer hadn't tried to hire someone in Manila. Murder was cheap here; no profit in outsourcing it. *What comfort.*

Or maybe he had? Anthony's story could end with a bullet to the head, delivered by a motorcycle-riding assassin, who silently slithered his way through choking Cebu traffic, then, like a viper's strike, delivered a lethal blow before Anthony even realized danger lurked. A quick and painless death it would be, but what comfort was there in that ending? Not the one he had envisioned for himself.

Perhaps he was overreacting, but that's the way the mind works when faced with imminent death. This was probably how animals at the lower end of the food chain lived, in a perpetual state of fear, death forever stalking them, every corner hiding a potential predator, every rock obscuring a killer who could pounce and deliver an instant death. Except for man, just about every living creature knows it had a mark on its back. Today, Anthony realized how desperate a life like that could be. This was not what he had signed up for when he agreed to run Exegesis's Asian operation a year-and-a-half ago. Not by a longshot.

CHAPTER THREE

Anthony caught his flight to Cebu. As the plane descended towards the Mactan-Cebu International Airport, the window framed a hallucinogenic mix of glowing cadmium reds, brilliant orange hues, and cool cobalt blues that battled it out for dominance in a war of fading attrition in the dying twilight. Small silhouettes of black skirted over waves of shimmering indigo as fishing boats and Bangkas returned from their daily trawls. L.A. might have its gorgeously diffusive magic hour, but Cebu had its mystical one, which offered more than a touch of the spiritual.

Once Anthony landed, he took a cab to Ammo Nation, where a generous $1,000 tip or "consideration" as they sanitizingly dubbed it in the Philippines, got him a Colt M45A1 Marine Pistol, with a filed-off serial number. The gun was tucked in his backpack, wrapped in a towel to minimize the weapon's telltale 'L' shape. The weight, however, was impossible to ignore. Along with the feeling of invincibility, comes a foreboding sense of inevitability, not only does the finger pull the trigger but the trigger also tempts the finger. However, any argument won at the barrel of a gun is a short-lived victory as the consequences of settling scores with a bullet are some of the harshest penalties society exacts.

After purchasing the gun, Anthony took a cab to the marina, where he loitered around, watching the action, sweat beading across his brow from the suffocating humidity. Several fishermen unloaded their double outrigger Bangka boats, oblivious to the squawking seagulls divebombing around them. The birds' shrieks added to a cacophony of disquieting sounds; engines throttling down as trawlers eased into assigned slips; sails flapping about in the blustery wind; sweaty, thin-as-a-rail fishermen yelling at each other in singsong Tagalog while unloading their daily catch. In the nearby seafood market, auction bidders shouted their offers in metronomic fashion while studying their competitors with stony eyes.

Analyzing each fishing crew carefully, Anthony tried to figure out who would be the least nosy, the small groups of fishermen unloading their double outrigger Bangka boats or the charterers with their sleek schooners. Always on the lookout for sucker tourists, those charterers would probably pepper Anthony with a slew of questions he'd refuse to answer. That would draw unwanted attention.

Anthony chose the crew of a brightly colored blue and white Bangka whose all-seeing eye on the bow was a clone of the U.S dollar's *Eye of Providence*. He approached a group of short, skinny men, whose weathered skin was dark from years of toiling in the scorching Philippine sun. These fishermen were probably direct descendants of the merchants and sailors who had plied their trade in these waters for centuries. Their discretion was probably cheap and easily bought. They would know the surrounding Cebu waters better than any tourist flytrap schooner.

The captain's green eyes radiated from his taunt-tanned skin while his sunken cheekbones stenciled his face in a way that would leave New York City modeling agents drooling. When Anthony struck up a quick conversation about the day's catch with the captain, he got vague answers. At that point, he decided to be direct and asked if the boat was available for hire. The captain shook his head and pointed at the charcoal black clouds swirling in the distant east, threatening rain.

"Typhoon's coming," the captain said.

Point taken. Anthony acknowledged the climatic threat with a nod, then pulled out the ArgoTrak and showed off the coordinates for *The Gambler*. "You know where this is?"

The captain nodded.

"Can you take me there?"

The captain rubbed his chin and shook his head slightly. "Cannot. Cannot."

Anthony countered with five crisp hundred dollars bills.

The money vanished as quickly as a buzzing fly gets snapped out of the air by a chameleon's hungry tongue. The captain's curling smile revealed a picket fence of yellowing teeth that lacked a few slats. *There goes that modeling contract.*

"Five o'clock, we come back, with or without your friend," the captain said in a strident tone that left no room for negotiation.

Anthony nodded acceptance of the terms.

The captain jumped aboard. Anthony followed, explaining that his brother had rented a boat and probably got lost in the waterways around Cebu. The crew nodded sagely as the captain kicked the boat into high gear while smiling broadly. This was probably the easiest five hundred he'd make all year.

The trawler's diesel engine sputtered to life. Thick plumes of black smoke belched out of the engine's exhaust and wafted across the rickety jetty, dissipating quickly in the humid breeze. The fishermen jabbered away in Tagalog while the captain navigated the ship into the busy channel.

Anthony assumed they were discussing how to celebrate tonight after this perfectly timed haul. He didn't care. He'd overpaid for the boat. He was on course to find a yacht filled with millions of dollars aboard. What he was going to do once he got there, he had no idea, but the weight of the gun in his backpack reminded him this was no typical Sunday afternoon cruise. He was looking for an answer to the most important question of his life.

During the ride, Anthony dangled his legs over the bow, letting the splashing waves kiss his ankles, while trying to ignore the sputtering engine behind him. For the first time, he noticed the incredible beauty of the Pacific around him. An ocean of turquoise stretching across a calm horizon, interspersed with explosions of iridescent aquamarines above a seabed dotted by coral reefs of white. Banks of deep green seagrass drifted in the languid tide like lazy octopus tentacles reaching up to the sky. It was as if some knowing hand had thrown a festival of dazzling Diwali colors across the crystal-clear waters of Kinatarkan Reef and the pigments had drifted down into the undulating depths, dissolving across the salty waters in a million hues of intermingling yellows, greens, and blues.

When looking for material to adapt into screenplays, Anthony had found a few good novels that focused on twins, but real life stories of twins killing twins were rare. Statistically speaking, it was far less likely to occur than murder amongst siblings or other relations, even with ratios taken into account. Anthony found about ten stories. Wael Ali supposedly strangled his twin, Wasel, although jurors failed to unanimously agree on a verdict. Shawn Wachter stabbed his twin, Shane, to death. After weighing the evidence, the prosecutors agreed it was self-defense and dropped the murder charges. Jeff Henry shot his twin, Greg, with a 12 gauge shotgun after a drunken argument. Wealthy heir, Timothy Nicholson, killed his twin brother supposedly in self-defense, but the jury disagreed, coming back with murder in the first. Trenton Henry was shot to death by his twin, Brenton, who later surrendered to the police, and murder was the conviction.

For the male twins, it was the standard fare of jealousy, drunken accidents, and inheritance chasing. For the fairer sex, however, things got a little weird. Anastasia Duval died in a mysterious car crash when her twin sister, Alexandria, deliberately drove off a Hawaiian cliff. The sisters were seen fighting before their SUV careened off the road and crashed onto a rocky shore 200 feet below. Alexandria was cleared of murder, though, getting off scot-free, but she claimed she'd lost a part of her soul.

But the Duval twins were nothing compared to the "silent twins," June and Jennifer Gibbons. Although of Barbados descent, the girls grew up in England, communicating mostly through a speeded up version of Bajan Creole. After being gifted a pair of diaries, June and Jennifer developed a passion for creative writing. They wrote a novel about young, attractive Americans committing grisly crimes in Malibu, California. Their work about a young teenager seduced by his high school teacher, *The Pepsi-Cola Addict*, was self-published and is still available on Amazon. However, the silent twins grew bored with fiction and soon their crimes became all too real. While in their late teens, the girls experimented with drugs and alcohol. Petty larceny led to arson. The twins were soon caught and convicted, then sent to Broadmoor Prison, a maximum-security hospital for the criminally insane in Berkshire, England.

The twins spent twelve years at Broadmoor. While there, they decided one had to die for the other to go free, so Jennifer accepted the martyrhood. When the twins were transferred to a lower-security prison in Wales, doctors found Jennifer unresponsive. She had drifted off to sleep during the ride and never woke up, dying of a sudden inflammation of the heart, a death that still defies explanation today.

Jennifer was just 29 years old when she died. Her twin was released shortly thereafter and has since lived a normal life. Once two became one, June suddenly found her tongue and started speaking to everyone as if she had been talkative her whole life.

Many of these twin murders made no sense, few were premeditated, one brought about by an all-consuming rage that seem to flare up out of nowhere. One wasn't even a murder, just a weird, unexplainable death. Passions run hot with twins, but rarely did it lead to murder, which made things all the more mysterious with his twin, Cyrus. Was Anthony being led down this dark path by another? Maybe. Hiring a hitman was certainly the coward's way, but was it also the Cyrus way?

After sailing for an hour-and-a-half, *The Gambler* came into view, an-chored a mile off Kinatarkan Island. At first, a pinprick on the distant horizon, the boat grew rapidly as the fishing trawler chugged in. Antho-ny's stomach churned at the sight. The crew avoided him as the engine throttled back, then the trawler glided towards *The Gambler*.

Anthony ordered the fishermen to steer cautiously, then slung his backpack over his shoulder. Once close enough for the boats to almost touch, Anthony leaped aboard *The Gambler*, landing in the aft with a thud.

With his hands scaling along the boom to keep his balance, Anthony hurried across the deck, eyes scanning for any sign of life or indication of threat. When Anthony reached the cabin, he took a deep breath and steeled himself. Anthony inched open the door. "Cyrus, what's going on?" The stench of urine hit him like a punch in the face. A dim blue light flickered somewhere inside the cabin. He unzipped his backpack, slipped his hand inside, released the gun's safety, then slid his finger onto the cool metal trigger.

CHAPTER FOUR

Eight months earlier…

THE CALM AND distant drums of a dragon boat sculling across the placid waters of San Vai Lake echoed around the seven towers of Macau's prestigious One Central condominium block. The wicked roar of a Lamborghini's engine shattered the serenity. Fat tires squealed on rain-soaked cobblestone streets as Cash Cheang's lime green Aventador screeched out of the condo's entrance, Johnny Cash's "Ring of Fire" blaring in its wake.

With his hair slicked back in a 1950s pompadour style, Cash Cheang didn't seem the country music type, but the lyrics rolled off his tongue as if he'd sung them a thousand times before. Snug in the car's bucket seat, Cash focused on the road ahead. His fingers flipped between the paddles with the precision of a skilled F1 driver who knew exactly how to make his engine purr. With expressive Tony Leung eyes made shadowy under a black L.A. baseball cap, Cash exuded a hip weirdness that was engaging in an odd and charming sort of way. He turned the music down, then glanced at Anthony, who struggled to lock the seat belt in place while trying to hide the disgust plastered on his face.

"You like color?" Cash said, his ear-to-ear smile revealing a mouthful of pearly whites.

"More into muted tones myself," Anthony said, trying the diplomatic route with a flashing smirk as he finally locked the seatbelt. He found the color rather garish and completely tasteless. Why would anyone spend half a million dollars on a sports car in such a vaingloriously ugly color? But that was the point, Anthony would later learn, do it because you have the money to piss away and piss off those who judge.

"You bring passport?" Cash asked.

"Both my Yankie and British ones. Perhaps I should use the British? Memories of the UK's atrocities might be far enough in the past for China to forgive and forget us by now."

"Wishful thinking. China's a master at playing the victim. They'll never forgive England for sacking the old Summer Palace or forget you started a war that got millions of their countrymen addicted to opium."

Anthony laughed. "From what I've read, they were pretty addicted to the stuff before we came along. And no disrespect, but I think addiction's in your nature. And Macau's enormous financial success proves the Chinese just traded one addiction for another."

Cash tapped his wheel in agreement. "Where do you think this came from?"

Anthony chuckled.

Cash slowed the Lambo down, checked Avenue Sun Yat-Sen for cars, then hit the accelerator. The engine growled with another wicked roar as Cash maneuvered the car onto one of Macau's main thoroughfares, empty in the dying twilight. "We have a saying in China, how can you tell if you're lucky if you don't gamble?"

The car went from zero to sixty in three seconds; stomach meet throat time for Anthony as the G-force hit him hard. Nothing like a Lambo's wicked roar and the road speeding by you at seventy miles per hour to dispel jetlag.

Macau was Anthony's kind of place; irreverent, mysterious, and utterly nonsensical. A third world country living a first world life because it sat upon a never ending pot of Chinese gambling gold.

The Chinese believed their skills came from providence, that fortune coupled with character and presented unforeseen opportunities, and luck was something experienced with an equal chance of success or failure. So, with a fatalistic attitude like that, why not roll the dice? This mindset enriched Macau enormously, and within a year or two it was projected to eclipse Monte Carlo as the richest place on earth. The perfect place for a man like Anthony to discover his fortune.

Cash glanced at Anthony. "Cyrus say you used to be in movies."

"No, I used to write them. It was Promethean work, though, for little or no pay," Anthony said.

"Promethean?"

"Hard work, with little reward. After Prometheus, the Greek god who pissed off Zeus because he gave man fire."

"Ah. Greek mythology. We have a casino called that here. Over there," Cash said, pointing across the Pearl River in the direction of the airport. "You see Macau's *Casino*?"

"Most of them, yeah. Quite impressive," Anthony said, glancing at the massive casino resort, Galaxy Macau, in the distance.

"No, the movie *Casino*."

"Scorsese's?"

"No, Broken Tooth's?"

"Whose?"

"Gangster who ran Macau in the Eighties and Nineties."

"Never heard of that one. Or him for that matter."

"Check it out, it's on YouTube. He was 14K triad boss running Macau about fifteen years ago. Mr. Charisma. Beat up a lot of people. Killed a few others. He loved the spotlight so much he made a movie about himself."

Anthony's ears pricked up. Stories about moviemaking always intrigued him and his eyes swung to Cash, who pointed at the Governor Nobre de Carvalho Bridge across the way. "He shut that bridge down for a day to shoot a scene where his character killed an informant."

"Police didn't arrest him for blocking the bridge?"

"Not for that. They did later, though, after he tried to blow up Macau's undersecretary of security."

"At least he aimed high."

Cash laughed.

Glancing through the Lamborghini's convertible top, Anthony marveled at the new face of China: on the left, massive integrated resorts lit up the sky like a Vegas wonderland; on the right, the towering and glass-encased skyscrapers of Henquin Island, backed by row upon row of modern condos that would fit comfortably in Manhattan's glitzy skyline. An endless loop of animated Chinese commercials played on giant *Blade Runner*-esque LED screens fronting several fifty-story commercial buildings.

Cash pointed to Henquin Island on the right. "The Chinese government sunk billions into what used to be barely inhabitable land. It's now exploding into a mini megalopolis. The CCP's singular goal, turn it into another Hong Kong."

"Looks like they're well on their way."

Cash shook his head. "Looks can be deceiving, especially Chinese looks. Henquin Island will never be Hong Kong. CCP can dictate where developers build, but, as many Chinese ghost towns have proven, economic reality trumps all."

"That's why we let the invisible hand of faceless corporations make our city planning decisions in the West."

Cash laughed. "But we will have entertainment, today's bread and circuses. They're opening up a Lionsgate Entertainment World there."

"Lionsgate, the film studio?"

Cash nodded. "It's an amusement park filled with rides based on *The Hunger Games*, *The Twilight Saga*, *Divergent*, even the TV show *Prison*

Break."

"You gotta take your hat off to a company that can make a ride out of a film about children being forced to fight to the death because a dictatorial government can't feed the masses."

"Especially since families not far from here were trading kids for the kids of their neighbors, so they didn't end up eating their own children."

"Jesus," Anthony said, recoiling at the thought. "That's about the most horrendous thing I've ever heard."

"Became known as 'starvation cannibalism.' Cannibalism wasn't taboo in China. That's a Western thing. The emperors used to eat humans at the imperial courts. If your emperor eats human body parts, there's nothing wrong with it, right?"

Anthony shook his head. "Wrong."

"Agreed."

"But then again, who are we Americans to judge? We named our most famous cannibalism incident a party."

"The Chinese have a saying, *Níng wèi tàipíng quǎn, bù zuò luànshì rén,* meaning, better to be a dog in times of tranquility than a human in times of chaos. You translate it as the Chinese curse, may you live in interesting times."

"I don't know about that. Who wants to read about the life of a boring dog?"

A reverent smile played across Cash's lips. "The question of a true writer."

It was all extremely impressive, Anthony had to admit. Perhaps Bloomberg was right and the 21st Century did belong to Asia, although he found the surroundings all a little soulless.

"Where is everybody?" Anthony asked.

"No one's moved in yet," Cash said.

"Really? Then why all the lights?"

"Why not? Makes a pretty picture."

So soulless, it literally was, Anthony thought, as Cash entered a highway pointing towards Zhuhai, a city of a million people a little north of Henquin Island. And Cash was right, it did make a pretty picture. China might not know how to populate a city yet, as so many ghost towns throughout the country proved, but it sure knew how to take a shiny and impressive-looking picture. At least from a soulless distance.

Once in Zhuhai, Cash took Anthony to the Hermes junket operator's office, a two-story, nondescript building located in the New Xiangzhou district. He introduced Anthony to his small IT staff, all Chinese men in their late twenties, all unremarkable beyond their profound geekiness. They looked as if they'd been quarantined for years in a room perfecting code and had missed out on the social benefits of female companionship and life. They greeted Anthony with excited smiles and warm handshakes. Although the halitosis was a little off-putting, Anthony smiled throughout the overly friendly introductions.

Afterward, Anthony got down to business. He called Simon Wagle, the head of Exegesis's casino practice, and introduced him to Cash's lead developer. Simon's thick southern drawl complicated the discussion but, within minutes, Simon was surfing through the Hermes Junket room's servers, scouring their contents as if he were in the room next to them, not sixteen thousand miles away connected via Zoom and a remote desktop access software.

As Simon worked remotely, Cash showed Anthony around the office, which included a crypto-currency mining operation set up in an air-conditioned back room. Servers mining Ethereum altcoins hummed in the background, while a bored black cat wandered around them, looking for a warm place to snooze. Cash handed Anthony a marketing one-sheet about a cryptocurrency investment in the White Tiger ICO.

Anthony glanced at the bullet points. He knew about Bitcoin and the Blockchain revolution that was going on in FinTech, but his knowledge was superficial at best.

"We're creating an ICO," Cash said with a smile.

"A what?" Anthony said.

Cash walked into his small office, opened a safe, then grabbed a few duffle bags from inside. "An initial coin offering. Our coin will be exchangeable for chips in a floating casino, backed by junkets like mine."

"A floating casino? That legit?"

"Will be once the Macau gaming board approves it. If not, we float down to Singapore or over to Manila. Many location options. You want to help us set it up? Plenty of work to do. Maybe you help sell the coin? Take some of your consulting fees in coins? Could make you filthy rich, like owning Amazon stock when it IPO'd or Apple before it made the iPhone."

As Anthony pondered, Cash strode out to the Lamborghini and tossed the bags into the front trunk. While he watched Cash strut around the car, he recognized the gait as the confident trot of a honey badger on the prowl for a late afternoon snack of King Cobra.

Five minutes later, Cash barely waited for Anthony to strap into the Lamborghini's passenger seat before he stomped on the gas and squealed away from the office. "What'd Simon say?"

"Your systems are ancient; they'll never handle what you want to do," Anthony said.

"Send me the specs. I'll have my team buy some new computers. How quickly can you start on the facial recognition work?"

"Let me check with Cyrus but probably within a few weeks."

"Sooner would be better."

"If that's the case, we can probably get someone on it ASAP."

"My favorite time."

Cash sped through the quiet Zhuhai streets as if he were late for an appointment. At the China-Macau immigration checkpoint, a guard in his mid-twenties waved Cash over to the side of the road. The guard was slight with a face as grave as a man who'd just lost a loved one minutes before. He first took Cash's Macau ID card, glanced it over, and handed it back. Anthony's passport required a deeper look, but it, too, was quickly returned after the inclusion of a red stamp.

The guard inspected the car from every angle, doing his job with way too much enthusiasm for Anthony's liking. He made Anthony nervous for good reason. He fired off angry volleys of Mandarin invective at Cash while motioning towards Anthony in subtle but obvious ways. A language that sounds like gunfire in the best of times is especially intimidating coming from the mouth of an irate mainlander who carried a gun and had the power to introduce Anthony to the draconian and highly unjust Chinese justice system. Here people could disappear into a legal system as labyrinthian as Dante's seven circles of hell and probably just as torturous. Or end up on an operating table for organ harvesting, if some of the more brutal accounts of its treatment towards the Falun Gong could be believed.

Cash complied to all the strident orders with nonchalant ease. He popped the hood, all the while offering soothing words of apology with a playful smile. At least that's what it sounded like to Anthony. Cash hadn't a care in the world about all of this.

Anthony saw the guard grab a small envelope from the trunk, then slip it into his sleeve. It was a bribe. Plain and simple. The standard way of doing business in China and many other countries in Asia. This had all been kabuki theater for the CCTV cameras above, which weren't angled to see deep into the car's hood.

Anthony chuckled to himself. He was stuck in no man's land, a place between two strange countries; one run by an unforgiving totalitarian dictator who thought nothing of wiping entire families off the historical record; the other, a subservient slave state to a totalitarian master, but he didn't feel threatened. Kabuki theater played by a ham-fisted actor mitigates the fear. Anthony studied the young soldier, mentally capturing details about the man's persona that might prove useful for a character sketch in a future novel or screenplay.

But everything went like clockwork. The guard's steely resolve vanished, and the hint of a smile flickered across his lips. That's what a bribe worth about a month's salary can do, even if there's an additional witness to the felony.

Cash slammed the car hood shut and returned to the driver's seat. He settled in and smiled at Anthony as if this was a common occurrence, which it might well have been. The ignition cranked. The engine roared. Johnny Cash's "The One On The Right Is On The Left" blasted from the Blaupunkt speakers.

As Cash pulled away from the border gate, he turned the stereo down and looked over at Anthony. "Guanxi." The word was said nonchalantly as if it fully explained the events of the last few minutes.

Anthony stared at Cash in confusion, his brow furrowing.

"You know Guanxi?" Cash asked.

"No."

"Cyrus no tell you?"

Anthony shook his head.

"Look, nothing happens in China without something called Guanxi. It means network of favors. I help you here, you help me there. I get Macau to give you a gaming license here, you give me shares in the casino that monetizes that license there. In the West, you know it as you-scratch-my-back, I-scratch-yours, but, in China, where the banking system is archaic and the courts are fixed, Guanxi is hugely important."

"We call that bribery in the West," Anthony said.

"No, no, no, no, not bribery, it's consideration."

"Consideration?"

Cash nodded, adding, "But Guanxi must be paid back. You refuse to return a favor once, there will be no second."

As the Lamborghini raced along Avenue da Ponte da Amizade lining the Pearl River, Cash looked over at Anthony and shared a joke, "You know the difference between paying a bribe in China and paying a bribe in the Philippines?"

"No."

"In China, they want you to get your money's worth," Cash deadpanned, a wicked smile playing across his lips.

Anthony broke into hearty and somewhat relieved laughter. The joke wasn't that funny, but the situation was. Anthony was sitting in a God-awful lime green Lamborghini, with a Chinese Johnny Cash fan speeding through the streets of one of the tiniest principalities in the world. A place that also happened to be the money laundering capital of the world, something he now had firsthand knowledge about, if the money sitting in the back was illicit, and the odds of that were quite high. As a writer, this was the kind of direct experience that raised insipid prose to inspired fiction, the kind of work that drove sales and caught the critic's eye in a fawning way. But he wondered if Cash explained all this because a favor request was headed his way and one would soon be expected in return? Or was Cash innocently explaining the quirky ways of doing business in China? Either way, this fascinated Anthony.

When offering Anthony the managing director position, Cyrus said it would be a great opportunity for Anthony to start seeing how the real world worked. Sitting in the passenger seat of one of the ugliest and most beautiful cars he'd ever ridden in, Anthony couldn't quite believe his luck. This episode alone could seed an interesting scene in a script or the entire chapter of an international thriller.

Cyrus had been right all along; Anthony needed to get out of L.A.

Venture into the real world to understand the true madness of life. And then write about it. Although Cash had unquestionably broken a few laws, this experience had the feeling of a cop ride-along. Anthony never feared for his safety. Maybe it was Cash's unbridled confidence that seemed to ensure everything would turn out fine? Either way, it was infectiousness. He was powerful in the eyes of those who mattered. That power can rub off on, Anthony noted. It can envelope you in a protective layer that seems to keep trouble at bay.

Cash nodded towards the Hong Kong-Macau-Zhuhai Bridge on the left, a six-lane highway rising twenty feet above the water and running far into the distance, towards Hong Kong. "Longest sea crossing in the world."

"Impressive," Anthony said.

Cash's mouth turned down. "Probably the biggest red elephant the world has ever seen. Opened late last year, but it's hardly ever used except by buses loaded with gamblers running back and forth to Hong Kong as well as Mainlanders looking for Duty-Free shopping in Tung Chung. The Hongkies call it, 'The bridge leading to the edge of the underworld.'"

"Really not handling that handover well, are they?"

"Can you blame them?"

Anthony shook his head. "Not really. Freedom's seductive."

Ten minutes later, Cash's Lamborghini raced down Avenue Sun Yat-Sen. Cash took a left by the 30 foot gold MGM lion and screeched to a halt before the casino entrance.

Cash glanced at Anthony. "Start Monday." It wasn't a question.

Anthony climbed out of the Lamborghini. "I'll send over a contract tomorrow."

Cash grabbed one of the duffle bags from the back seat and offered it to Anthony. "No rush."

Anthony took the bag.

"You seemed a little worried back there," Cash said, a playful smile dancing across his lips.

"Confused more than worried."

"Don't be concerned about what happened back there. In China, rich people don't ever go to jail. They just hire poor people to do their time for them. Usually works well for both parties involved."

Anthony opened his mouth to ask a question, but the Lamborghini's throaty roar drowned out his words.

"Welcome to Macau. They say what happens in Vegas, stays in Vegas, well what happens in Macau, never happened," Cash yelled over the roaring din. Tires screeched as Cash hit the accelerator. Johnny Cash's "Ring of Fire" filled the air as the car peeled out. Cash's voice faded into the cool night air as the whiff of burnt rubber drifted into Anthony's nose.

Anthony turned, then strutted into the casino and across the floor as the jangly whir of slot reels spun through the air, offering the promise of glorious riches to any sucker willing to drop a dime or two into the heart of the ravenous wagering beasts that go by their much more alluring names of '88 Fortunes', 'Aztec Treasures', 'Fa Fa Fa', and 'Koi Princess'.

"A fool and his money are easily parted," so the saying goes. A gambler and his money even more easily so, thought Anthony as he strode past the banks of vibrantly colored slots filled with symbols reflecting Asian-themed icons like red dragons, happy pandas, and seductive Han dynasty princesses.

He smiled at the phony sound of coins dropping into a tray. He knew these were losses disguised as wins. Dollar signs here, ringing bells there, and blinking lights everywhere were all cues designed to trick the player into seeing potential riches all around. They made any win more memorable, motivating the player to return sooner than he otherwise might. What the gambler didn't realize was all this noise was just that – noise – and all these lights were just lights flashing to stimulate the brain while taking the mind away from the fact that these slots were mosquito traps set to zap away a gambler's money as quickly, painlessly, and seductively as possible. The casino's modus operandi: hit 'em with a dopamine high while pickpocketing the money away as slickly as a thief lifts a wallet from an ignorant mark.

"How do you walk out of a casino with a small fortune? Walk-in with a large one." It was a joke Anthony had used often on industry executives. Today, he'd be walking into and out of a casino with a small fortune, at least that's what it felt like to him. But he couldn't shake the feeling he was some kind of sucker caught in the early innings of a long con orchestrating around him. This money was too easily gained.

Or maybe this was just how the rich lived? His twin, Cyrus, had been gifted with the Midas touch; just about every business venture he touched turned to gold. Maybe teaming up with Cyrus put Anthony into an orbit that meant easy riches materialized? But he somehow doubted it. Business was a zero-sum game often leaving the rule followers choking on worthless sand, while the corruptible few walked away with the millions and even billions on offer.

CHAPTER FIVE

STARING IN SHOCK at the ¥200,000 in cold, hard yuan laid out before him, Anthony calculated the money's worth in good old U.S. dollars at $30,000. Not a huge sum, but not the kind of money you tossed at hired consultants in the middle of the street, at least not any American street.

Business was done very differently in Asia. Especially in China, where cash seemed to slosh about in large amounts, working its way through a whole host of vague intermediaries, some legit, some sketchy, some bordering on the edge of illegality. Others were straight-up money-laundering fronts. In China, Hong Kong, and Macau, money was easily attained if you were willing to gamble away your soul.

That was the weird thing about carrying around huge sums of cash in Hong Kong and Macau, you never felt anyone was going to try to steal it from you. Anthony had stood in line at HSBC a few times and seen ten-inch stacks of $1,000 notes emerge from Hermes purses or D&G handbags and dumped on bank counters as if they were empty packets of cigarettes. The people handing over crisp packets of Hong Kong dollars seemed oblivious to the fact that this currency was negotiable anywhere in the world and could be separated from its owner with a quick, lip-numbing pistol-whip. No one seemed to consider the obvious risk.

Anthony guessed there weren't too many thieves in Hong Kong or Macau. However, he would later recognize the special administrative regions of Macau and Hong Kong were infested with crooks, but these people didn't waste time on such slim pickings as $30,000 and such uncivilized methods as pistol whipping. These people stole on epically grand scales, not bothering with amounts less than a million Hong Kong. They also took to heart Oscar Wilde's quip that "A true friend stabs you in the front, not the back."

Anthony grabbed his phone, and called Cyrus, who answered on the second ring with a groggy "Hello."

For thirty seconds, Anthony paced across the floor, relaying the border bribe story, finally adding in concern, "Who knows where this money comes from?"

"Who cares where it comes from? Where it's going is all that matters. And that's into our bank account."

"You're not worried about its provenance?"

"It's what?"

"Where it comes from."

"No."

"They're junket operators, Cyrus."

"Hermes is a publicly-traded company. On the Hong Kong stock exchange. Like a lot of other junket operators," Cyrus said. His cool, calm, and comforting tone seemed to say, "Everything's fine, everything's under control, nothing to see here, move along, go your merry way."

And it eased Anthony's mind, his frown instantly disappearing. "Oh."

"Look, this is the murky world that is Macau. I thought you said you wanted some raw, unvarnished life experiences."

"Sure, I want that."

"I thought you wanted to get out of your Hollywood bubble and see how the world really worked, warts and all?"

"Of course, I did, but I didn't want to go to jail."

"You're not going to go to jail. Trust me, they'll be rounding up the junket operators before they arrest any Westerners. I've got your back, man. If there's even a hint of legal trouble, let me know and we'll Seal Team Six you out of there, or I'll hire the best lawyer available to bribe the judge."

"Glad you see the humorous side in all of this."

"I do. And you should, too. Anthony, it's the Wild, Wild East out there, a place where normal rules don't apply. Look, there's a huge opportunity to make a small fortune with our services. And sounds like you've already got a great story to tell or write. Cash's quite a character, no?"

"That he is."

"You've got money and inspiration, two birds, one money launder."

"As long as there's no jail time."

"Foreigners don't go to jail in Macau, they just get deported."

"Comforting."

"Look, everything'll be fine. Deposit the cash in our bank account. Make four deposits over the course of ten days, all in differing amounts, just to be safe. Open a safety deposit box and put $7,500 in there. Take $5,000 for yourself, as a bonus for your great work and your Houdini-like ability to avoid jail time," Cyrus said while howling to himself.

"Hey, it's my neck on the line out here."

The dial tone cut off Cyrus's howl.

"Shit," Anthony said, turning off the phone.

As Anthony set aside his cut, he felt the adrenalin rush that comes with a big win at the track, this one more enticing as it contained an illicit quality. Like hitting a 100-1 longshot, a win that comes with the knowledge you got one over on just about every other gambler at the track. Like you were momentarily walking on air and tapping into a financial secret eluding everyone else.

Cyrus's detailed strategy to avoid any potential money laundering red flags troubled Anthony. If nothing else, it proved consciousness of guilt. The good news was Macau's banking system was highly secretive, working far beyond the IRS's prying eyes, but still nothing was completely beyond their probing gaze.

Anthony jumped to his feet and stepped into the kitchen. He grabbed the Ultimat Vodka decanter from the freezer, then stuffed ice cubes into a leaded glass tumbler. He poured the pricey vodka over ice that crackled and snapped apart. He cut a slice of lemon and squeezed it into the drink.

Anthony looked around the large kitchen, with its subzero fridge, and stylish Gaggenau appliances, and the brushed stainless steel Gaggia Classic Pro Espresso Machine. He picked up the bottle of Ultimat Vodka and eyed it critically; its cobalt blue crystal bottle was a beautiful decanter in its own right. This kitchen was ten times the size of his former kitchenette in Los Angeles if you could call what he had there a kitchenette. This was stocked with much pricier appliances, much tastier food, more expensive juices, more indulgent cheeses, much more extravagant alcohol, along with some ludicrously overpriced caviar, a leftover from Cyrus's last visit to the apartment a few weeks ago.

Anthony chugged the vodka, then poured another. He walked into the bedroom, then slumped onto the bed. Pulling the goose feather down comforter over his body, he sank into the soft memory foam mattress that hugged his body in a way no other mattress ever had. He'd sleep well tonight.

He turned on the TV. A CNN reporter wearing a gas mask ducked an incoming projectile and then hurried up the street while barely avoiding an angry mob of Hong Kong protestors armed with colorful umbrellas, mops, street cones, and tennis rackets. The Umbrella Revolution of 2014 had rolled into 2019 after Carrie Lam decided to allow the mainland authorities to legally extradite Hong Kongers for any crime it wanted to weave out of thin air. Molotov cocktails spiraled down and exploded in a shower of flames twenty feet from a line of policemen marching across Queensway Road.

Anthony shook his head at the sad sight, then flipped the channel to CNBC, where Jon Najarian offered up his latest useless take on the options market.

Choosing to leave the questions of ethics and morality for another day, Anthony wiped away any troubling thoughts with a few more slugs of mind-numbing vodka. So smooth, it went down like water, while the lemon squeeze added a nice refreshing tang.

As Anthony drifted off to sleep that night, pangs of guilt set in. Was this money collected from human trafficking or, possibly, child slave labor? He couldn't shake the image of a five-year-old girl hunched over a sewing machine, stitching up fake Gucci loafers while slaving out a grueling fourteen-hour shift at some grim Dongguan factory.

🪙 CHAPTER SIX

A PHONE TRILLED, rattling Anthony out of his drunken stupor. It was 12:35 p.m. Much later than he normally awoke, but last night's first celebratory vodka turned into a second, then a third as the smoothness made them all go down like chilled water in a parched throat on a blistering summer's day. If making $5,000 for doing little more than writing up a proposal wasn't worth a night of drunken revelry, what was? Especially since Anthony had never seen so much money in his bank account before.

But now, a price was due. A pounding head, spent muscles, a touch of vertigo, and a mouth as arid as the Kalahari Desert. Anthony lifted his head off the pillow. Peeled open his eyelids. Blinding white light seared into his bloodshot eyeballs, bleaching his retinas. His eyelids snapped shut. Refused to reopen. Slapping his hand on the bedside table, Anthony groped for the screeching phone. Once his fingers hit the squealing device, he pulled it under the duvet, then answered the call with a groggy, "Hello" that barely escaped his parched lips.

"Is this Exegesis?" Mary Liew asked in the oddest accent Anthony had ever heard. A cross-pollination of Singlish and English tinged with a tone of firm German directness.

The sternness of the voice sobered Anthony up in an instant and he answered, "Yes, this is Anthony Wilson, the company's MD."

"This is Mary Liew, from City of Dreams, you available to talk?"

"Yes."

"It's your consultant. His training is useless."

"Okay. I'm in Macau now. I can come over to your office later today if you'd like."

They agreed to meet at four o'clock in the café in the Hard Rock lobby. Once Anthony hung up, he popped out from under the covers, something he immediately regretted as light screamed into his retinas. "Shiiiitttt."

Right on the dot of four o'clock, Mary Liew marched into the café and immediately spotted Anthony, which wasn't hard to do as he was the only white person in the place. She strutted the few steps to Anthony's table and, even though the distance was short, the impression was immense. It was one perfectly orchestrated and graceful move, executed by a woman who knew she drew attention wherever she went.

Her flawlessly tailored blue pin-striped suit clung to her body in a way that threaded the line between sophisticated formal business outfit and hinting at way too sexy club attire. Barely threading the right side of professionalism, the suit conveyed a touch of eroticism that would tweak any breathing heterosexual's libido but would ultimately make them embarrassed that the thought of sex was the first thing crossing the mind when so much respectability was also on display.

Mary played a fine style game. As a man who took his style seriously, his sartorial eye knew its way around a notch, a shawl, and a peak lapel, Anthony respected that Mary played as well to the Milan runway crowd as she did to the VIP bouncer meatheads. The folio she carried was an afterthought, barely spotted by Anthony before she placed it on the table between them.

"You charge me a thousand dollars a day for someone so useless my staff teaches him how to do his job," Mary said, her words as swift and direct as a hollow point bullet. Her perfectly groomed eyebrows shot up, elongating her diamond-shaped face. Her pupils seemed slightly off-center, but this was a flaw that intrigued rather than put off. It was a picture-perfect illustration of imperfections producing perfection.

"Sorry, I had no idea. This was all set up before I arrived," Anthony said.

"Understood. But we don't need him anymore."

"Of course not. And we won't be billing you for his time."

"We wouldn't pay even if you did."

Anthony nodded, trying to suppress a laugh. He liked this woman's directness, to say nothing of her sexiness. "Can I ask you a personal question?"

"Sure," she said, his eyes sweeping away, turning guarded.

"How did you get that wonderful German-slash-Singaporean accent?"

She smiled and her eyes returned to Anthony's face. "I was born in Hong Kong. My father is German. Mother Chinese. We moved to Dusseldorf when I was five. I was educated there until I was eighteen, at which time I moved to Singapore for college. I guess what you learn in your youth sticks with you for life."

"When I say 'water,' people hear my English accent from my days at a British boarding school."

"Anyway," she said, slapping the table, "I'd love to chat, but I have a new trainer to find."

"Indeed. But would you be willing to give us a second chance? I have the head of our gaming practice coming to Macau for another client. I'm sure I could make him available to you."

"Send me his resume. I'll review it, we'll see."

"Sure."

Mary pulled out a couple of sheets of paper from the folio and slid them over to Anthony. "I asked your Miami office to send me some resumes for a potential SAP consultant I need for an upcoming CI project, and this is what they sent me."

Anthony glanced the sheets over, seeing they were two resumes for the same person.

"Can you tell the difference?" Mary asked, her eyes squinting displeasure.

Anthony looked closer, was this a trick question?

"I'll give you a hint. The second one shows Rehann Leghari has the experience I specifically asked for *after* I rejected her first resume because she lacked those required skills."

Anthony spotted the added expertise. He couldn't believe his HR department could be so stupid as to add a skill after the fact? What amateurs.

"Must be a mistake. Let me look into this," Anthony said with a tight smile.

"Yes, must have been a mistake," Mary said, repeating the words slowly, with a sarcastic curl of the lips. Then she rose.

Anthony dug into his bag and pulled out the book he had ghostwritten for Cyrus. "I have a gift for you."

"Oh?"

"Don't be too excited. It's all about how to use analytics and AI in the casino industry, not the most captivating of reads."

Mary took the offered book and glanced it over. "Thank you. Thank you, very much."

"It should be useful to your team. If you like, let me know, and I'll get you more copies."

Mary nodded, then strutted away. Anthony watched her departing figure, an approving smile curling his lips. She was a weird and unique amalgamation of smoldering Asian sexiness and profound German seriousness. She spoke in short, clipped, economical sentences that were weirdly erotic. It was easy to envision her as a dominatrix who charged high and mighty men high and mighty prices to parade around in a skimpy leather outfit atop six-inch heels while smacking her palm repeat-edly with a cat-o-nine-tails whip that promised to beat the naughtiness out of them.

She was certainly one who got the creative and other juices flowing. Anthony jotted down a few short sentences describing her looks and her commanding presence; personality sketches for a character study, per-haps? A muse, she certainly could be.

CHAPTER SEVEN

Donning a sharp suit that was way too warm for these humid early autumn days, Anthony strode through the lobby of the Macau Roosevelt Hotel, enjoying the streams of cool air-conditioning hitting his face. The hotel was a sister property to L.A.'s Hollywood Roosevelt Hotel and it wanted everyone to know about its colorful, star-studded past. Pictures of the first Academy Awards lined the lobby walls. Nameless stars of yesteryear showed off their little gold Oscar statutes while beaming brightly for the flashing cameras.

Anthony glanced their way as he passed through, remembering his time living across the street from the famous place and wandering around the dark halls, trying to catch sight of Marilyn Monroe's ghost; an apparition supposedly still haunting the shadowy corridors and, every now and then, revealing herself in a mirrored reflection. Before he had moved to Macau, he had driven by the Macau Roosevelt several times during its construction and chuckled at the *Historical Landmark: Coming Soon* sign out front; another one of those lost in translation signs that seemed omnipresent in China.

Anthony wandered out to the pool, where the blast furnace of Macau's heat made him instantly forget about the air conditioning. Cash sat at a table near the pool with two junket girls, who swayed to the beat of a chillout tune Anthony recognized but couldn't place.

Cash jumped to his feet, grabbed a racing form from his table, and approached Anthony. "Come, let me show you the view."

Anthony followed Cash up a small flight of steps to an infinity pool overlooking the Macau Jockey Club. The large racetrack covered several acres of land in the shadow of Galaxy Macau's massive integrated resort containing both a dirt track and an outer turf track. A grandstand that accommodated thousands of spectators appeared to be a quarter full.

Anthony marveled at the view. "This is world-class. And I should know because I've been to a few of the world's greatest racetracks."

"Only one with an overlooking infinity pool, I'm sure."

Anthony nodded.

"You like racing?" Cash asked.

"My preferred form of gambling, actually. That and betting against England at every major football tournament."

"Football is a game in which twenty-two men kick around a ball for ninety minutes and England loses on penalties."

"You follow it too. Self-flagellation at its finest."

Cash handed the racing program to Anthony. "One of my horses is running in the fifth. I thought this would be a great place to watch him. Guess which one's mine."

Anthony flipped to the fifth race and looked over the horses' names.

"Here's a clue," said Cash as he dug out a handful of betting slips from his pocket, then offered them over.

Taking the tickets but not looking at them, Anthony spotted the obvious horse in the program and said, "Cowboy's Sweetheart?"

Cash nodded with a smile.

"Tell me, Cash, what's with the country music fascination?"

"How can you ask, a screenwriter like you?"

Anthony shot Cash a questioning look, his brows squeezed tightly together.

Cash explained with a smile: "Every song tells a story. And don't you just love the wit, 'I'm So Miserable Without You, It's Just Like Having You Around', 'Live Like You Were Dying', 'Man, I feel like a woman'? Someone as literate and irreverent as you should respect titles like these."

"I respect the titles, it's the music underneath I find problematic. Shania Twain, really?"

"I was making a point about the song titles, not the songs, but you're right, she's trite, like most of today's alt-country acts."

A junket girl approached with a pair of binoculars in hand. This was probably the one duty she had to do all day, make Cash aware his horse was about to run and she did it with absurd aplomb, adding a few words in Cantonese while offering Cash the binoculars in a dramatic flourish.

"Ah, the race is afoot, almost literally," said Cash, grabbing the binoculars. He trained them on the track below. After a few moments, he announced, "They're off."

Anthony had done a little research on Macau the previous night before the vodka introduced him to dreamtime. *Time Magazine* had once called it a "mini replica of 1920s Chicago," complete with machine gun assassinations orchestrated by gangsters with colorful names like Broken Tooth and Fatti Pui. Broken Tooth gained notoriety when he commissioned a movie about his life, *Casino*, then illegally shot it in Macau's warren-like streets, dinghy restaurants, seedy apartments, and shabby hotels. When the undersecretary of security's unoccupied car blew up in his driveway one night, the Macau authorities arrested Broken Tooth. Two lengthy trials ensued. Broken Tooth and his cronies were charged with the bombing, but the cases fell apart. One judge abruptly resigned. Fearful witnesses quickly developed debilitating bouts of amnesia. A second trial centered on Broken Tooth's association with triad organizations. This one also lacked witnesses. At the trial's conclusion, however, a three-judge tribunal presiding over the case left the courtroom to view *Casino* privately. To everyone's astonishment, the judges declared the depiction of Broken Tooth's life as a mafia leader in a fictional film an accurate representation of his life and his crimes. They sent him to prison for 15 years. This may have been the first and only time a film of fiction convicted a man of a true-life crime. The apparent authenticity of the film's cinematic depictions in a city where nothing was as it seemed proved to be Broken Tooth's downfall.

"Macau, only place in the world where you can go to jail based on evidence that is a fictional movie," Anthony said.

Cash nodded. "Was a dangerous place back then. But we cleaned it up with the help of a little fiction."

"Seems to have turned out okay."

A crooked smile broke across Cash's lips while his hand swept across the track. "At least on the surface."

Anthony nodded.

"Cyrus says you're a pretty good screenwriter."

"Not good enough to get produced, unfortunately."

"Not an easy business, the film business. Maybe one of the hardest."

"If you're not Broken Tooth, of course."

"Cowboy's Sweetheart's seventh, but he's a plodder," said Cash, using the horseracing lingo for a thoroughbred that hangs back in the early stage of a race, saving its energy for a burst of speed in the stretch run. He handed over the binoculars.

Anthony checked out the race below. A distant but intense roar rose from the crowd as the horses sprinted into the first turn.

"You want to write my story. Growing up on the mean streets of Macau, that how you say it?" Cash asked.

At first, Anthony didn't get the reference. After a moment, however, he understood, silently amused this slick junket operator was so enamored by movie gangsters. "Like the Scorsese film?"

Cash nodded, then continued with his story: "Rising to success in Macau's modern-day gambling industry."

"Sounds fascinating, but there's an old adage about biographies and autobiographies, 'Everyone has a book in them, but for most people, that's where it should stay.'"

Cash laughed. "I tell you my story. You decide, but I don't think it should stay here," Cash said, tapping his left pectoral.

"You're not worried about leaving evidence?"

"Of what? I think you have the wrong impression of me. I'm not triad."

"Too bad, that might make it more interesting."

Cash laughed and smirked in agreement.

"But how do you know I'm a good writer?" Anthony asked.

"Cyrus told me."

"I'll let you in on a little secret about brothers, sometimes they bend the truth. Especially twins. And especially a born salesman like Cyrus. How about I send you a copy of one of my scripts? You can read it, then decide."

"No need. I go with my gut. It's worked for me for forty-five years. You want to write my story or what?"

Anthony lowered the binoculars, then handed them back. "I'm kind of busy right now with Exegesis and your facial recognition project, to be honest."

"A true artist would jump at the chance."

Anthony knew Cash was right. A true writer and artist would jump at the opportunity to write a story like this. Who knew where it would lead?

Cash raised the binoculars and tracked the horses around the last turn. "How about we make a bet? This is Macau, after all, the gambling capital of the world,"

"What kind of bet?"

Cash pointed at the betting slips in Anthony's hand. "How about if one of those bets comes in, you agree to help me?"

There's no such thing as a free lunch or a free bet, Anthony knew, but this offer had little downside. "This is the way you negotiate?"

"Always good to add a ticking clock, no? Increases the inherent dramatic tension of the scene."

"You've watched too many movies."

"No doubt. Look, I'll pay you two thousand an hour, MOP. We do about five-to-ten hours a week for a month. You hear my story, then decide."

Anthony mentally calculated MOP into dollars. With the current rate of exchange of about eight MOP to one U.S. dollar, it came to about $250/hour. Not a bad payday, not a bad payday at all.

Cash threw out his hand. "The finish line approaches."

Anthony shook the offered hand. "Deal."

Cash raised the binoculars and watched the race unfold as the crowd cheered the head-to-head stretch run.

"Ten, seven, and maybe Cowboy in third," Cash said, a disappointed smile playing across his lips.

Cash took the tickets from Anthony, handed them to the junket girl, and fired off a couple of sentences in Cantonese. The girl quickly searched the tickets for a potential winner. After a few moments, she squealed in delight and thrust the winning ticket into the air. Cash gestured for her to hand the ticket over to Anthony. She did with an endearing pouty display.

Anthony checked the ticket, a trifecta bet that included a bunch of horses in the first slot and a field bet for place, with Cowboy Sweetheart the lone third horse. He had come in third by a nose.

"What are the odds of the winner and the place horses?" Anthony asked.

Cash raised the binoculars and read the tote board. "First went out at forty-to-one, second was fifteen-to-one."

"This'll pay massive," said Anthony.

"Congratulations," Cash said as he lowered the binoculars.

"It's your ticket."

"My gift to you."

Anthony was speechless. The ticket was worth thousands of dollars. He offered it back. "I can't take this."

Cash pushed it away. "Take it as an advance."

Anthony nodded, at a loss for words.

"Stick with me, my friend, and we'll be hitting longshots forever," Cash said as a broad smile took over his entire face, wrinkles around the eyes and all.

CHAPTER EIGHT

YOU NEVER FORGET your first kiss, your first lay, or your first flight on a private jet, especially if that private jet's in-flight service features include champagne poured from $500 bottles of Cristal, Beluga caviar eaten off a bed of crushed ice, and three spectacular Hermes junket models keeping the food, booze, and entertainment endlessly flowing.

Most of the large Macau junket operators had private jets. It was simply the cost of doing business with the rich and the powerful. For high rolling whales accustomed to a lifestyle that included traveling in the rarefied air of private jets, rubbing shoulders with the great unwashed to scratch their gambling itch just wasn't on. If the junkets wanted to make their fortunes on these high rollers, they'd have to pay for it in free private jet flights and complimentary hotel suites. They'd have to serve the finest food man could hunt down, kill, then serve up by whomever Michelin deemed this week's most important addition to the Culinary Arts since grunting caveman slapped raw zebra meat on roasting savanna fires. Obscene amounts had to be spent on the finest forever-aged, single malt Highland Scotch whiskey or wines from the renowned French region of Bordeaux; sipped from super thin, hand-blown, light as a feather stemware that almost hovered in the air untouched, of course.

It all somehow worked. A hundred high rollers drove a third of the revenue at one of the Cotai Strip's massive integrated resorts. Ensuring these high rollers were kept happy was not only imperative, but a bottom-line necessity for a business that spent billions of dollars on eye-catching properties, which were some of the biggest buildings in the world. Anthony didn't know what was rarer than rarified air but whatever it was, he was traveling in it.

"So, where we headed?" Anthony asked, immediately recognizing the absurdity of a question like that coming from someone headed skyward on a Bombardier Challenger 850, not from a friend joining his buddies in the backseat of an Uber Black for a drunk boy's night out.

"To the WeChat World Series of Poker finals in Sanya. I'm one of the two hundred finalists," Cash said. He sat catty corner from Anthony and wore a Nudie Cohn-inspired outfit, this one topped by a $5,000 white Stetson cowboy hat made from 100% beaver and completed with a 14-karat gold buckle set with 26 sparkling diamonds. It glittered now and then when it caught the sun streaming in through the windows.

"Congratulations. That's impressive," Anthony said.

"Not really. I sponsored one of the satellite winners. Now I'm taking his place."

"That legit?"

"It's China. No one checks or cares. Least of all my player, who was handsomely rewarded for his work. I'll be representing Wuxuan, a lovely little city of five hundred thousand in southeastern China."

Anthony pulled out a notebook and flipped to the first page. "You ready to get started?"

Cash nodded.

Anthony had spent the night before reading up on the history of the junkets. The Hong Kong City University had published a recent paper claiming, "A gangland reputation, financial clout, and the ability to recover debts by whatever means necessary are what is needed to run a high-rolling junket in Macau. The report says they are still dominated by triads, who no longer kill but still loan sharked like crazy."

"Our business differs little from the money-lenders whose tables Jesus overturned a couple of millennia ago," Cash said. He scooped out half an ounce of caviar with a mother-of-pearl spoon, then added it to a toast point, eating it with a loud crunch. He closed his eyes and smiled while immersing himself in the exquisite experience. A sip of champagne followed.

"But who owns these rooms?" Anthony asked.

"Some retired and inactive triad members still run some of the junket rooms, but triad membership, though sufficient, is no longer a necessary condition. What is necessary, above all else, is access to huge sums of money and you need to have good relationships with the troika of power in Macau, the casinos, the triads, and the police."

"An unholy alliance if ever there was one."

"Our very own Axis Alliance."

Anthony chuckled. "How'd you get into the business?"

"My brother-in-law loaned me the money to get started. He had a good relationship with the triads."

"He still backs you?"

"Gone. Like the ex-wife."

Anthony laughed, but then wondered how the woman became an ex-wife. "She worth talking to for the book?"

Cash shook his head. "I made enough money to buy my brother-in-law out. Once a junket room has enough capital for growth, it can be turned into a formal business. Like a bank, the junkets solicit deposits from investors, who then receive a fixed monthly dividend for their investment. Then the junket will be strong enough financially to extend credit to its gamblers as well as serve as the bookmaker."

"Banks loan against baccarat tables?"

"Banks loan against anything that generates positive cash flow. I think it was your Bob Hope who said, 'A bank is a place that will lend you money if you prove you don't need it.'"

"Their generosity is topped only by casino loan sharks."

Cash nodded. "These tables might be the most valuable real estate in the world. Millions of dollars pass over and under two meters of felt every day."

Anthony wrote the quote down.

Cash motioned to the bowl. "Try some of the caviar. This is what we serve our best customers, Beluga. You want?"

Although he wasn't a big fan of caviar, Anthony took the mother-of-pearl spoon and glanced it over, impressed.

Cash noticed Anthony's inquisitive look, and explained, "To avoid tainting the exquisite taste of the caviar with metal knives, of course."

Anthony added caviar to a toast point, then ate it. He followed it with a sip of champagne. It tasted exquisite, salty as hell, but in a good way, containing a subtle essence of the ocean along with a buttery and nutty flavor.

"We prepare it in the true 'Malossol' way. Caviar should never be strong or overpowering. Caviar eggs should be distinctly separate globes, with a firm, lustrous appearance. They should pop in the mouth, releasing a flavor that flows over the tongue," Cash said.

"I'm not usually a fan of caviar, but this is delicious."

"Finest in the world. Our clients demand nothing less."

On the tarmac before the flight, Cash had introduced Anthony to the three young Hermes junket girls. They were almost clones of each other, all sharing the typical Han Chinese features of porcelain skin, slender body, oval-shaped face, and double eyelids that made their brown eyes appear large and round in their perfectly made-up faces.

These women were like doppelgangers, almost duplicates in natural beauty, but there was one who truly stood out, Vivian Liu. She was a notch above the rest in both beauty and style. The black cashmere cardigan draped over her toned and muscular shoulders blended well with the dark, monochromatic dress she wore underneath. She immediately caught Anthony's eye when she extended her cashmere-gloved hand. Her long, sleek, and slender fingers slipped into his palm with ease. It was the softest cashmere Anthony had ever felt. Maybe Loro Piana? The grip underneath was strong, yet softly padded. Warm to the touch. Once Vivian broke the handshake, Anthony pulled his hand back, but immediately missed the warmth of her touch. A memorable introduction. She had lips that always seemed ready to break into a smile as well, endearing as hell to him and all the men who saw it, he'd bet.

When first looking into her bold, brown eyes, Anthony recalled how the stars of sitcoms and network dramas often wore cashmere on set because the eye tended to recognize something special in the luxurious fabric. It always projected well on film. Even if the viewer wasn't completely aware of it, cashmere framed a character in soft edges that made them richer, more interesting, and more worthy of empathy. More of a star.

Vivian would fit perfectly in front of a camera. She had that feature so few embody yet all desire – star quality. One's eye constantly wandered to her perfectly symmetrical face, as if directed by something beyond their control. It was something Anthony had seen in very few women before, and he'd been in the room with A and B listers, so it wasn't for a lack of proximity to them. He'd seen stars up close and personal and had conversed intelligently with a few of them. Vivian had that appeal, in spades, and he wanted to get to know her better. A whole lot better.

Back on the plane, Anthony's eyes locked onto Vivian's as she glanced his way. The rush of electricity that comes with deep attraction and sexual desire coupled into one momentarily energized him. But the line of sight was broken by a junket girl stepping up to refill Cash's champagne glass. Anthony focused on Cash, shook off his fanciful reverie, and turned serious.

"How does a dead chip program work?" Anthony asked.

"A player puts money on deposit with the casino, which gives him chips that can only be used in their casino or junket room. When the player wins, he gets his dead chip back along with a normal casino chip. When the player loses, he loses the dead chip, of course. The player is incentivized to use the dead chips because he earns a commission on each chip rollover. The player's buy-in must be turned over at least four times to qualify for the program. The chips are called 'dead chips' because they have no value beyond the casino's dead chip program. The most important thing about a dead chip program is a mainlander can deposit money with a junket operator in China, collect the chips in Macau, roll them, and then send the winnings anywhere in the world, including to countries with highly secretive banking laws."

"A convenient way to get money out of China."

"The single most convenient. Junket rooms are all about power. And power is measured in manpower and financial capital. And being the fiercest and most aggressive junket in the city helps."

"Like a honey badger."

"A what?"

"A honey badger. Baddest animal on the planet, according to *The Guinness Book of World Records*. It snacks on king cobras and all sorts of venomous snakes. Takes down animals twice its size."

Cash nodded while repeating the word honey badger, liking the sound of this new English term on his tongue.

A few hours later, the Hermes jet skidded across the Sanya Phoenix International Airport's tarmac and taxied into the private jet parking area, which was filled with about ten other expensive jets.

"Welcome to the Hawaii of China," Cash said.

Anthony glanced out the window. The waters of the South China Sea shimmered in the warm, late afternoon sun beyond the airport's runway.

The Bombardier eased to a stop before a delegation of immigration officials. The plane's door opened. A short staircase descended. Cash appeared in the doorway, then bounded down the steps. His entourage followed. Passports were reviewed. Everyone was cleared without delay, even the standout American.

Nice to have friends in high places, Anthony thought, following Cash into an awaiting Bentley.

The Hermes junket girls piled into a Shangri-La Resort & Spa Escalade, giggling as they disappeared one-by-one into the black SUV. The driver grabbed their luggage and stuffed it into the voluminous trunk. Anthony's eyes crossed with Vivian's again and she smiled sweetly, inducing another fluttering in his chest. He smiled back, then turned his attention to Cash, who stared at him, brow pinched together in a questioning look.

"So, I re-read part of your proposal last night. I like your idea of tracking a gambler's bets to find out who our most profitable players are. Very interesting. How much to implement such a system?" Cash asked.

"Not cheap. There are baccarat tables that track chips and bets, but they cost a million bucks each, U.S. There is cheaper technology that can track the colors of the chips and the height of the chip stacks, probably a couple hundred grand each. It's substantial work but it'd probably be worth it knowing your turnover."

Cash nodded, mulling the idea over. "You're good at explaining things. That might come in handy tonight."

"Thanks," Anthony said, taking the compliment in stride, but with a fleeting, opaque smile of confusion.

Cash noticed the disquietude. "You're going to help me sell my ICO tonight. To some very rich men, who are also high-ranking members of the CCP. Remember my floating casino idea?"

"Sure, but I don't know anything about ICOs."

"You heard of Bitcoin?"

"Sure."

"Blockchain?"

"Of course."

"Then you know enough."

"But I hardly know anything about them."

"Neither does anyone. Have you read a crypto white paper recently?"

"No."

"Then you're in the majority," Cash joked with a disarming smile.

Anthony smirked.

"Look, they're an alphabet soup of acronyms and made-up terms," Cash said. "Just talk analytics, like you do in your book. Throw in a bunch of technical jargon, that always impresses."

"But my book has nothing to do with cryptocurrencies."

"I know that. You know that. But *they* don't know that."

"But—," started Anthony.

"Look, you're white. Trust me, in China, that's enough."

CHAPTER NINE

TWENTY MINUTES LATER, the Bentley's recently waxed tires crunched on white gravel while easing to a stop in the Shangri-La Resort's expansive driveway. One of Sanya's finest resorts, the Shangri-La Resort's grounds stretched across several acres of manicured lawns before the glistening Haitang Bay.

When Cash and Anthony emerged from the Bentley, the hotel manager, a dignified-looking American man in his late forties, greeted them with a warm, engaging smile, a slight bow, and a few words in Cantonese.

"So glad to see you again, Mr. Cheang," said the manager. He led Cash and Anthony into the hotel's entrance, striding with strong, powerful steps like a man who owned the place. They strolled through a pastel-hued restaurant decorated with large Chinese lanterns and an abundance of Jiangnan-styled wooden furniture, before entering a large private dining room flooded with natural light. A group of three men and three women stood at attention, smiling in recognition once they saw Cash.

The men, Bohai Sòng, Jiayi Li, and Zhen Zhao, were in their mid-forties, dressed in expensive and rather ostentatious clothes. Zhan's short-sleeved shirt had 'Balenciaga' in big bold letters screaming across it. Bohai's dark red pants, lighter red shirt, and matching red velvet designer loafers could hardly be deemed modest, but gaudy they were not. A stylist would certainly approve of the nice tonal flourish that contained a color that had so much political significance in China. Jiayi was clad in a black Chinese tunic suit. The women behind the men were secretaries, in their thirties, their lithe and attractive bodies outlined nicely in their conservative blue suits.

Cash introduced the three men to Anthony, who shook the offered hands. Jiayi presented the secretaries. Anthony expertly hid his nervousness behind a pleasing smile, remaining on the periphery of the group, only engaging when asked a question.

Bohai sat down at the head of the table. His underlings followed in hierarchical order around him; the two lieutenants flanking him on either side. The young female secretaries took seats strategically around the table.

Cash sat down directly across from Bohai with Anthony to his right.

Vivian entered the room and slid into a seat beside Anthony. She leaned into him and said, "I'll be your interpreter. Chinese dining norms can be very formal, and we don't want anyone to be embarrassed, now do we?"

"We certainly do not," Anthony said. And he made a silent "Thank you" to Cash for finding such a pretty and classy woman as his interpreter. However, having a woman that made his heart go flutter was the last thing he needed at a time like this. He was about to be presenting to some extremely powerful people under some seriously false pretenses and he needed to focus exclusively on the task at hand. There was no room for lascivious thoughts that so often crowd everything else out.

Vivian leaned in to subtly explain the seating arrangement, "Bohai is in the 'boss seat', the chair facing the door."

Anthony nodded subtly. Chinese business meetings were deeply formal affairs and hosts were sticklers about hierarchy and norms. He should pay attention here, get the thought of his hand slowly sliding her panties down those long, slender legs out of his mind.

Within moments, Vivian rose, pulled out four leather-bound folios from her Prada bag, and then placed them before Bohai, Jiayi, Zhen, and

Anthony. Intrigued, he flipped it open and saw it was a prospectus for the White Tiger ICO.

Cash stood up and rattled off some things in Mandarin. Anthony caught snippets of English, words like Bitcoin, Blockchain, MantraDao, PolkaDot, and cryptocurrency. They were interspersed with Mandarin words that were unique sounds to his brain. Anthony knew a little French and could get by in the language, but so many words in French contain corresponding English sounds. This language was so utterly unique that there wasn't even a frame of reference for some of the sounds in it.

Vivian leaned in to translate Cash's pitch, "Whether in U.S. dollar notes and coins, shells, or precious stones, all of which have been used as money at one time or another. The instrument only works if everyone trusts it."

The effect was mesmeric. Vivian's perfume, a sweet mixture of vanilla, lavender, and bergamot, had an exhilarating effect on him. He marveled at how she could make some of the most unsexy words imaginable thrilling and sexy. If she didn't have acting aspirations, she should get them quick. It's been said that Morgan Freeman can make the phone book interesting to listen to. Anthony had no doubt Vivian could make it sexy to hear too.

Cash paused to let the words sink in. Vivian glanced at Anthony. For a moment, he thought he saw her pupils dilate, one of the more subtle and involuntary signs a woman makes when interested in a man. As if being coy, she averted her gaze down, then Cash continued with his pitch. Vivian's translation followed. Anthony heard little but his thumping heart.

Cash pointed at Anthony and fired off something in Mandarin that must have intrigued the three CCP members as they all glanced his way in unison, eyebrows raised.

"He wrote a book on all of this stuff," translated Vivian. She then corrected herself, "*You* wrote a book on all of this stuff." She smiled sweetly at him, then mouthed, "impressive."

"Ghostwrote," Anthony said, correcting Cash. It was an attempt to temper enthusiasm, as he commonly tried to do when people oversold his talents, which happened all too often. He was about to learn Cash was a master salesman. Hyperbole was his only modus operandi in meetings like this. For a moment, Anthony worried he'd made a faux pas and caused Cash to lose face by correcting him in front of these most important government officials.

However, Cash didn't seem bothered by the correction and implicitly stated so when he relented with a smile, "Ghostwrote, I stand corrected."

"You own cryptocurrencies?" Bohai asked.

The question threw Anthony slightly off balance as he hadn't. He wasn't ready to lie. Not for Cash. Not for anybody. "You know, I attended a conference a few years ago and one of the sponsors was a Bitcoin exchange. That was when Bitcoin sold for $275. Today, I just can't convince myself to pay $10,000 for the same asset."

Bohai and his lieutenants nodded sagely.

Anthony had cleverly threaded the needle of truth. All the best lies have a touch of truth to them, as do all the best deflections. "One of my biggest investing mistakes. But I'd buy the Bitcoin miners over Bitcoin any day. Or, of course, find a new crypto coin to invest in."

Anthony could hardly have made a better pitch. He noticed a satisfied smile flicker across Cash's face.

The sommelier, a robust and handsome French man in his forties, wearing an immaculate blue, pin-striped suit, brought over a bottle of 2008 Château Lafite Rothschild. He cradled it as carefully as if it were the King of England's newborn son being presented to the nation for the first time.

Without so much as a cursory glance at the bottle, Bohai nodded consent. The sommelier pulled out a wine opener and expertly slid out the cork. He poured a taster for Bohai. Forgoing a wine sniff, Bohai took two quick sips, then nodded curt approval.

The sommelier went around the table, filling glasses. Once Anthony brought the wine glass to his lips, he sniffed subtle notes of graphite, black currants, licorice, and camphor. He drank. It was the best wine he'd ever tasted, and he savored it slowly.

"You like red wine?" Vivian asked.

"Yes. Especially French Bordeaux, which I believe this is," Anthony said.

"You don't prefer to add a little coke to yours?" the sommelier asked while discretely nodding at Bohai. Sure enough, Bohai was bastardizing the pricey wine with slugs of cheap, sugary *Coke*.

"*Sacré bleu,*" Anthony said under his breath as his mouth dropped open in shock.

"Although I guess this is good news. Means more for the rest of you," the sommelier offered with a wink.

"Good point," Anthony added. Then he glanced at Bohai and said, "Mix away" under his breath.

Vivian explained this was the vintage the Chinese had gone apeshit for because Lafite pulled one of the cleverest marketing tricks in modern winemaking history. Lafite embossed the Chinese symbol for eight – '八' – onto the bottle. The fact that 8 or '八' was also a symbol of good luck in Chinese culture meant the bottle instantly became the go-to gift for businessmen looking to start successful corporate relationships or family members bestowing good luck upon one another. The vintage's appearance here meant Bohai was pulling out all the stops to impress Cash.

"Just be aware it's not drunk like wine in the West. We often do a bottoms-up style," Vivian said, motioning as if she were taking a shot of liquor.

Once he saw everyone's wine glass had been filled, Bohai raised his glass in a toast.

"*Gan Bei*!" said Bohai. Then he downed the wine in a few quick gulps.

Everyone followed suit, thoroughly not enjoying the coveted, pricey, and quite rare wine the way the vineyard had intended.

What a waste. Anthony downed his glass in a quick shot.

"Best you drink up, you'll probably enjoy the dinner more. Trust me, you'll understand once the food arrives. In China, we eat everything, and I mean everything, and tonight, you're going to have to eat some things you would never eat just to gain face," Vivian said.

"Like?" Anthony asked.

"Chicken head."

"Chicken head? How on earth do you eat that?"

"You just suck on it for a while."

"Sounds disgusting."

"It is."

A Chinese waitress handed Anthony a menu. He glanced at it and saw nothing but simplified Chinese.

"Don't bother trying to read it. They just offered it to be polite."

Anthony shut the menu and set it on his plate.

Bohai addressed the table and Vivian translated, "Since we're in China, we're going to order one thing that walks, one thing that flies, and one thing that swims. Here, we say, anything that walks, swims, crawls, or flies with its back to heaven is edible."

The table laughed politely at the joke.

"Leaves plenty of room for some pretty weird creatures in between," Anthony whispered on the sly to Vivian, who chuckled and nodded in agreement.

Several waiters entered the room with trays of chilled bottles of Tsing Tao, which they placed around the table. Beer was poured for each guest.

At the head of the table, Bohai turned to Cash and asked in halting English, "How much money do you want to raise?"

"Five hundred million US."

The amount meant little to Bohai, but it shocked Anthony, who had to quickly stifle a "Damn!"

"Twenty percent of that goes toward the construction of the three hundred-million-dollar White Tiger Hotel Casino, which will float in the sea next to Macau. The Norwegian government is picking up the rest of the tab. Everything should be completed by 2022," Vivian translated.

"The Norwegian government wants in on the Chinese casino business?" Anthony whispered to Vivian. "I've heard everything now."

"Why floating?" Vivian translated from Bohai's question.

"Because we can move it if we want to. Economic problems arise in China, we move elsewhere," Cash said.

Bohai vehemently shook his head, then chided Cash with a few short words in Mandarin.

"That won't happen," Vivian translated.

"And big question – is legal?" Bohai asked in halting English.

Cash returned to Mandarin, and Vivian translated that the ICO was a bet on the liberalization of gambling licenses in Macau. The Macau Government would be extending the current six casino licenses after 2022, perhaps even adding a seventh. If Hermes didn't win one of those licenses, it could always tap into the licenses already held by its casino partners. This money raise, however, put them in a very powerful position to win one of those licenses, because as most people know, money talks.

Especially when it's stuffed in briefcases and slipped into a corrupt politician's hand, Anthony thought.

With his index finger, Bohai tapped his cheek repeatedly. His lieutenants joined the conversation, shooting off a few questions in Mandarin. Cash answered them with ease while carrying the relaxed countenance of a salesman who knew he had plenty of buyers for a limited product. His biggest problem, settling on a price that maximized profit.

Vivian again translated the discussion. It soon became clear the questions were small and insignificant. Where the ICO would be registered? What exchanges it would be listed on? How many casinos in Macau were involved? The questions were intelligent, revealing buyers who understood the ins and outs of the crypto world, which wasn't surprising as many in China saw it as a way to circumvent the CCP's strict cross border capital outflow rules.

During the Mandarin question and answer session, the food arrived.

"Dongshan Lamb in coconut milk, which is goat, not lamb," Vivian said as she served Anthony.

He took a bite, then smiled, savoring the creamy taste. "Will we get some fish later that's really beef?"

"No, but we will get some chicken that's Trump."

"How does that work?"

"We call it a Trump chicken," Vivian said while pulling out her phone. She browsed to Baidu and typed in Trump Chicken. Soon an image of a chicken with a helmet of golden hair that was the same color and similarly odd shape as Donald J. Trump's mane popped up. Vivian showed the picture to Anthony. He laughed at the incredible similarity between the two.

"Quite a resemblance."

"It's an endangered species, so don't let anyone know you ate it here, okay?" Vivian said, a cheeky smile playing across her lips.

"A dinner of so many firsts."

At the end of the table, Bohai cut off his chattering lieutenants' questions, then shot Anthony a look, asking, "You think this good investment?"

Caught off-guard, Anthony's heart jumped. The probing look momentarily froze him. However, after a few moments of self-reflection and a sip of water, he answered as matter-of-factly as he could, "Religion, Karl

Marx said, was the opium of the masses, but I think he was wrong. I'd argue sports is. Sports and gambling. And for the record, gambling isn't just a human trait. Studies have shown both pigeons and monkeys love to gamble." He stopped for Vivian to translate his words. As she did, he thought through his next lines.

Bohai's eyes focused on Vivian, nodding on each point.

Once Vivian finished, Anthony continued, "You've got a billion addicted gamblers on this side of the China-Macau border, and you'll never be able to change their behavior no matter how much you try to legislate it. Prohibition never works as America found out when it tried to prohibit liquor. So, why not profit from the Chinese's insatiable desire to make a bet? After all, sports and gambling have been with us forever. The Ancient Greeks loved to play a game of chance. Romans gambled on gladiator fights. Gambling will be with us long after we're all gone, probably even longer than the rule of the CCP," Anthony said.

Vivian's eyes widened in surprise at Anthony's derogatory remark towards the CCP, but she translated his words in a way that was considerably shorter than he thought it would require. After about a sentence, she gave Anthony a nod.

He continued: "I believe it was your Sun Tzu who said, 'Victory comes from finding opportunities in problems.'"

Vivian translated. Bohai mulled over Anthony's words for a few moments, then spoke. "I don't think our greatest general was talking about gambling addiction when he spoke of problems," Vivian said, adding, "But why not profit from the weakness of our fellow comrades, as Sun Tzu says?" He raised his beer in a toast.

Anthony seconded Bohai's raised glass and toasted Vivian with a "*Gan Bei*!"

Everyone in the room joined in the jovial and relieving toast.

As Anthony swallowed the last sip of his beer, a waitress slid a plate containing a chicken head before him.

"They honor you," Vivian deadpanned.

"No need. Really," Anthony said through gritted teeth. He knew he had no choice but to shove the chicken head into his mouth, so he slugged his beer to work up his courage. He had taken Vivian's advice and drunk quite liberally throughout the evening, so he was quite tipsy, but, still, this was gross. Steeling his resolve, he picked up the chicken head and plopped it into his mouth. Unsure of what to do with it, he simply sucked on it for a few moments.

"Mmm, tastes like..." Anthony mumbled, extending the pause for a few seconds to play out the obvious joke, "...chicken."

Uproarious, drunk laughter erupted from the table. Several glasses raised up in another roaring toast. Cash smiled a satisfied smile at him, then raised his glass, adding a cheeky wink as well.

After about twenty seconds, Anthony removed the chicken head from his mouth. He placed it on his napkin and mouthed "Delicious," with a sarcastic eye-roll. He downed several gulps of beer to wash away the lingering briny taste.

"This is the special Trump chicken, by the way," Vivian said.

The sommelier appeared behind Anthony and refilled his glass with a full slug.

Anthony leaned into the sommelier and whispered, "Must be hell to see a Lafite desecrated like this?"

"*Comme planter des fleurs dans du fumier de vache,*" the sommelier muttered.

"Like planting flowers on cow manure," Anthony whispered to Vivian. Both shared a furtive laugh. "I can be your translator, too."

The sommelier nodded cordially, then moved on.

After the dinner plates were removed, the lights dimmed, and a stage in the back of the room came alive. A rumble of percussion and the poke, poke, poke of a snare drum beat out a steady rhythm, while a Chinese

Zither plucked out a few distinct, high-pitched notes.

Vivian leaned into Anthony. "Now, we will have a performance of the ancient Chinese dramatic art of the Sichuan opera. *Changing Faces* or *Bian Lian*. Have you seen it before?"

Anthony shook his head.

Three actors dressed in beautifully embroidered flowing black robes and colorful silk masks that contained exaggerated facial expressions ran onto the stage. A fourth actor who looked like the devil in red entered behind them, carrying a candle in one hand. He stepped to the front of the stage, lifted the candle to his lips, and then exhaled a large flame toward the dinner guests. Although twenty feet away, the fire warmed Anthony's cheeks. It reminded him of a few sets he'd been on that used explosives.

Cash glanced at Vivian and fired off a volley of Cantonese while nodding towards Anthony. Vivian listened in, thinking for a few moments as she interrogated Anthony with a questioning look. Then, she shook her head in disagreement.

After the third comment from Cash, Anthony said, "What's he saying?"

"He's testing out your Chinese name," Vivian said.

Anthony laughed. "Anything sticking?"

"Nothing so far," Vivian said.

"What are they?" Anthony asked.

But the question was lost in a round of rowdy cheers led by Bohai. Glasses clinked in another raucous toast, spilling expensive Maotai and cheap beer all over the carpet and table as laughter lifted into the rafters.

On stage, the actors surrounded each other like jackals circling prey, now and then stepping to the front. With a dramatic hand flourish of their costume and the pulling of a lever somewhere under their garment, the actor's silk mask instantly changed to another mask, red turned to blue, then to yellow. Then white. Black. And back to red. A sweep of a hand and another actor's mask turned from green to blue. A swift turn of the head changed the red mask to white. Anthony watched the show in awe and almost childlike wonder at the instantaneous face changes and magiclike quality of the act.

After a minute of faces changing faster than the eye could see, the devil character stepped forward and exhaled a burst of flames that momentarily lit up the room like a film set, then everything plunged into silent darkness. Raucous drunken applause soon followed.

At the end of the night, Vivian sauntered down the hotel hall, Anthony at her side. His eyes focused on her face as he placed his hand on her back in a non-threatening way. She seemed to approve of the touch with a slight smile.

"Skilled opera stars can change about ten masks in twenty seconds," Vivian said.

"That should be in a film," Anthony said.

Vivian nodded.

"Maybe one of mine," Anthony said.

"Maybe. Are you writing anything now?"

"Researching."

"By the way, one subject you should avoid in China is politics. Way too sensitive. Bohai and his people think the party will last five thousand years."

"A Third Reich to the fifth. God help us all."

Vivian arrived at Anthony's hotel room door, then nodded at it. "You have WeChat?"

"Yes."

WeChat and WhatsApp numbers were exchanged. Anthony moved in for a kiss, but Vivian's slender fingers pushed him away.

"I'm here on work," Vivian said. She took his hand, gave him a quick sterile handshake, then turned 180 degrees and stepped over to the room right across from his.

Anthony entered his room, which had a chic safari vibe to it. When his head landed on the pillow, he quickly drifted off to sleep. Between vague consciousness and an illusory dreamland, visions of Vivian appeared. She approached him, then kissed him, slowly unbuttoning his shirt. She stepped back and removed her cashmere wrap, then her dress. Soon, she was down to only her black cashmere gloves, but he didn't let her take them off. Instead, he took her hands in his, pulled her towards him, and kissed her softly on the lips.

CHAPTER TEN

THE NEXT DAY, after a lie-in and a late lunch, Cash and his entourage checked out of the hotel and left for the airport. On the drive through Hainan, Anthony noticed massive red posters filled with Xi Jinping in a black suit surrounded by images of planes, rockets, and satellites, as well as a long list of quotes in simplified Chinese. Xi's thoughts about the country becoming a leader in artificial intelligence, Cash explained. Xi's headlong push into AI had a sinister edge because Xi wanted to use AI as a powerful surveillance tool that could identify potential dissent in real-time.

"Xi's making himself chairman of everything. Dictator for life," Cash said, narrowing his eyes in displeasure.

Anthony shook his head. "If there's anything the twentieth century taught us, it's dictatorships are bad."

"Not for the dictator. Xi's making himself as powerful as Mao, but creating a lot of enemies, too, so there's hope."

Anthony relented with a nod. "Antagonists never see themselves in a bad light. Always the heroes of their own stories, no matter how many bodies they bury."

"It'll be interesting to watch this play out, but safely, on the other side of the Chinese border," Cash said. "But maybe nowhere is safe. And what's incredibly sad about Xi is his father was one of the architects who helped push the reforms that built Shenzhen and enriched the Guang-dong region enormously. Some say his father deserves more credit than Deng. Instead of pushing to open up China further, Xi embraces the dictator Mao, who once banished his father from the party.”

“Like I said before, talent skips a generation, they say,” Anthony said.

A sad smile crossed Cash’s lips as he nodded in agreement.

An hour later, the Hermes jet was wheels up over the South China Sea, leaving Sanya behind in its contrailed wake.

Once the plane touched down in the SAR, immigration was a breeze. Inspectors met Cash’s entourage on the tarmac and quickly cleared everyone through, even the one with the American passport. As Anthony took his documents back from the immigration officer, he noticed several customs inspectors waving through the plane’s luggage, which had noticeably grown by a few bags. They were placed in the large trunk of the Hermes’s Rolls Royce Silver Shadow.

Fifteen minutes later, Cash dropped Anthony off at One Central. Cash and Anthony climbed out of the car. Cash collected a designer leather duffle bag from the trunk and handed it to Anthony.

“Your next payment,” Cash said.

“Perhaps a wire next time?” Anthony said.

Cash laughed. “Cash is king, I hear.”

Anthony took the offered bag.

“If you’re interested in helping me sell this ICO, let me know. I’ll pay you in coins, could be very lucrative,” Cash said.

“Let me think about it.”

“Don’t take too long. Time is of the essence. We go public in eight weeks.”

“What about Bohai and his team, they in?”

“What you’re holding says yes,” Cash said, pointing at the duffle bag in Anthony’s hand. “You did well.”

“What if I’d screwed up?”

“We lose three potential customers. Bohai gets a chuckle. No big deal. You know how many communist party members there are in China?”

"No idea."

"Ninety million. Plenty of them would be interested in this opportunity, even if Bohai isn't."

"You could have warned me."

"Where's the fun in that? Plus, I didn't want you to be nervous. Sometimes is better to be thrown into the deep end. Now you know what you're made of. You can rise to the occasion, even if that means selling an ICO to a room full of high-ranking CCP members. We all have hidden talents. Maybe yours is selling ICOs to CCP VIPs?"

"Some men are born great salesmen, some men become great salesmen, and some men have great salesmanship thrust upon them."

Cash's brow furrowed in confusion.

"Shakespeare," Anthony explained. "Paraphrased."

"Ah, you literary man," Cash said, climbing into the Rolls, then nodded for the driver to leave. "Just keep selling."

"And writing?"

"And writing, yes."

CHAPTER ELEVEN

ANTHONY GRABBED A late evening flight to Manila to meet up with Cyrus in the Philippine capital. He had a few hours to spare for work but exhaustion from the previous night's entertainment meant sleep consumed him once the plane rolled off the runway and lifted into the sky.

When the plane's wheels skidded across the wet Manila airport tarmac, Anthony awoke. Rain lashed the window. Another steamy summer storm passing over the city gave the lights of Resorts World Manila across from the landing gate an otherworldly glow in the dying twilight.

An American passport meant a quick passthrough immigration into the former U.S. colony. Since he only had a carry-on, Anthony breezed through baggage claim, which was a relief as he was carrying more money in his backpack than he had ever seen in his life. Admittedly, it wasn't that much, a fact that also reminded him how pathetically low his bank balance had been for about as long as he could remember. Even though what he carried was fractionally under the legal limit, he still felt as if he was doing something illegal. He might well have been. That's the thing about laundered money, it's always dirty, no matter how many washing cycles it goes through. Of course, knowing money is from illicit activity and proving it are two completely different things. He had to admit money had both a calming and empowering effect. He could see the allure – it smoothed out life's harsh edges.

Upon entering the arrival hall, a full choral rendition of that joyful Christmas tune "O Come All Ye Faithful" sung by a choir of thirty dancing Catholic parishioners assaulted Anthony's ears. Trying to ignore it, he searched for a familiar face in the thick crowd of Filipino families expectantly waiting for their loved ones. Kids darted about, beaming brightly, barely able to contain their excitement as their aged relatives tried to temper their enthusiasm with sharp Tagalog words delivered in strident, impatient tones. Anthony soon spotted Cyrus at the edge of the crowd, heading his way, smiling ear to ear.

Cyrus approached, pointing at the Philippine tourism department's advertising slogan plastered on the walls above them. "Welcome to Manila. And never forget, it's more fun in the Philippines."

Anthony laughed as he embraced his brother in their usual awkward hug. He motioned toward the choir belting out the final bars of one of his least favorite Christmas carols. "Correct me if I'm wrong but it's October 27th, right?"

"Christmas comes early in the Philippines," Cyrus said, then he glanced down at Anthony's small carry-on luggage. "This all you got?"

"I travel light."

"As do I. Best for quick getaways, right?" Cyrus said, with a cheeky wink and a sly smile playing across his lips.

Anthony laughed.

"Follow me," Cyrus said. He led Anthony through the terminal, up an escalator, and onto the sky bridge connecting the airport to Resorts World Manila, all in splendid, air-conditioned comfort. "You know, this airport has a macabre claim to fame?"

"Yeah?"

"Only airport in the world named after someone murdered on its tarmac."

"Really?"

"Ninoy Aquino. He was killed after his return from exile in the eighties. Marcos warned him not to come, but Aquino insisted. He was walking across the tarmac when a peasant from the provinces shot him in the back of the head. Aquino's death sparked the People's Revolution and ended Marcos's reign of terror. And now there's democracy in the Philippines, however tenuous that might be."

"I kind of remember something about that. But mostly about Imelda and her shoes."

"'The greatest robbery of a government ever committed,' *The Guinness Book of World Records* called it. Amazingly, there seems to be a growing fondness for that corrupt family again."

"How quickly people forget, once the stench of rotting bodies dissipates."

"Don't ever let them tell you crime doesn't pay. You just have to steal big. Like the Marcoses here, the Hos in Macau, the Keswicks in Hong Kong."

"The Trumps in America?"

"U.S. politics we should probably avoid."

At the entrance of the Manila Marriott, Anthony handed his bag to a security guard, who put it through a metal detector. Another security guard scanned the brothers with a metal-detecting wand. Once cleared to pass, the two headed into the lobby, then up to Cyrus's room.

Once in the large, comfortable suite, Anthony handed Cyrus the thick manila envelope that had been burning a hole in his backpack. "That's a signed copy of our shareholder agreement, along with the 65,000 yuan you asked for."

Cyrus placed the envelope into the room safe. "You hungry?"

"Starving. I never eat airplane food."

"I'll introduce you to one of the best restaurants in Manila with some of the freshest seafood you'll ever taste. Can hardly get it any fresher."

After a fifteen minute taxi ride with a soundtrack direct from a '90s A&R station, Anthony and Cyrus arrived at the Hongkong Master Cook restaurant, a one story strip mall on the edge of Manila Bay. The twins jumped out and Cyrus led Anthony into a bustling fish market situated right next to the restaurant. The day's catch of parrotfish, giant prawns, tuna, snapper, and a whole colorful assortment of fish Anthony had never seen filled beds of crushed ice. Tanks filled with crabs, shellfish, scallops, and lobsters demarcated each stall.

Cyrus led the way, smiling at the vendors. "The one place in Asia it doesn't pay to be white, a market. Prices probably just went up twenty-five percent because of our pasty white skin."

Anthony laughed.

"So fresh it doesn't even smell fishy," Cyrus said, sniffing the air. "You buy it here, then take it across the street and they'll cook it for you however you want. Only way to get fish fresher is to sushi it out on the boat."

Cyrus stepped over to a tank filled with large red Cruzan crabs. "Maybe we can have them do it in a Singapore Chilly Crab style way? Memories of youth, right?" Cyrus pointed at the largest crab in the tank. The smiling vendor, an attractive, skinny Filipino woman in her early twenties, pulled it out of the tank and then plopped it onto a scale.

"We'll take ten scallops as well as a squid. And some snapper," Cyrus said, pointing at a large red snapper on a bed of ice. "About half of that."

The fish vendor grabbed the snapper and whipped out a large cleaver. Fish decapitation came in one shift stroke. Then the vendor filleted the fish with the skill of an experienced chef twice her age and a decade of culinary school experience behind their slicing.

Like an itch that just needed to be scratched, Anthony couldn't let something that was troubling him go, "You're not bothered where Cash's money comes from?"

"No, I'm not. And neither should you be," Cyrus said, glancing at Anthony, who was opening his mouth to say something before Cyrus cut him off: "You know, it's easy to be moralistic when you have few responsibilities in life. You have any idea how much Brandon's medical bills cost?"

"You can't help him if you're in jail."

"You worry too much."

"I have to. My life hasn't been nearly as charmed as yours."

"You have considerably fewer financial demands than I do. Some of us don't have the luxury of ensuring every dime we make is as clean as a wire coming in from the Queen's Bank of England checking account."

Anthony sighed. "You're not going to give me another one of those patented Cyrus life lesson lectures, are you? Lectures that are notable only for their naïveté."

Cyrus handed the fishmonger some money, then grabbed the two plastic bags filled with his order. Cyrus gave the fishmonger a sweet smile and a "*Salamat*," the Filipino word for thank you.

"Come back again, we're here every day," the fishmonger said with a sweet, inviting smile. "And every night."

Cyrus winked at her. "Hey, boss, can you help me with something?"

"Name it," the fishmonger said.

"You know the Tagalog translation for conflict of interest?"

The fishmonger thought for a few seconds, her brow furrowed quizzically as she searched for a word or a phrase that might fit, but she couldn't so she shrugged it off. "Not that I know of."

"Thanks," Cyrus said, walking away. He turned to Anthony following beside him. "That's kind of weird, don't you think? Just about everyone around here has a hand out for a handout. Just about everyone you meet here is a corrupt, walking-talking conflict of interest, yet Tagalog lacks words for it."

Cyrus led Anthony out of the fish market, across the way to the HongKong Master Cook restaurant, which was a bustling madhouse of activity. Cyrus muscled his way up to the cashier, handed over his plastic bags filled with seafood, then placed his order by pointing at the Singapore crab dish on the large menu plastered on the wall. Once done, a waiter in his thirties led Cyrus and Anthony to a table on the patio, overlooking the calm waters of Manila Bay.

"You been following what's been going on in the business world lately?" Cyrus asked while settling into a plastic seat.

Anthony sat down across from Cyrus. "Sure, I own a few stocks, so I keep up with CNBC."

"Blue chip companies like Boeing and Wells Fargo turning into cesspits of white-collar criminality. Elite universities selling coveted admission spots to the highest Hollywood bidder. Silicon Valley unicorns, like billion dollar Theranos, turning out to be long cons run by beautiful, blue-eyed sociopaths. And then there are the supervillain corporations, like Facebook, who mine our personal data and sell it to the highest bidder, so they can convince you to buy something you neither need nor want. It's a company as evil as the Tyrell corporation."

"Kudos on the *Blade Runner* reference."

"Guess how many white-collar criminals were convicted in federal court last year?"

"I don't keep up with those kinds of statistics. It's troubling you do, to be quite frank."

"Less than fifty. Today, the criminal justice system doesn't care about the crimes of the rich. The only elites going to jail are the idiotic ones victimizing their fellow elites, like that pharma frat boy fool, Martin Shkreli."

"Your point is?"

"We're in the golden age of impunity."

"Sorry, you can't theorize your way out of this one," Anthony said, chuckling. A wry smile crossed his lips. "You've put a lot of thought into this, haven't you?"

A young Filipino waiter stepped up and placed a couple of beers onto the table. Cyrus and Anthony grabbed the bottles, toasted each other, then drank.

"Yes, I have. You ever heard of the Offshore Alert Conference?" Cyrus asked.

"Not my kind of conference."

"Mine either but hear me out. It's a bi-annual event, held in London and Miami, that's why I know about it. Basically, tax lawyers learn about what the feds are planning to crack down on in the coming years. Imagine a yearly picnic where cops give drug dealers tips on how to hide baggies during pat downs."

"You been?"

"No, but my attorney has, and he told me investigators can crackdown on almost any offshore account if they just have enough time, money, and resources. But that's the problem. They only have enough time, money, and resources for a few cases every year."

"I don't know, I believe there's a moral imperative here."

"Is there? We'll submit our legitimate tax returns at the end of the year. Everything will come out in the wash."

Anthony glanced up at the TV, where a CNN anchor cut to a reporter on the ground in Hong Kong.

"You know, we're working in the most regulated industry in the world," Cyrus said. "As a vendor, Exegesis has been authorized by the New York Gaming Commission to work with the casinos there. That's no small feat. I, personally, had to be approved by the commission, and getting that kind of approval felt like I was getting clearance to work for the CIA. They wanted a breakdown of my assets, my stocks, bonds, options, property I own in any and every country around the world. They wanted everything itemized. Get this, they even wanted to know the value of my wardrobe."

"Your wardrobe?"

"Exactly, the clothes off my back. They also wanted the names and contact details for Cathy's parents."

"Cathy, your ex-wife?"

"Yeah, Cathy, my ex-wife. It's no joke working in this industry. These casinos are regulated like banks, which they kind of are."

"That's obsessive."

"Isn't it? Look, Anthony, you're too sensitive a soul. You need to start being more selfish."

Anthony shot Cyrus a condescending look. "Sometimes I think you've got enough of that for the both of us."

Cyrus shook his head. "Look, don't be so concerned about all of this. It's just the way business is done in China, and they've been doing it this way for thousands of years. Who are we to try to change them? Honestly, you should focus on yourself and your financial situation because let's be frank, it's pretty dire for a man your age."

"Why do you think I moved to Macau?"

Another waiter arrived and dumped a plate full of scallops and the chili crab on the table.

Cyrus breathed in the pungent aromas with a wistful smile. "Brings me back to Singapore circa 1990."

Anthony nodded then picked out a claw and a double jaw lobster cracker. He split open a claw and pulled out the cartilaginous fin-shaped strip in the center, then removed the meat from the base and ate it, smiling at the sweet, savory taste.

Cyrus grabbed a claw, twisted it until it cracked open. "We live in a moral cesspit. Even if you want to rise up out of it, your nose will still be filled with the stench of shit we all have to smell. Plus, you've got it all wrong. Why would a junket operator do anything illegal? They can pretty much print money. Why risk going to jail for what must be a pittance compared to what they make on their baccarat tables every day?"

"Because, apparently, even if they get caught, they don't go to jail."

"Really?" Cyrus said, his eyebrows shooting up in pleasant surprise.

"According to Cash, when the rich get in trouble in China, they don't do time, they just hire a peasant to do it."

Cyrus shook his head and broke into a wide grin. "Oh, shit, that is clever. The inventiveness of the Chinese."

"No moral dilemma there," Anthony deadpanned.

"You see, it's much worse – or better – than I thought."

"You're right, it sure is," Anthony said, with a judging side-eyed glance at his twin.

Cyrus caught Anthony's disparaging look. "Hey, no one said life was fair."

"Nice to hear that from a man who's seen far more than his fair share of luck."

"Hey, I've worked extremely hard for what I have."

"Few would fail in life with all the advantages you've had, Cyrus. Be objective."

"Well, I believe in the saying, the harder you work, the luckier you get."

"Of course, you do, but that's what psychologists call confirmation bias."

"Losers blame their failures on luck."

"Just as winners too often credit their successes on skills they don't possess when pure luck is probably a better reason for it."

"Cathy left me because she said I was on the road too much. Working too hard. I was never there for her."

"Look, calm down, I'm just teasing you," Anthony said in an attempt to placate Cyrus's ego, which he often viewed as fragile as a butterfly's wing. "What you've done is very impressive and that AMEX Centurion card you carry around with you says so. But maybe this is fate. Brandon having this disease and the cost of his medicine is your bad luck. You've scratched and clawed so much for money since you were a kid and now you have a child whom you love more than anything in the world and he costs you a fortune to keep healthy. Maybe Brandon is fate telling you what's important in life?"

Cyrus reflected for a few moments as if the words were hitting home, but then he broke into a wide, shit-eating grin. "Bullshit, it's just my wife's bad genes."

Anthony chuckled. "You said it not me."

"You know that money's probably legit, right? Probably just from some Dongguan factory owner who desperately wants to funnel his hard-earned cash out of China, so he can have a hard-on weekend of fun with his mistress in Macau, or maybe take care of his family and offshore some of his wealth beyond the eyes of the CCP. They're making life pretty difficult for their citizens to get money of out China these days."

"Fifty thousand a year doesn't add up to much, even in twenty-five years."

"Exactly. And look, the great political fight of the twenty-first century is going to be between the U.S. and China, our beloved U.S. The more we do to bleed the CCP financially dry, the better it is for all of us, right, including the Chinese people?"

"So, it's my patriotic duty to take the money?"

"Yes, it's *our* patriotic duty as God-fearing Americans. The more we get out, the less China has to enslave its people. And maybe even ours at the rate they're going."

The world was a complex place. Anthony had always envisioned himself as someone who could successfully navigate the tricky morass of human morality and higher purpose ethics, but perhaps his self-assessment was a bit naïve? Morality takes on a vastly different shade and hue when the green was stacked up high around you, and it could be secreted away sight unseen, no questions asked, then disappeared into a bank account invisible to the prying eyes of America's almighty IRS.

"Well, you'll love this story then. Some of that money came directly from several high-ranking party members in Sanya," Anthony said.

"Really? That is a juicy detail," Cyrus said, an intrigued smile cracking his lips.

"Cash is pitching them a floating casino and a cryptocoin that helps the Chinese get their riches out of the Mainland. Buy my coin, which is tradeable anywhere in the world."

"We need to be a part of that."

"Good, I wanted to discuss this with you."

"Things are changing fast in China right now and not for the better. You need to close some deals quickly. All of these Macau casinos have to be relicensed in a couple of years and there's no guarantee the American casino operators will get their licenses renewed, especially in today's anti-US political environment. If they don't get relicensed, we're frozen out. Smash and grab should be our mentality and our motto. Got it?"

"Smash and grab," Anthony said while nodding. He raised his fist in the motion of political solidarity.

"Remember what I said in L.A. when I asked you to come out here? About the starving artist persona?"

"Sure, it loses its appeal to the opposite sex once a person turns forty?"

"Bingo. Remain a moralist all you want, but, if you do, you should expect life's greatest opportunities to pass you by. And don't forget China's been stealing from us since we let them into the WTO, so why shouldn't we steal a little back?"

CHAPTER TWELVE

DEATH BY POWERPOINT is a phenomenon known to many an executive who struggles to stay awake during a presentation so tedious and lacking in emotional depth that the brain shuts down. Struggling to keep his eyes open at times, Anthony watched the team from his software partner make its listless presentation. Now and then, he glanced at the ten Melco executives pitched around the board room table, seeing vacant stares and flickering eyelids that revealed a level of disinterest that didn't bode well for a potential sale.

Their software partner had made the fatal error of using examples from the finance, manufacturing, and even the oil and gas industry to help explain their highly sophisticated software. These cases meant nothing to the veteran casino executives sitting around the large conference table, who were only interested in knowing how analytics could help increase their casino and hotel revenue.

Anthony wanted to cut in, but he knew it would be inappropriate, so he silently sat through slide after slide, dull anecdote after dull anecdote, bad joke after bad joke while struggling to stay awake. Throughout the presentation, the company's managing director, Honesto Cruz, sat in emotionless silence. Now and then, he smoothed out a crease in his formal barong Tagalog, the long-sleeved, embroidered shirt often many Filipino men don in formal meetings instead of the standard suit and tie of the West. It probably helped with an audience of mostly Filipino executives, but Melco's senior managers were a mixture of people who had cut their teeth in Vegas or Melbourne, or atop a gambling mountain in

Malaysia. Honesto had introduced his team at the beginning of the presentation but had contributed nothing since, which Anthony found odd.

When one person from Honesto's team had referred to slot machines as slotting machines, Anthony realized their vendor partner knew little about the industry. He exchanged a caustic smile with Cyrus.

After fifteen minutes of a limp, non-informative, and straight-up boring presentation, the reins were handed over to Exegesis. Cyrus plugged the wireless presenter into his laptop. His presentation popped up on the 55-inch screen dominating the front of the room, opening up on an image of a baccarat table.

"We're working on what I think is an idea that could help the house legally increase the odds on baccarat. I thought this was something City of Dreams might be interested in hearing about and potentially partnering with us on," Cyrus said.

"Not only would City of Dreams be interested in hearing about something like that, but every casino in the world would be," said the CTO, a tall, handsome Aussie in his sixties, with a warm and engaging smile dancing across his thick lips.

"Baccarat's a game where you want the same amount of people playing both sides of the bet, right?" Cyrus said.

Around the table, all heads nodded. Before the meeting, Cyrus took Anthony to a section of the casino floor filled with what looked like a spaceship. Banks of monitors surrounded an area where five croupiers dealt several games of baccarat at once. Two other croupiers spun the ball into two roulette tables. A scattering of players filled the seats, switching between several gambling games at once. This set-up allowed the casino to speed up play considerably and that was the goal for every casino, get customers in, extract their money, then send them back into the world to find more money they can bring back to the casino, then gamble away. It was a practice that hadn't changed in centuries.

"So, why don't you aim to fill your stadium seating areas with as equitable a ratio of gamblers who play the banker side as well play the player side? I believe if we can get this ratio right, let's call it the golden baccarat ratio, you'll increase your hold. And, most importantly, do it all legally."

The CTO's eyebrows rose. He shot a look at his team that told them to pay close attention to the presentation.

Cyrus pointed at the first slide, the picture of a baccarat table, specifically at the trend indicator, a digital sign above the dealer that tracked which baccarat side had won the previous hand; blue lights for banker, and red for player. "You're currently tracking the trend, right?"

"Have been for years," the CTO said.

"First in the industry to do it, I know. But why not also track a person's unique trend propensity? You could build a segmentation model to break your gamblers into groups of players, those with a high propensity to play banker, those with a high propensity to play player, and everything in between. You can use that data to fill up the stadium seating areas so that everything is equitable, fifty percent banker gamblers, fifty player gamblers. We can create a gambling propensity profile that gets added to a customer record. Easily done if the player is using a patron card, which most people are, right?"

The CTO nodded. "I'd have to check with Williams to see if that can be tracked, but it could easily be added, I'm sure."

"Once you know a player's preference is to play the banker side, you can, theoretically, get him onto a table that contains an abundance of gamblers who like to take the opposite side to equal out the table odds. You can set up baccarat tournaments where you not only invite a fifty-fifty split of players but also have designated seats where they're invited to sit. Incentivize them to take a particular seat that, unknown to them, will even out the table play. We could create a real-time indicator of a table's at that moment split. Any time the ratio gets too out of whack, your hosts can send out mobile offers to the players who would bring your stadium seating area back to odds parity."

"Your software can do this?" the CTO asked.

"We wouldn't be here if it couldn't."

After the meeting, a smiling Cyrus led Anthony across the busy casino floor. "It's amazing, we've been implementing their analytics solutions in this industry for eight years now and they still show their finance examples. I know today's casinos are kind of acting like banks, but please."

"Maybe we should let them know they're called slot machines not slotting machines?" Anthony said.

Cyrus chuckled. "Nah, the dumber they look, the smarter we look in comparision"

"Good point."

"Half the shit they said in there can't be done. There was more fiction in their thirty minute presentation than in most two hour Hollywood movies. We often have to reel back their promises. Let the clients know they're embellishing. They sell, we implement, and they always, always, always overpromise in the sale."

"It's like that Wanamaker quote, 'Half the money I spend on advertising is wasted. I just don't know which half."

Cyrus chuckled. "Exactly. Half the money I spend on IT is wasted; I just don't know which half. And we should keep it that way."

"So, you liked my baccarat idea?"

"I like my baccarat idea."

"I wrote about it in our book."

"You ghostwrote it in *my* book, ergo my idea."

"That the way you going to play it?"

Ignoring the question, Cyrus nodded at the baccarat table. "Talking about baccarat, you ever played it?"

Anthony shook his head.

Cyrus glanced over the baccarat tables on offer. "Don't let the fact Bond played it fool you, it really is rather dull. We'll have to break my Vegas rule, however, never play at a table with a hot, female Asian dealer. They always slaughter me in Blackjack, so I've learned to steer clear."

"Here, you have no other choice."

Cyrus sat down at the baccarat table with the prettiest dealer, a Filipina in her mid-thirties with flowing dark tresses that framed a perfectly symmetrical face filled with Asian features but hints of a mysterious Spanish heritage. He placed a thick wad of pesos on the table before the dealer. "Seeing these dealers, it's clear why the Philippines is the only country in the world that has swept all five of the world's beauty pageants."

"Who knew there were five?" Anthony said, sitting beside his brother.

"Miss Universe, Miss World, something called Miss Superlative, and I don't remember the other two."

The dealer dumped Cyrus' crisp notes into the table dropbox, then handed over a large stack of 1,000 peso chips.

Cyrus slid one chip onto the Banker side. "The goal is to a get as close to nine or an iteration of nine as possible. So, you have one big betting decision to make, banker, player, or tie."

Two cards were dealt facedown for Cyrus. Two for the dealer.

Cyrus slowly lifted the right corner of his top card, bending it to the point where he could see the 'K' for King on the downside face. "The Chinese love to do what's called, squeezing the cards."

"First time I've seen a *gweilo* do it," the dealer said with a sweet smile.

"We can be superstitious, too," Cyrus said.

Cyrus lifted the second card in the same 'squeezing' fashion, soon revealing an eight. "There's a reason for this squeeze, you see. The longer the squeeze, the more likely you'll turn over a good card, so it adds some nice dramatic tension to the gambling process. As a writer, you should appreciate that. The position of the nine on the card is further from the top than a king or a queen, you see?"

"That makes complete nonsense, but superstition is often the victor when pitted against common sense."

"Often? Always."

"So, a king isn't good, but an eight is?"

"Exactly. We're pretty close to a nine. These are good cards."

The dealer flipped over her cards, revealing two eights.

Cyrus threw up his arms in a touchdown signal motion. "We have a winner."

The dealer slid over Cyrus's winnings, which he pocketed. "Money won is twice as sweet as money earned, right?"

"Tis the reason why we gamble," Anthony confirmed, with a beaming smile.

The dealer laid out another hand. Cyrus squeezed the cards, revealing an eight and a seven. The dealer turned over her cards, revealing another losing hand. She paid out the bet. Cyrus took his winnings but again left the initial bet.

Another two cards were dealt. Cyrus squeezed his cards, revealing two jacks. "Oops, wrong game. If only we were playing blackjack."

Anthony nodded.

"Listen, I might need some help with our Singapore entity," Cyrus said.

"What kind of help?"

"Might need you to be a director for me down there, for some corporate governance shit. Need someone local to oversee the operation."

"I'm not exactly local. That's fifteen hundred miles from Macau, although I wouldn't mind moving down there."

"At least you're in the same time zone."

"Sure..." Anthony said, extending the word out, waiting for some kind of financial incentive to be offered in return for this new, higher level of responsibility. But nothing came. Anthony jumped in, "Gonna make it worth my while?"

"It's not much. You gotta sign a few documents, that's all."

Anthony agreed with a reluctant nod. "Sure."

"Another thing, I'm making Jada the majority shareholder of the U.S. company."

Anthony recoiled at the news. He couldn't quite fathom this; what was a part-time real estate agent who had no experience running a software company becoming the majority shareholder of his twin brother's software company?

"Why?" Anthony asked.

"With her as a majority shareholder, we can apply for minority-owned government contracts."

"That makes giving half your company away worthwhile? Can't you just start another company?"

"It's not that easy. We get the longevity factor this way."

"What if she decides to divorce you like Cathy did?"

"Not going to happen. She'd never leave me."

"Love is fickle, my friend, you sure you want to risk banking your company's future on a woman remaining loyal to you for the rest of your life?

"You gotta problem with this?"

Anthony stared into his brother's eyes. "I just thought…" Anthony started but didn't finish.

"Thought what?" Cyrus asked with a genuine look of interest.

"I don't know, I thought I might take a more active role in all of the companies."

"You seem to have your hands full out here."

"Because I'm cleaning up a lot of your messes."

"Look, the twenty percent you got for the Asian operation was pretty generous. Let's revisit this in a year or so, okay?"

"Hey, it's your company, you can do whatever you want with it," Anthony said. This corporate shuffle kneecapped any chance of him rising to a leadership position in the U.S. company; however, he was vaguely suspicious it might even threaten his standing in the Asian one as well.

"We're also worried about something happening to me. You never know. This is a pretty serious operation," Cyrus said

"I know and understand, I'm here for you. Whatever you need."

"I know, and that means a lot to me."

Anthony smiled. "And look at it this way, you obviously don't need two kidneys, and now, if someone kidney punches you, there's a fifty/fifty chance it's not gonna hurt."

♦ CHAPTER THIRTEEN

ANTHONY RETURNED TO Macau on the late afternoon flight from Manila. Once he arrived home, he quickly unpacked and ordered a pizza. He pulled out his phone, connected the Bluetooth to his speaker, and hit play. The jangly guitar strumming of Billy Bragg's folk-punk anthem "Help Save the Youth of America" energized Anthony as he sang along to the lyrics he knew so well. Halfway through the song, a pounding on the front door caught his attention. He turned the music down.

"This is Detective Fonseca. Macau Police, please open up," came a strident, gravelly voice from the other side of the door.

Any thoughts of inordinately quick pizza delivery times disappeared, replaced by foreboding concern, even a hint of fear. Macau wasn't China, but it was still a place as corrupt as any Third World banana republic. One wanted as little contact with law enforcement as possible.

Anthony cracked open the door. "Can I see your badge, please, detective?"

The suit-and-tied detective pushed his way in. Detective Fonseca's eyes scanned the place with the deep attention to detail of, well, of a detective investigating a fresh crime scene. The detective spotted several framed pictures sitting on the bookshelf. He grabbed one of Anthony climbing the red carpet in Cannes with a lithe attractive woman a decade older than him on his arm. "Don't be so concerned, Mr. Anthony. I'm not here to arrest you."

The words did little to ease Anthony's mind, however. He felt awkward, not knowing what to do with his hands so he shoved them into his pockets.

"Would you like a coffee?" Anthony asked, thinking this was what you did when an uninvited detective landed in your house. Be polite and offer refreshments to stay on their good side.

Detective Fonseca ignored the question.

Perhaps refreshments weren't enough. Perhaps only money moved these people. Anthony had plenty of yuan in a safe inside his bedroom, but he knew this wasn't quite the time to start throwing consideration around.

"And I'm not the Hong Kong police. I won't drag you out of your very fine, two-bedroom apartment in one of Macau's finest residencies and toss you in jail," Detective Fonseca said. He nodded towards the verandah and added, "Or throw you off the balcony, as many of my Hong Kong colleagues have been accused of doing to some of those poor, confused protestors."

"Freedom isn't very confusing, detective."

Detective Fonseca offered a fleeting smile, which was more threatening than if he'd muscled into Anthony's face.

"How can I help you, detective?"

"You know a junket operator named Cash Cheang?" asked Detective Fonseca as his eyes scoped out the apartment again.

"Yes, I'm doing some business with him."

"What kind of business?"

"I'm not at liberty to discuss my client work, detective."

Detective Fonseca turned to Anthony and eyed him with a stern look. "You're confused, Mr. Wilson. You're in Macau, you're at liberty to discuss everything because you're here at our grace."

"I need to check with my lawyer," Anthony lied.

"This isn't the United States, Mr. Anthony. Rules are different here. We have no secrets amongst ourselves in Macau."

It was a line that almost brought a guffaw to Anthony's lips. Macau was the exact opposite of transparent; it was riddled with more mysteries than the Vatican library's secret archives. It's why the government didn't allow the data of its casino players to be uploaded to any cloud provider, even Alicloud, a Chinese company now controlled by the CCP. It's why the CEOs of the Macau casinos were threatened with jail time if any of their patron data escaped Macau's porous borders. But Anthony knew he had to play along, so he held his sarcastic tongue. "I'll check with my lawyer and get back to you in the morning, detective."

"Are you familiar with a man named Broken Tooth?"

"The Macau triad boss. Sure, I've heard of him."

"Have you heard of his latest endeavor?"

"I don't keep up with the exploits of former triad bosses, detective."

"Yet you know of him?"

"He's part of Macau lore, isn't he?"

"Macau law?"

"Lore as in Folklore."

"Ah. Sadly, yes. He was a major headache in the past. Today, however, he's involved in something else, an ICO your client is selling."

This was news to Anthony. Cash had implicitly stated Broken Tooth was safely ensconced in Hong Kong, enjoying whatever retirement a former triad member banks up after incarceration. He certainly wasn't in the cryptocurrency business. Or so Anthony had been led to believe.

The detective pulled out two pieces of paper from his inside jacket pocket. A quick once-over revealed they were part of the prospectus for the White Tiger Hotel and Casino, as well as an invitation to a seminar looking for investors. Exegesis was listed as a company involved in the event. Anthony's name and likeness appeared in a list of advisors, which surprised him. He hadn't authorized this.

"The picture was taken from the Internet and crudely slapped on without my consent, detective. I've never seen this before and I certainly didn't give Cash permission to add me to any of his marketing material," Anthony said.

"You mean a liar lied to you? How shocking," said the detective, while leveling Anthony with a harsh glare. "Have you heard of a company called Sky Mining."

Anthony shook his head.

"A man named Le Minh Tam?" Detective Fonseca asked.

"No."

"How about a company named Modern Tech or the cryptocurrencies iFan and Pincoin?"

"I don't know too much about cryptocurrencies."

"Yet Cash has your face and company prominently displayed in his marketing material?"

"Once again, detective, I didn't approve."

Detective Fonseca pulled out a notepad, opened it, then read from it. "Le Minh Tam, the CEO of Sky Mining, disappeared from Vietnam last year with $35 million in investors' capital and assets. The company had promised a profit of forty-eight percent per month. Surprise, surprise, a Ponzi scheme. Unsurprisingly, however, it quickly collapsed. About thirty-two thousand people lost their life savings, including many from Macau."

"What does this have to do with me, detective?"

"Maybe nothing. Maybe everything. You see, Macau has had its own cryptocurrency scandals, some reaching into the highest levels of government. Rather embarrassing for the legislators involved."

"As I said, I didn't okay this, detective. I'll take it up with my client tomorrow."

"You know the saying, 'A fool and his money are easily parted?'"

Anthony nodded.

"Cryptocurrencies seem to bring out both the scammers and the fools. Be neither, Mr. Wilson, is the best advice I can give you if you want to stay safe in Macau," Detective Fonseca said.

"As I said—" started Anthony, but the detective cut him off with a wave of the hand.

"You're new here, aren't you?"

"Been here a few months."

"You're working under a blue card, right?"

Anthony nodded.

"That's a privilege Macau bestows upon people it believes contribute positively to its society. And it can be revoked at any time. For any reason whatsoever."

"As I said—"

Again, Detective Fonseca cut him off: "Have you heard of the term White Monkey?"

Anthony shook his head, but he figured it was probably a racial put-down.

"Look it up, it might help you figure out what's going on here."

"Detective, with all due respect, there are some cryptocurrencies that are legitimate investments."

"Maybe so. But ninety-seven percent of ICOs are now trading below their initial offering price and will probably never go above them. Cryptocurrencies are the perfect instrument for scammers in so many ways. Personally, I'll never understand the idea of using real money to buy fake money from a decentralized Blockchain, then hope my fake money increases in value, but that's just me."

"Every investment carries its own risk. And a lot of people have made a fortune with Bitcoin and Ethereum, which is, I'll agree, a little like gambling, but so is investing in the stock market, if you ask me."

"As an American, I believe you are taught to pursue life, liberty, and happiness," Detective Fonseca said.

"That and money above all else. Like the Chinese."

Detective Fonseca smirked but retained a grave look. "It'd be a shame if something got in the way of those pursuits? Especially that most coveted of all – freedom. But, I guess, you'll have free room and board for a few decades, right? I hear the food isn't that great in our prisons, but our prisoners are inventive. They use the lights to cook a good sausage. Although we are looking at ways to replace those bulbs with greener, less heat emitting ones."

Detective Fonseca handed Anthony his card and stepped towards the door. "Check with your lawyer, Mr. Anthony, and get back to me in the morning."

And with those words of warning, the interrogation was over. Detective Fonseca gave Anthony a quick, opaque smile, offered a curt "good night," and then was gone.

With a shaking hand and a deep sigh, Anthony locked the door. He beelined it to the kitchen and poured himself a vodka, which he chugged down in one gulp. He made another and hurried into the bedroom.

Anthony fired up his laptop while mouthing the term "White monkey." He soon discovered the term wasn't pejorative. Quite the opposite. Many Chinese equate Caucasian faces with business success and felt a touch of internationalism could help drive sales. They used white people to give their products or services a touch of cachet. There is a foreigner-worship mindset in China that is both weird and the complete opposite of racism. Lucrative work was available to Westerners simply because they were white. Anti-racism at its finest.

Had Anthony unknowingly been used to legitimize the cryptocoin? Honestly, he had no idea. He had his suspicions. Perhaps Anthony had been roped in to give Cash's project a sense of international legitimacy? Maybe the banquet in Sanya had been an innocent dinner, but he somehow doubted it. Now there was a smartass detective on his tail and the idea of going down the crypto road was far rockier than he had initially thought, as if the land of crypto wasn't rocky enough to start with. The addition of a detective never bodes well in either fact or fiction. Like the principle of Chekhov's gun, a detective's presence in a narrative usually means arrests for some, prison for others, and death for an unlucky few. It was time to move a little more cautiously, perhaps as carefully as a mine-sweeper navigates through waters laced with bombs.

Another knock at the door caught Anthony by surprise.

"Shit," Anthony said as he stomped over to the door and yanked it open. "Can I help you, detective?"

But the detective was nowhere to be seen. A delivery boy with eyes flitting about in angst lingered in the doorway. The open pizza box revealed a pie missing a slice. The delivery boy flipped the pizza box shut and added a shrug that included a one-handed palm raised to the sky gesture that said, "There was nothing I could do." A few defensive words in Cantonese followed, then some broken English. "Detective say friend. He say you friend."

"No worries," Anthony said with a disarming smile. He reached into his pocket for some cash. "No worries."

CHAPTER FOURTEEN

SITTING IN A Chinese restaurant overlooking the mall at the old Lisboa Hotel, Cash and Anthony watched as a bevy of statuesque Chinese beauties strutted up and down the hall in groups of twos, threes, and fours. Now and then, a Chinese man approached one of the women and offered a hushed price. When propositioned, the women glanced the men over, then did one of three things, accepted his proposal, negotiated for more money, or simply declined the offer outright with an annoyed shaking of the head that said, "Why are you wasting my time?" When terms were agreed, the women led the Johns, or Chens, to the elevator, their high heels clicking loudly on the tiled floor as they departed. In the space of ten minutes, Anthony had seen four pairs couple, then head to the upper floors to get busy getting down.

After their meal, Anthony decided the time was right to confront Cash, so he pulled out Detective Fonseca's ICO flyer and laid it out on the table. "Do you know what this is?"

Cash picked it up, looked it over, then shook his head.

"Why is my name on it?" Anthony asked.

"I have no idea." Cash replaced the flyer on the table, then added, "Look at the quality, I'd never produce something as shoddy as that. Where did you get it?"

"A detective gave it to me. You think he made it?"

"Maybe someone involved on my side got a little carried away?" Cash said with a flurry of hand movements, but a vagueness that seemed to open the door to the possibility he might have some culpability in the flyer's creation. "What does it matter. You want in, right?"

"Possibly."

"What else did the detective want?"

"To give me a history lesson on Macau's cryptocurrency scams. Apparently, some politicians got caught up in one recently, caused a lot of problems in town."

"OneCoin," Cash said, almost spitting out the word in annoyance. "That scam, which wasn't even an ICO, ruins it for the rest of us. When is a cryptocurrency not a cryptocurrency? When it's a Ponzi scheme wrapped inside an ICO."

"OneCoin?"

"They didn't even have a Blockchain. All smoke and mirrors. There were no tradeable coins. Nothing but a long con. The creator and mastermind disappeared with hundreds of millions of dollars a year ago. No one knows where she went. Many of my friends lost tens of thousands of dollars on OneCoin. We're not OneCoin. We're a legitimate block-chained ICO."

"He also mentioned some crypto scams in Vietnam."

"Bohai and his team were very taken with you. They want copies of your book, by the way. They were impressed to see it on Amazon."

Most were, even though it wasn't particularly impressive to sell on Amazon as anyone can self-publish there.

"Must have been my white monkeyness that impressed them," Anthony said. The sarcasm, however, went over Cash's head.

"Your knowledge of Sun Tzu helped. Most just quote the favorites; about knowing yourself and your enemy. You're a natural ICO salesman."

"I hope not."

"Why not?"

"Never saw myself selling ICOs."

"Don't sell yourself short. And we're all salesmen. Or saleswoman," Cash said, nodding towards a thin woman in a black pencil skirt chatting up a potential Chen nearby. An inviting smile played across her full ruby lips while her wandering fingers slid across the man's cheek. "You know, these women pay twenty thousand to be a part of this operation."

"Dollars?" Anthony asked, his brow shooting up in surprise.

Cash nodded. "They use the rooms upstairs at no cost, work when they want."

"But the work."

"Better than doing it in China."

"It's all legal?"

"Prostitution's legal in Macau. But operating a brothel isn't."

"So this place is flouting the law?"

"Who's going to tell? The women?" Cash said in a dismissive tone that almost stated the idea was ludicrous, and it probably was. Any woman ratting out the controlling syndicate would instantly be unwelcomed in Macau and probably in the entire Guangdong region as well. They might even find themselves face down in a ditch with a bullet in the back of their head just to send a message to others who might suffer from loose lips. "What are the police going to do? Crackdown on an operation they're making a fortune on?"

"You involved here?"

"No. One of Stanley Ho's nephews runs the place," Cash said, referencing the former godfather of Macau gambling. At 90, Stanley was now whiling away his days at the Hong Kong Sanatorium & Hospital in Hong Kong's Happy Valley, right next to the famous racetrack where the cream of Hong Kong flocked to gamble every Wednesday night. It was a thoughtful gesture for the family to put him so close to one of his loves, horseracing. The multimillion-dollar donation convinced the hospital administrators that a man should be free to pursue his hobbies into the golden years of his life.

"Macau untouchables," Anthony said.

"Maybe, but maybe not for long. Beijing wants this place shut down, but nephew Ho's ignoring their orders. Not smart, if you ask me. Xi will soon call his bluff. Business is off big time as well. Visits to Macau by CCP officials and wealthy businessmen are scrutinized more than ever. Because of these travel restrictions, Chinese whales cannot come to Macau freely. The junkets have had to adjust."

One of the prostitutes recognized Cash and sashayed over, giving him a sweet and knowing smile. He fired off a volley of Cantonese at her, then turned to Anthony. "You interested?"

"She is beautiful, but I don't pay for sex," Anthony said, giving the woman an apologetic smile.

"I pay for you," Cash offered as nonchalantly as if he were picking up a cheap café tab.

"Very kind, but no thanks," Anthony said, trying to refuse the offer as diplomatically as possible, which wasn't easy as the stunning woman's eyes gave him a provocative once-over. "I have a date tonight, actually."

Cash shrugged. "No problem. They prefer mainlanders anyway. You *gweilos* take too long." He fired off a few words in Cantonese at the woman, who shrugged and sauntered away, flashing a sweet smile over her shoulder at Anthony that said, "Maybe another time?"

Anthony smiled back, enjoying being the center of female attention.

"Same price for service, whether it's five minutes or fifteen or forty-five, as some of the *gweilos* demand," Cash said.

Anthony chuckled to himself, amused at the idea of prostitution as a business comparable to the restaurant business, where turning tables over as quickly as possible was the goal. The quicker the diners or lovers were in and out, the more money passed through the till.

"This date tonight, anyone I know?" Cash asked.

"Yes, actually. Vivian," Anthony said as matter-of-factly as he could.

"So, my matchmaking worked?"

"We'll see."

"Where you taking her?"

"Ristorante Il Teatro."

"Most romantic restaurant in Macau. I know the maître d'," Cash said, pulling out his phone. He scrolled through his contacts, then made a call. It was immediately answered, and Cash fired off a few directives in Cantonese, all the while smiling and eyebrow flashing Anthony. After a few moments, he hung up. "Set for eight-thirty. That work?"

"Perfect."

CHAPTER FIFTEEN

A CYMBAL CRASHED. The five emphatic brass notes of Frank Sinatra's "New York, New York" strutted out of the restaurant's speakers as Performance Lake sprang to life before Anthony and Vivian, who sat at a table perched on a balcony overlooking the lake. Jets fired water twenty meters into the sky, then segued into a perfectly choreographed dance of undulating streams that swayed and strutted to Sinatra's brash and triumphant anthem, mirroring in movements the song's staccato tempo and bold beats. Above it all, Sinatra's voice rang out as if to say New York might be the toughest place to succeed, but succeed there is what I'm gonna do. Ironic since Hollywood was where he truly made it big.

Eyes wide with excitement, Vivian stared in wonder at the dancing water show, then glanced over at Anthony, who broke into the smile of a man whose best-laid romantic plans were just realized. When he'd entered the room, he caught just about every male eye in the place tracking Vivian's saunter through the restaurant; an ego boost if ever there was one.

"It's beautiful," Vivian said, staring out at Performance Lake, an illuminating smile filling her face.

"I hear the food is amazing, too," Anthony said.

"It is," Vivian said, then glanced at Anthony. "Cash gave me your script, by the way, and I read it. It's pretty good, pretty funny. What happened to it?"

What happened to it? Good question. For Anthony, Hollywood proved to be the most frustrating place in the world. After writing seven scripts, attaching directors to each one, and even making a little money selling options on a few of them, Anthony's road in Hollywood led to a decade-long frustration and a bank account as empty as a studio head's soul. Anthony would probably be rich and turning down projects left and right had any one of those projects been produced.

"There's nothing like being gifted at something you can't monetize," he'd often lamented. It was like the gift was a curse. Like the universe was tormenting you – here, see what you can have. You can rub shoulders with the rich, the powerful, and the famous, but at the end of the night, after walking the red carpet, you get to return to your tiny single apartment. You'll dine on instant noodles and drink cheap vodka, just so you can remember how different your life is compared to the truly successful. Anthony fell silent for a few moments. He knew a first date wasn't the time to be too honest about one's failures.

"What happened to it? It never got made, obviously. It's based on a book I optioned, and the rights reverted back to the author a few years ago, so I can't do anything with it now. I can always re-option the book, but it's been around so, in Hollywood's eyes, it's tainted. Like a woman in China who's over thirty, it's unwanted, like a chicken leg."

"So, you know about them?" Vivian asked.

"Such a dichotomy, in a culture where men outnumber women by considerable margins, women over thirty are considered used and unwanted."

"Big problem for us. And you're right, makes no sense. At all."

"I doubt you'll have a chicken leg problem."

Vivian smiled sweetly.

"What about you? What are your dreams and, more importantly, your ambitions?" Anthony asked.

"When I was young, my teacher asked me to write down my top three dreams. My first dream was to marry a rich man. I got slapped. My second dream was to sell offal, cow intestines, because I saw my local street vendors selling offal for twenty dollars a shot and I thought you can get rich this way. I got slapped. For my third dream, I asked my teacher what dream she'd like me to have. I got slapped again."

Anthony laughed, unable to stop himself. For a moment, he was self-conscious about chuckling at her woes, but when he saw her smiling, he knew it was okay to laugh at her story of childhood heartbreak.

"And there, in a nutshell, is the difference between the Chinese and the American cultures. We Americans live in an ethereal dream, filled with crazy conspiracy theories and outright lunacy, while your dreams, which are filled with unabashed honesty and concrete ideas, get slapped out of you. If more Americans were treated the Macau way, we'd probably have a much better society. But talk about destroying a kid's future," said Anthony.

"In Macau back then, we didn't have dreams, we had survival."

"Times have changed. Macau is one of the richest places on earth now."

"It's still dead-end Macau. We were so poor back then, four people lived in a two-bedroom apartment. My parents couldn't even afford one of those red rabbit lanterns during Chinese New Year. I wanted that more than anything."

A waitress arrived and placed an appetizer of smoked salmon in the middle of the table.

"How'd you meet Cash, by the way?" Anthony asked.

Vivian's joviality flickered away momentarily, then she glanced at the dying water show beyond the windows. "I was working as a hostess here, at Wynn. He came in with some customers one night. We started talking. He heard me speak in English, then Portuguese, then Mandarin with his customers, and he took my card, said he might need some help with an English-speaking client."

"How long have you been working for him?"

"A few years now," she said, her voice trailing off. But then she veered the conversation away from Cash. "Let's not talk about me. I want to hear about what it was like working on a film set. I wanted to be an actress once."

"Acting is never a one time in my life passion. It's like writing, you're either bitten by the curse or you're not."

She chuckled. "You know what it means to be an actress in China, even a famous one?"

"What?"

"You're a high end prostitute for the CCP. You'll get rich, but you get tossed between the beds of the high-ranking party members who get excited by seeing your image two stories high on a movie screen. It's a nice notch in their sexual belt, something to brag about at the next KTV night."

"What's a KTV night?"

"Karaoke TV. Singing and dancing. Like a strip club but without the strippers, just a lot of female entertainment."

"What is it about Asians and karaoke?"

"It's ingrained in our culture. Asians like to be loud when they drink. We socialize with our co-workers and Karaoke is popular. We're all closeted entertainers."

"You sing?"

Vivian shook her head.

"The first time I met you, I thought, there's a woman who belongs in front of a camera," Anthony said.

"It's what all men say with every attractive woman. You're so beautiful, I'd like to take pictures of you."

"I didn't say beautiful."

"You don't think I'm beautiful?"

"It takes far more than beauty to make it as an actor. There's a quality stars have that captures the eye and doesn't let it go. I saw that when we first met on the tarmac, and I see it every time I'm around you."

"To be watched, huh?" Vivian said, pronouncing watched like watch-ched.

"Your English is very good except when you speak in the past tense. We usually have a more silent ed at the end of our verbs, while you tag it like it's the English name Ed. The way many people around here do."

"Maybe because I studied in Portugal. When Macau was a Portuguese territory, its citizens had the right to receive free university education there. I got that, along with my EU citizenship."

"Nice."

"Many in Macau did the same. It's one of the reasons why Macau's citizens don't rise up like they do in Hong Kong. Many have a get out of Macau free card – EU citizenship. The ones who don't are mainlanders who came here decades ago. They still show undying loyalty to the party. But they spy on each other and then report back to the CCP. Doesn't make it a great place to live."

After dinner, Anthony invited Vivian back to his place for a nightcap. He had created a playlist of music that would dovetail well with the Rat Pack standards from Performance Lake and Dean Martin's "Sway" played softly in the background as he prepared two glasses of wine in the kitchen.

Vivian perused the living room, glancing at the framed pictures of Anthony's moviemaking days Detective Fonseca had also found so interesting. A tuxedoed Anthony climbing the red carpet in Cannes, not looking out of place amongst the elegant actresses and well-dressed actors and producers around him. In another image, Anthony was pictured on the set of a low budget flick. An actress smiled his way as a gaffer and the director of photography prepared lighting around her.

"I have some Bordeaux, but, sorry, no coke to mix it with," Anthony said in a raised voice from the kitchen.

"Oh, you're missing the best part," Vivian said.

Anthony emerged from the kitchen with two glasses of red wine in hand. He offered one to Vivian. They toasted, then drank.

"That's my co-producer," Anthony said, pointing at the woman in the picture. "She's a member of the academy. She offered to take me to the Oscars once, but I said, 'No thanks, I'll go if they invite me.'"

"You didn't?" Vivian said in shocked disbelief. "I couldn't imagine turning down such an invitation."

"I know, arrogant, but I always thought the best way to fail in Hollywood was to get caught up in all the BS, the parties, the drugs, the pretty people, all the delusions. It's a vacuous place that can quickly suck you dry. Perhaps I had it all wrong, should have gone all-in on the partying."

"We Chinese see entertainment as an important part of business,"

"So, I've seen, but explain 'face' to me and why it's so damn important to you."

"Face is your position and standing in the eyes of others. Face can be like money in the bank, saved up over time, and used to achieve things later on. If you can accomplish something through personal contacts that others can't through normal channels, you have face. A boss praising you gives you face. If you succeed at a difficult task at work – face. However, if you greet others warmly at social events, and are given the cold shoulder, you lose face. Questioning someone's ideas or opinions in a public setting would diminish that person and cause them to lose face."

"So, another word for respect?"

"Yes, but more. You don't want to lose the face of the boss. My friends have told me horror stories about foreign businessmen who had, unknowingly, disrespected a host. They were then served dog or cat or even worse in retaliation."

"They probably deserved it then, arrogant *gweilos*."

"Sometimes giving face to a contact simply means complimenting them, but one always needs to show the proper amount of face to those who feel they deserve it. If not, they will be judged as having bad character."

"Bad character?" Anthony said, moving to kiss her cheek softly. "You don't want a bad character."

"No, you don't," Vivian said, her eyes closing, mouth curling into a smile. "Can wreck potential business deals and ruin relationships."

"Wouldn't want to ruin an important business relationship."

"No, you wouldn't. So, when it comes to face, tread extremely carefully."

"I will," Anthony said, his lips reaching her lips. "Does a beautiful face give you good face?"

"It helps," Vivian said, chuckling. "But we believe that someone's inner character is reflected in their outer appearance. If someone is ugly on the inside, they are probably ugly on the outside, too."

"Some would say that was superficial," Anthony said, his lips moving down her neck. "But great for people as pretty as you."

"And you," she whispered. "In Mandarin, we have a saying, *Yŏuyuán qiānlĭ lái xiānghuì*, Fate brings people together from far apart."

"Far apart is not good," Anthony said pulling back and staring deeply into her eyes. Then he moved in for a kiss, softly at first. Before he knew it, they were tearing at each other's clothes, stumbling towards the bedroom.

A few hours later, his mind hazy from the wine, his eyes drowsy with sleep, Anthony stared at the silvery moonlight dancing across the Pearl River beyond the windows. Lights from the dredging barges creating more Macau flickered as reclamation work continued deep into the night.

Were most Chinese women as easy as Vivian or did the ease with which her clothes slipped off her beautiful body have more to do with an order from Cash than his inherent sex appeal? The thought flickered through Anthony's mind as he drifted off to sleep.

CHAPTER SIXTEEN

FACTORY, UPON FACTORY stretched out as far as the eye could see. Riding shotgun with Cash in his Lamborghini, Anthony watched the nondescript buildings pass endlessly by, hour after hour, mile after mile, song after song. It was an impressive sight, but how many factories housed kids stitching out counterfeit Gucci loafers or phony Burberry handbags twelve hours a day to feed the insatiable demand for cheap fakes in the West and in China?

Johnny Cash's remake of Nine Inch Nails' "Hurt" rumbled out of the speakers, rising to a slow and methodical march as Johnny focused on the pain.

Nice changeup, thought Anthony, although he much preferred the original. But hurt could also be how his wallet felt if Cash's ICO turned out to be a Ponzi scheme, like the ones Detective Fonseca had so pointedly warned him about.

"How was your date, by the way?" Cash asked, glancing at Anthony.

"I don't kiss and tell," Anthony said as a wide smile broke across his face. The dying sunlight glinted off his new designer shades as he caught Cash's inquiring look.

"That smile's a hell of a tell," Cash said.

Anthony laughed, then changed the subject, "Seeing these factories pass by hour after hour makes you understand how China mints a billionaire a week."

"Before the trade war with the U.S., each one of these factories was pumping out products as fast as their lowly paid worker and unpaid assembly line robot could churn out. Now, half of these factories are empty, their machines sitting idle, their factory workers back in the fields."

"You feeling it in Macau?"

Cash shook his head. "The Chinese will give up food and water before they give up gambling."

Anthony laughed. "A lot of wealth here."

"No one in the West understands what's going on here."

"About what?"

"Beijing's establishing new security offices in Hong Kong with their own law enforcement personnel, neither of which comes under Hong Kong's authority. Soon, Hong Kong's judicial system will look just like the kangaroo courts of China. Trust me, Hong Kong's dead after this. It becomes just another Chinese city, like all the rest. What gratitude for a city that once created a quarter of China's GDP? Hong Kong should be a lesson to every civilized nation that wants to do business in China. Engage at your own peril."

"First they came for the capitalists."

Cash shot Anthony a querulous look with eyebrows raised.

"Famous poem about the Nazis," Anthony explained.

Cash nodded. "Hong Kong should be a wake-up call to all who think China is going to evolve into a functioning and functional democracy."

"I don't think anyone's foolish enough to think that now. And we, in America, have our own, self-inflicted political wounds to deal with."

"No kidding, but you can wash away all your electoral sins in the next election. China has no democratic elections. Our sins just fester forever."

"I guess the CCP figures they have no choice. Squash democracy now or run the risk of it metastasizing across the mainland?"

"The saddest part is the mainlanders don't even realize how much better off they'd be with a government like Taiwan's or Hong Kong's that doesn't force its people to live in servitude. Look at Taiwan, their standard of living is five times that of China's. Hong Kong is fighting for the mainlander's freedom, but these idiots don't even realize it." Cash said, pointing at the cars passing by. "'Put a Communist in charge of a desert and eventually you run out of sand,' as the old saying goes."

Anthony laughed.

As the Lamborghini crested a peak, Dongguan appeared below them. A generic-looking city, with only one skyscraper dominating the dreary landscape, and one color shading the palette. A vast wasteland of dull graphite structures surrounded by nondescript factories lay under a charcoal sky peppered with foreboding clouds of swirling black.

"Lenin would be so proud of what China has become," Anthony said with pointed irony. "Communism more ruthlessly capitalistic than even America's cutthroat capitalism."

Cash points to the sky. "Air pollution's still a big problem here. They're even using drones to catch polluters now. Not sure it will do any good though. Corruption's too rampant. Laws too weak. A leopard can't change his spots, after all."

"Ah, but an octopus can."

Cash laughed a deep, throaty laugh. "You're right, an octopus can. Never thought of it that way."

"He can change his spots, his stripes, his colors, as can a chameleon," Anthony said. He wanted to bring the conversation around to the ICO. Anthony spent the previous night researching ICOs and discovered it was a pretty straightforward world. They were just funding instruments using cryptocurrencies, although with a lot more flash and social media pizazz than an Exchange Traded Fund. "So, give me the elevator pitch for White Tiger's cryptocoin."

"White Tiger reduces standard junket commissions rates from five percent to one percent. We're developing a social wallet that holds digital currencies, so players can withdraw fiat currency from a Bitcoin ATM, which are getting more and more common these days if you hadn't noticed."

"I had."

"We'll be providing liquidity on our exchange, as well as listing on multiple crypto sites, like Coinbase, Binance, Kraken. There will be digital exchanges in Hong Kong, maybe Thailand, as well as in a few other places where token owners can cash out."

"Any financial commitments from the casino operators?"

"We're in discussions, but the casinos have to follow stricter rules than the junkets."

"What about online gambling, sports betting, you plan to get into that market? The Macau license comes up in '22. Seems like a lucrative play."

Cash shook his head. "The CCP calls sports betting the opium of the twenty-first century, so I don't think they'll be legalizing it anytime soon, which means we steer clear. At least for now."

Cash turned the car off the highway, onto a busy side street filled with bustling bars, overflowing restaurants, and well-attended hair salons. He parked the car and cut off the engine, silencing the last, longing wail of Johnny Cash's "Hurt." He jumped out of the car and led Anthony to a hotel across the street.

Anthony pulled up the collar of his wool coat to keep the chilly winter wind at bay. He breathed in deep, but immediately regretted it and coughed from the acrid and tinny smell hanging heavy in the air.

"Like breathing soup, right?" Cash said.

Anthony nodded, then followed Cash up the hotel steps.

"You know the one golden rule foreigners must follow when visiting China?" Cash asked.

Anthony shook his head.

"Don't interfere. Ever. You see a man on the street hitting a woman, walk on by. You see a baby lying in the street, walk on by. I know, tough for Westerners, but if you don't and you do get involved, you will be blamed for whatever the Chinese man or Chinese woman wants to blame you for. And you will be arrested and, trust me, you don't want to have anything to do with the Chinese justice system."

"Like Dante's seventh circle of hell, I'm sure."

"And put your phone away. It's worth a month's salary for most of these people around here."

Once Cash entered the hotel, the staff greeted him with warm smiles, then fell in line as he bounded up the steps, heading to the first floor conference room. Meeting rooms lined the well-lit hallway. Cash headed straight into room 20. Anthony followed. Four rows of neatly lined up tables were set before a modest stage that contained large White Tiger ICO posters. Each table included a name tag and a thick white envelope emblazoned with the White Tiger logo.

Cash looked over the place, displeased. Then he left the room, barking orders at the hotel manager and her nervous underlings.

Anthony took his designated seat, then opened his package and read the cover letter, containing an offer of 250,000 White Tiger coins. What that equated to in dollars and cents, he had no idea, but even if each coin was worth ten cents, this was a decent chunk of change.

An hour-and-a-half later, the White Tiger ICO's upper brass, a group of fifteen of the most diverse people Anthony had ever met, filled the seats, staring up at an animated Cash on stage. All had introduced themselves to Anthony before Cash's speech. The group was an odd mixture of tech nerds, sketchy-looking junket operators, rotund and ponytailed Eastern European men, and a few engaging women whose short, insightful discussions with Anthony revealed a knowledge about Crypto more than all the men combined.

On stage, Cash raised the mic to his lips. "Hundreds of high rollers venture to Macau every day to play baccarat and other games of chance in high stakes junket rooms like mine." He proceeded to lay out the case for a cryptocoin that could save the player money. The rolling turnover of about US $250 million a day turned some heads, as did the revelation that when the White Tiger ICO went live, transactional turnover was expected to be around $200 million.

"That'd be bigger than any other ICO in the world," said an impressed Dr. Bouneoues, the director of business development and finance, to Vickyle Delera, the company's chief technology officer, sitting beside Anthony in the front row.

Watching Cash on stage, Anthony recognized the man's innate talent for oration. Although his English was a little rough around the edges, Cash was a naturally gifted speaker, his pacing perfect, his voice rich in life and deep in understanding. Had he been born in America's Deep South and turned to religion as a young man, he might have found his calling in the evangelical ministry. He might very well now be asking his flock of Christians for donations to pay for the ministry's second private jet because a super light plane just wasn't good enough when Jesus really wanted the church to have an ultra-long-range jet that could truly spread the *Word* far and wide, even internationally. And his parishioners, with their cult-like devotion, would fling their hard earned ducats into overflowing collection plates, safe in the knowledge their generous charity greased the wheels for their ultimate ride to heaven and a life of immortality sitting beside their beloved Jesus.

"We will quickly build an international community of White Tiger Coin holders, who will help power the White Tiger eco-system," Cash preached, his voice dropping into baritone territory. "Three hundred and sixty million coins will be sold through the White Tiger coin sale, out of which seventy percent has already been committed. If the White Tiger coin sale continues at this level, and we expect it to, it will become the largest token generation not only of its kind but ever!" Cash paused, opening his arms up to the crowd.

Rapturous applause erupted from the crowd.

This man can sell. Anthony clapped along in the raucous ovation. He caught the multi-level marketing undertone of the talk. I need you to sell this coin for me and, if you do, trust me, there will be lots of coins in it for you. But it was subtle, not too over the top. Cash needed help selling the coin from the people in this room, but if there was one thing that came through from Cash's presentation, it was that this product sold itself. Or maybe Anthony was watching one of the world's greatest salesmen in action. It was hard to tell which one it was, but Anthony knew one thing – he was on board to sell the hell out of this coin.

CHAPTER SEVENTEEN

THREE WEEKS LATER, at the Macau Fintech and Blockchain Summit, Anthony held the White Tiger prospectus open to his official White Paper. Feeling proud of what you've accomplished is easy when your work is wrapped in a glossy brochure that looks as slick and professional as a listed company's stock report. Anthony skimmed through the prospectus and smiled at the first-class presentation.

Around him, the summit teemed with the usual mix of geeks, freaks, and weirdo nerds these events attract. Blockchain, crypto, and DeFi devotees, they called themselves, but abject loser was a fitter description. Mixed amongst them were the statuesque models hired to add a sexiness that would titillate the testosterone-heavy audience. It was like looking at the best and worst phenotypes available to mankind; curvaceous embodiments of exquisite female beauty matched up against bloats of roving male oddity. Potbellied men in stretched-to-the-max Metallica, Atari, or Foo Fighter T-shirts wandered amongst a thick crowd of pencil-necked geeks, sickly-looking techies, and scraggly teenaged boys. The phenotype comparison was not kind to man.

The White Tiger ICO booth dominated the west end of the floor. As Anthony approached, The Charlie Daniels Band's "The Devil Went Down to Georgia" reached its fighting fiddling climax, which brought a smile to his face. The Faustian meaning of the song obliviously lost on the coin's potential buyers, subtext not big in Macau or among the naive crypto crowd. That was one of the things Anthony found amusing about living in Asia, all those lost in translation moments like the Hollywood

Roosevelt's "*Historical Landmark, Opening Soon*," or the "*Thanks for your coming*" signs above the exit of a local grocery store, or even the menu that offered "Gruel" in its selection of breakfast items, not knowing this was anything but a complimentary term for food. The erroneous signs and lost subtext never failed to amuse.

Models of giant white tigers coiled and ready to strike loomed over the booth, giving it the air of a movie set. Floor-to-ceiling LED screens covered the back wall. Slickly produced advertisements for the coin played on a loop, featuring interviews with famous ICO investors, gurus of the Blockchain, attention-seeking junket operators, and photogenic tech evangelists. Several extremely fit techies, muscles bulging through their too-tight White Tiger T-shirts, answered questions from a sizable crowd of potential investors overflowing out of both ends of the booth.

Even at an event brimming with beauties, the three White Tiger girls stood out. An Asian, a Russian, and a Brazilian, all three women towered over six feet tall and had chosen faces and bodies sculpted by the hands of a skilled plastic surgeon rather than the sometimes clumsy paws of God.

Vivian hovered around the booth, translating questions for intrigued Chinese investors. She exchanged a sweet smile with Anthony when he glanced her way.

Sam Slater, a CNBC journalist, lingered by the booth, anxiously checking her watch. A cute American in her early thirties, her tight blue suit captured her washboard stomach and bosomy curves. She saw Anthony approach and hurried over to him, then asked in exasperation, "Where's Cash? We go live in ten."

"He said he'd be here five minutes before the interview. By my calculation, he's still got four minutes."

"Look at this place, it's buyer beware if there ever was buyer beware. Every scammer for himself."

"The difference between this place and Wall Street is, here, every hustler is hiding in plain sight."

Sam shot an impressed glance at the White Tiger booth. "Crypto, the grift that keeps on giving. Amazing how you can take technology that was cutting edge in 1979, add a catchy name and some wonderful buzz-words, then market it as if it's the greatest thing to happen to money since Julius Caesar stamped his visage on a ducat two millennia ago."

"Little different to the music industry, which constantly has to devise new distribution methods to get people to buy that same old song."

"Looks like your coin's getting all the attention. You have no qualms about fleecing ignorant investors?"

"You know what J. Paul Getty said was the secret to success?"

Sam shook her head.

"Rise early, work late, and strike oil."

Sam chuckled. "The third one obviously the most important."

"You're looking at the oil barons of the twenty-first century. They might not be the prettiest bunch of people, but these entrepreneurs have their pulse on today's greatest get rich quick scheme, cryptocoins."

"You might be right, but you might be wrong. You could be looking at this century's tulip bulb mania as well."

"No doubt, but huge fortunes can be made before bubbles go pop."

"All I ask is for the chance to prove that money can't buy me happiness," Sam said, checking her watch. "Two."

Wearing a sparkly white suit that looked like it could have been hand-sewn by the famous country and western costume designer Nudie Cohn, Cash strode down the hallway like a domineering honey badger. Every person he passed noticed his presence with an impressed smile or an angled brow of respect. Embroidered motifs of the American West, lassos, horses, rolled dice, poker cards, and a stack of casino chips, filled the fringe-lined white jacket. A pair of brown cowboy boots completed the head-turning look. Although Cash's immediate audience was an audience of one, Sam, his suit would make a bold impression on the millions of viewers, and thousands of potential investors, watching on CNBC Asia later. Cash was playing to that crowd.

"Talking about timing. Showman's gotta show," Anthony said, nodding toward the approaching Cash.

The furrow on Sam's brow vanished when she saw Cash striding towards her. A knowing smile curved her lips as she clasped her hands in prayer. "Thank you, thank you, thank you, oh booking gods. If this interview doesn't go viral, nothing will."

Cash winked while sliding by Anthony. "Timing's everything, no?"

Anthony nodded. "No Stetson?"

"Fashion's as much about what you say as what you don't."

Anthony nodded.

Cash motioned towards the White Tiger Booth. "Like a movie set, no?"

"Yeah, like something from *Narnia*. It's more cinematic than most booths you see at the Cannes film market or AFM."

"AFM?"

"The American Film Market. You wanna be a producer, you better learn the acronyms and the lingo."

Cash nodded.

Sam introduced herself and then shepherded Cash toward the interview area. The two settled in as a sound technician added lapel mikes. Once done, the off-camera director gave Sam the action signal with a thumbs up and a laughing smile. She quickly introduced Cash, then dove into her questions, "So, tell me about the White Tiger ICO."

"This is the first time the public has been allowed to invest in a junket or become a shareholder of a casino. You're becoming an investor in a junket that utilizes Blockchain technology, getting revenues from the gambler who wants to reduce the high fees junkets normally take for moving money in and out of the casino. You also get the inherent staking opportunities of crypto. I might remind you that no one's ever lost money investing in a casino, except, of course, your president, Donald Trump."

An hour later, it was time for the main event. Anthony settled into one of the last seats available in the main ballroom, beside Vivian in the front row. He looked around and saw the White Tiger C-suite filling the other seats by the edge of the stage, jabbering amongst themselves with excited smiles plastered across their faces. A coin sale could rise or fall on its launch into the world, and this could be a lift-off to the moon moment or a fail-to-launch implosion that meant game, set, and investment, over.

The lights dimmed. Vivian and Anthony turned their attention to the stage. An animated 3-D White Tiger logo roared out from the LED screens covering the back wall.

The instantly recognizable strains of New Order's New Wave masterpiece "Bizarre Love Triangle" blasted from the speakers, assaulting everyone's senses. Its pummeling thirteen-note drum pattern cut through the song's sparkly synth notes. Bernard Summer crooned the first few lines, energizing the crowd in ways few songs can. Many sang along, but the song soon faded into silent expectations.

A deep, visceral, throaty growl roared from the speakers with a threatening clarity that sent shivers through Anthony's spine. If he'd been in the jungle and heard that, he'd know his time was up.

Cash bounded onto the stage as the roar died down, opening his arms to the crowd, which whooped, howled, and squealed in delight. "Welcome to White Tiger."

Behind Cash, the picture of a computer server farm filled the digital wall. "What is the Blockchain? The next generation of the Internet? The most important technology ever invented by man?" Cash paused for effect while glancing at each section of the audience. After a second, he continued: "What is White Tiger? And how do *we* work with the Block-chain? Well, sit tight, and let me introduce you to possibly the best investment you'll ever make. Trust me, your kids, grandkids, and grandkid's grandkids will thank you for being here today."

Muffled shouts directing everyone to "remain calm" rose from outside the room. A few seconds later, the doors flew open.

Anthony's eyes swiveled to the entrance. A stream of Macau cops flooded in, circling the crowd, while a squad of police rushed the stage.

Half the audience jumped to their feet and fled, many covering their faces as they sprinted for the exits. There were probably a few wanted characters in this sketchy mix. Others watched in utter confusion, frozen in their seats, their mouths dropped open in shock, their puzzled eyes staring blankly at the stage. Was this part of the act?

It was like a scene from a hostage drama, the police crashing into the house where the kidnap victim was holed up. However, this time the cops beelined not to some hostage, but to the stage, towards Cash. No guns were drawn, but the rapid-fire Cantonese ordering Cash to turn around sounded like gunfire. An enraged Cash returned volleys of Cantonese cuss words at the approaching policemen.

Several people swarmed the stage as if trying to protect Cash. Vivian jumped up and headed into the fray.

Detective Fonseca strode onto the stage, whipped out his badge, and thrust it into Cash's reddening, rage-filled face.

The Macau cops encircled Cash, blocking all escape routes.

On the wall behind Cash, the PowerPoint continued, reaching mid-presentation, when another tiger appeared and let out a guttural roar that gave the cops onstage a shiver of fright.

Anthony saw Vivian muscle forward, pushing people aside while desperately trying to get to Cash. He followed close behind and caught up with her at the edge of the stage.

As Detective Fonseca read Cash his rights, Vivian turned to Anthony, and translated for him in a shout, "He's under arrest."

"No shit. But why?" Anthony asked.

Vivian broke away to get closer to the stage, struggling to hear the detective's words. She pushed her way through the agitated crowd, who were now turning on the police and booing them.

Moving through the crowd, Anthony caught the detective firing off a few words that sounded like "Bao sa" and the way out-of-place "Dick ball." Or was it, "Chick ball"? Neither made any sense whatsoever. Cantonese wasn't the prettiest language on its best day, it's heavy on tones and the rapid-fire delivery often made it sound more like gunfire aimed to kill rather than language in which to communicate. Even "I love you" can sound like a brutish and short threat.

"What's happening?" Anthony shouted above the rising din.

On stage, Detective Fonseca pulled out a pair of handcuffs and slapped them onto Cash's extended wrists, a move that seemed practiced. Probably not Cash's first arrest. Two policemen flanking Cash stepped forward, grabbed him, and frog-marched him towards the exit.

The shocked crowd slowly dispersed, allowing Vivian to make her way back to Anthony.

Sam thrust a microphone into Anthony's face. "The man sure knows how to make a dramatic entrance. And an even more sensational exit. Any comment on the arrest?"

Annoyed, Anthony shoved the mic away and pushed Sam aside to let Vivian through.

"What the hell does 'Dick ball' mean?" Anthony asked Vivian.

Vivian's face cratered in despair; tears slid down her cheeks. "It's not Dick ball it's *t'sick ball*, which means live streaming, *Mao sa* means murder. Someone working for Cash just live-streamed a murder on WeChat."

CHAPTER EIGHTEEN

AT TEN A.M. the next morning, the Hermes Junket Bentley arrived at One Central to pick up Anthony. The chauffeur drove in silence to the Departamento Policial de Macau, a four story, beige building in the heart of main Macau. Anthony had seen it on TV a few times as this was where those arrested in Macau were taken for booking and charging.

In the backseat, Anthony glimpsed at the copy of The Macao Daily newspaper sitting on the Nappa leather upholstery. It was in traditional Chinese, as good as Greek to him, but a picture of the three arrested men filled the front page. Another of Macau's odd quirks was those detained were forced to wear hoods to hide their identity, but these hoods had oversized ears, which made the fugitives look more like hooded cats than anything else. *The cat burglar,* Anthony had thought whenever he had seen those arrested in the past. It wasn't hard to spot which "cat" was Cash, the hood with ears atop a white fringe-lined Nudie suit made him look absurd.

At ten-thirty, the chauffeur opened the driver's door, stepped over to the passenger side, and flung open the back door. Cash charged out of the police station, hurried across the street, then slipped into the Bentley without acknowledging Anthony. As the Hermes Junket Bentley pulled away, Cash leaned forward and told the driver to stop at the A-Ma Temple.

Cash turned to Anthony while picking up the newspaper. "Come, let's burn some paper. Starting with this!" He slapped the newspaper on the armrest divider between the leather seats.

"Let me translate. Murder in Coloanne Village. Two triad members beat up a gambler who owed them five thousand dollars and they live-streamed the torture on WeChat to the family in Zhuhai. On WeChat! They ended up accidentally murdering the gambler!" Cash said, his face reddening to the color of a beet.

"Who would do something so stupid?" Anthony asked.

"No one who worked for me, that's for sure!" Cash growled, struggling to contain his rage. "I look ridiculous, don't I?"

Anthony glanced down at the picture again. Ridiculous was being kind, but Anthony wasn't about to agree verbally. Silence was the best option now. Let the man vent. Anthony glanced at Cash, who glared out the window.

A few minutes later, the Bentley eased to a stop at the curb before the A-Ma temple, a Buddhist shrine dedicated to the Chinese sea-goddess Mazu, which was shrouded in a slow crawling mist. A smattering of Chinese tourists gathered to take photos and suck up an important part of Macau's illustrious 500-year-old architectural history.

Cash grabbed a thick cashmere overcoat from the seat beside him, slipped it over his wrinkled Nudie suit, then stepped out of the Bentley. Anthony followed, pulling his thick scarf tight around his neck. As they stepped across the beautiful Portuguese stone-tiled pavement laid out before the temple, several onlookers gawked their way. Anthony recognized the ogling from a time he wandered the back alleys of Rimini, looking for Federico Fellini's favorite haunts; on a trip to Italy, with a famous Italian actor who had hired him to write a script years before. At that time, he had found it disconcerting and was amazed at how strangers acted like stuttering imbeciles when confronted by fame in the flesh. Here, however, no one recognized Cash or anyone who recognized the junket operator refused to acknowledge the man who might hold their debts and the two entered the temple as humbly as a pair of celibate monks ascending Mount Athos.

As he walked past the rock wall lining the temple, Anthony noticed engraved inscriptions of poems that recounted the history of Macau etched into the rock. Ignoring them for now, he followed Cash into the Buddhist Pavilion. Cash purchased some joss paper from a monk, then the two men headed into the Prayer Hall.

Cash peeled off several pieces of thin joss paper and tossed them into the small fire pit. "An offering to the Gods."

Plumes of pencil-thin smoke drifted skyward, fusing with the fog in ways that made them indecipherable from each other; heaven and earth entwined.

"The Chinese aspire for social harmony above all else. This was not harmonic. Is that how you say it, harmonic?" Cash asked.

"Yeah, that's how we say it. And, no, this was not harmonic, not harmonic at all," Anthony said.

"So, obviously, the death of a gambler who comes here for a fun day of gambling does little for Macau's harmonic aspirations."

"Not many come here for a fun day of gambling, from what I've seen."

"Maybe so, but they certainly don't come to die."

"True that," Anthony said, mimicking the Portuguese slang he'd often heard in Macau. "But who killed him?"

"Some loan sharks who work out of my junket room, but they don't work for me."

"The police don't know this?"

"Of course, they do, but the gambler was playing in *my* junket room. *My* jurisdiction. One of *my* runners gave him chips, which he immediately gambled away. He wanted more. A triad I work with agreed to a loan, five thousand dollars, which the gambler immediately lost. He was soon escorted out, forced to sign a loan agreement, then the family was contacted. They refused to pay. Doctors in Zhuhai, plenty rich, but they had officially disowned their son years ago, claiming he was a degenerate."

"How do you officially disown a son?"

"You take out an ad in a newspaper in Macau and Zhuhai, let everyone know he's no longer your responsibility."

"You can do that?"

Cash nodded.

"How clinical," Anthony said.

"Yes. And many people do. As you know, gambling is a big problem in China. The family refused to budge. The beatings got harder, but once again, not under my direction. The family was adamant. Like you Americans, right? Don't negotiate with terrorists," Cash joked.

The attempt at humor fell flat as they were discussing a man's murder.

"This is the biggest problem with the gambling business. It ruins lives," Cash said, glancing down at the mainlanders below. "But you tell yourself if they weren't gambling, they'd be drinking themselves to death or shooting up. Or murdering themselves with some other slow-killing poison. Human nature is human nature. Some people just can't handle it."

"We all have our sins, and we all have the freedom to choose."

"And money won is twice as sweet as money earned right, as your brother wrote. That quote explains why we love to gamble, no?"

Anthony nodded.

"In China, family is considered the most important part of an individual's life," Cash said. "For many, their family provides them with a sense of identity and a strong network of support. In this case, obviously, not. It must have been heartbreaking for Heng's parents to disown him. Unlike many parents in your country, Heng was probably an only child."

"But what happened to the triad members who killed him?"

"They turned themselves in before the police arrested me."

"Then why arrest you?"

Cash turned to Anthony, stared at him hard. "Because Beijing wants to send me a message. Macau always wants you to know who's boss. *Always*. They had no reason to arrest me, except to embarrass me. To warn others about working with me. Maybe derail the ICO?" Cash fell silent while staring at the mainlanders below. A mirthful smile cracked his lips. "Ever been to the Bund in Shanghai?"

"Not yet."

"That's the way to answer. Don't say, no, say not yet, keep the opportunity open."

Anthony nodded.

"It's beautiful. You should go some time. But be warned, if you want to take a picture of the magnificent Shanghai skyline at night, the famous photo of the Oriental Pearl Tower on the river, it'll be you with and a hundred thousand of your closest friends. Five to ten people deep along the railings, all night long. That's China. A place where it's impossible to be alone. You know, we say, privacy is the American's love of loneliness."

"Privacy and individualism are ingrained within our culture. We'd go crazy without it."

Cash offered up the last pieces of joss paper. "You want to make an offering to the Gods?"

Anthony shook his head. "No, thanks, I don't speak their language."

"Neither do we. China is a nation of two hundred languages, you think these Gods speak Mandarin, Shanghaiese, or Cantonese? It's probably all grunts to them, like it is to you, but that doesn't stop us from demanding things."

Anthony took the paper and tossed it in the fire. It shriveled up, disappearing into a leaf of black ashes that dissipated into the flickering flames. "Most people don't pray. They just beg."

"True that. You know, this probably makes our book and the ICO more valuable. Loansharking, murder, junket operator gone bad, surely that will entice more potential investors?" Cash said.

"But what if you go to jail?"

"No chance, my alibi's airtight. You were there, right?"

Anthony remained noncommittal, neither agreeing nor disagreeing, his face a blank slate.

"Look, Huang will get a nice funeral, paid for by the junket. We'll wipe out his debt, give something extra to the family," Cash said.

"That's good, make some amends," Anthony said, although it seemed a little too transactional.

"I'll make sure his funeral is well-attended, I'll send some strippers."

"Strippers? At a funeral?" Anthony said, thinking that if there were two words in the English language that didn't belong together it was strippers and funeral, with Mariachis and childbirth a close second.

"It's common in China to have strippers at a funeral."

"It is?"

"Beijing's trying to crack down on the practice, but, yes, it helps with attendance. Extremely common in the provinces."

"Naturally, that would probably increase attendance," Anthony said, concurring with Cash in what was certainly the most ridiculous statement he'd made while arguing with another person.

"A well-attended funeral is an honor to the dead."

But strippers? Cash's intentions might have been good but sending strippers to a funeral seemed sacrilege. Not a good idea in any culture, no matter how ancient. Sure, the logic was sound – want to increase male participation, send in scantily-clad women, but surely the sacrilege wasn't. It was one of those wonderful conundrums China seemed to produce en masse: on the one hand, it made complete sense; on the other hand, utter nonsense. Perhaps that's what you find when your culture's 5,000 years old, a crossroads of the sensible and the ridiculous?

Cash shrugged. "And who said life was fair? Perhaps in death, we can even it up for Heng?"

Anthony agreed with a smirk and a raised eyebrow. "You a religious man, Cash?"

"Not the type of question you ask a man at a temple."

"Even atheists attend funerals out of respect for the dead."

"I believe in fate, the gambling kind and the spiritual kind. You?"

"Heaven for the climate, hell for the company."

Cash chuckled. "Who said that?"

"Twain by way of Machiavelli."

Cash's body stiffened. "Time to think more like him, Machiavelli, that is."

"What do you mean?"

"Time to go on offense," Cash said, then turned to Anthony and looked him square in the eye, slightly abashed. "I haven't been completely honest with you."

"How so?"

"That facial recognition technology you're implementing for me isn't to identify my high rollers for marketing purposes, it's for me to identify the money launderers playing in my casino. This technology gives me evidence of the crimes they've committed. Video footage of people playing with the kind of money they should never have access to. The names, numbers, dates of play, amounts of bets, as well as the wire transfer receipts showing the winnings going into a bank account in the British Virgin Islands, Switzerland, or the Philippines. Footage that would make many a corrupt Chinese politician extremely nervous. These videos and our book are my get-out-of-jail-free card."

The revelation hit Anthony like a bullet. This ventured deep into the blackmailing of foreign officials' territory, something that violated the foreign practices act he'd agreed to defend in writing with his other clients.

"You could be messing with the wrong people here," Anthony said.

"Yeah, well, maybe *they're* messing with the wrong person here," Cash shot right back.

"These are some pretty powerful people, Cash."

"I'm not a lowly baccarat dealer pulling in twenty thousand MOP a month."

"I know that, but—"

Cash raised his finger, then tapped Anthony on the sternum. "'Do not engage an enemy more powerful than you, right?' Sun Tzu. Unless it is unavoidable and you have to engage, then make sure you engage on your terms, not theirs."

Anthony shook his head, his eye flitting about in nervous anxiety.

"These are *my* terms," Cash said. He turned on his heels and marched back to the Bentley.

Anthony exhaled, cursed under his breath, then followed Cash. This wasn't what he signed up for when he agreed to join his brother's company as managing director six months ago, not by a long shot. Things were spiraling out of control and this dramatic turn of events could suck him down a rabbit hole of corruption and greed that dead-ended in a Macau jail or, even worse, a Chinese kangaroo court. Blackmail was now added to the mix. Anthony picked up his pace and noticed a couple of men avert their eyes as Cash strode by. Perhaps there was a loan or two outstanding from these worshipers. Their attempt to ask for heavenly assistance for their all too worldly debts got derailed at the sight of the physical embodiment of their debt, Cash, whose presence was surely a sign from above that their temporal obligations weren't so easily prayed away.

Although this might have been a "How the hell did I get myself into this kind of mess moment?" for most people, that thought never crossed Anthony's mind. Not only was he well aware of how he'd ended up at a historically important temple in Macau, but he also knew he was sitting on a story that might be the one he'd been chasing his entire life.

Slipping into Cash's Bentley, Anthony knew he was in for the wildest ride of his life. Write what you know is great advice, but for too many writers, their experiences prove to be anything but noteworthy, let alone book worthy. What was unfolding before Anthony was anything but boring. Everyone has a book in them, he had once told Cash, and he believed for most people that was where it should stay. However, the story now encircling him could prove to be the answer to his writer's block. If he could safely navigate through what was sure to be some of the craziest events of his life, he might even have one hell of a tale to tell.

CHAPTER NINETEEN

AFTER A 14-HOUR flight from Hong Kong to L.A., then a five-hour flight across the country, Anthony landed in Fort Lauderdale. He waited for Cyrus in the upstairs departure area. When Cyrus's new Porsche 911 pulled up, Anthony threw his large backpack in the tiny back seat, then jumped in.

"Nice car," Anthony said, settling into the passenger seat. "But it makes you look like you're going through a mid-life crisis."

"Mid-life crisis? I had that a decade ago. What do you think the Ducati was for when I turned thirty?" Cyrus said, with a chuckle.

Anthony laughed in a way that said he was being kind rather than truly amused.

Cyrus jumped into the driver's seat. "Finally bought something for myself, after years of busting my ass for the big ball buster and the little chains." Cyrus slid his hands over the steering wheel. "Feels really nice. You want to take her for a spin?"

Anthony shook his head. "I think my license expired."

"Fine," Cyrus said, stomping on the gas. He weaved his way through the few other cars dropping people off in the departures area.

Anthony pulled out an envelope from his backpack and shoved it in the glove compartment.

"Gets easier with each one, doesn't it?" Cyrus said, glancing over at Anthony.

"As long as it's under the legal limit, I'm cool."

Fifteen minutes later, Cyrus's 911 pulled to a stop in the Wilson residence's oversized circular driveway, surrounded by lush lawns and tall privacy hedges. The twins climbed out. Anthony grabbed his backpack and followed Cyrus into the white, bungalow-style house that spread across the large lot.

Anthony noticed the interior of the four bedroom house contained a strong feminine touch.

He pointed at the trim with a sour look on his face. "Pink, really?"

"When you're married, you learn to choose your battles," Cyrus said.

"Like fighting for your company?" Anthony said while cocking an eyebrow.

Cyrus shook his head and rolled his eyes. "You'd understand if you had kids."

"I'm not sure I would, even if I had kids."

"Drop it."

"Drop what?" Anthony asked. A smile broke across his lips, then quickly disappeared.

Cyrus showed Anthony the master suite, proudly pointing out the two custom built, walk-in closets, the dual sinks, the whirlpool tub, and a separate shower.

"Two people can get ready at the same time, a modern marvel. What will they think of next, a separate washer *and* dryer to speed up the laundry chores?" Anthony asked.

As Cyrus and Anthony wandered back into the living room, Cyrus's five-year-old son, Brandon, raced up to them, shrieking in delight, arms flailing about in uncontrolled excitement.

"What'd ya bring me? What'd ya bring me?" Brandon squealed.

Anthony dug into his backpack and pulled out a small remote control car. He handed it to Brandon, who grinned from ear to ear.

"Ask Marta to help you open it," Cyrus said.

Brandon nodded, then darted into the play area, a chaotic mess of upturned toys. Shelving units crammed with books and games of all kinds lined the wall.

"Honestly, does he need any more toys? There isn't room for anything else in there," Anthony said, glancing over the room.

"You know how we Americans are. Too much is just enough," Cyrus said.

"Does he grasp what's going on?"

"As much as a five-year-old can. He'll point to his back and say, 'Daddy's giving me a new kidney.'"

"Nice."

"Indeed, but 'new' is probably overdoing it. Some wine?" Cyrus asked as he stepped towards the bar.

"You sure? You're only a few days away from surgery."

"All the more reason to. One last hurrah, right?"

"I'm a little jetlagged actually."

"I find coming this way harder, so better you stay up late tonight, get a good night's rest, and, by the morning, you'll be back to normal."

"Sure."

Victoria Wilson's distinctively British accent rose from the dining room off the kitchen.

"Mom's here?" Anthony asked.

"Of course, she's reading to Julia probably."

Anthony walked into the dining room, where Cyrus's seven-year-old daughter, Julia, lay on Victoria's lap, her eyelids heavy, trying to hold off sleep.

"Hey, mom," Anthony said, then leaned in to kiss Victoria on the cheek.

When Julia heard Anthony's voice, her eyes popped open. She smiled in delight, wriggled off her grandmother's lap and rushed into her uncle's waiting arms.

"Uncle Anthony," squealed Julia, her face beaming brightly. "Daddy didn't say you were coming."

"Last minute trip," Anthony said.

"Was grandma putting you to sleep there?" Anthony asked with a cheeky smile and a playful side-eye at his mother. Then he added mockingly, "She used to do that all the time when your daddy and I were kids. Those stories were snoozefests."

"Brandon's been keeping her up," Victoria said. A stout woman of seventy-five, Victoria spoke in an English accent that had only grown stronger with age and still projected halfway across a room. It commanded attention everywhere she went, especially in the South, where Americans tended to correlate proper English accents with deep intelligence.

"Has he?" Anthony asked.

Julia nodded excitedly in an exaggerated reply.

"Brandon's been restless these past few nights, probably getting a little anxious," Victoria said. "He's a tough little cookie, but reality's settling in. For them both, I think."

Anthony sat down across from his mother. Julia jumped into his lap.

"It's great what he's doing," Anthony said.

"I'm proud of him," Victoria said.

In the kitchen, Anthony caught sight of Cyrus's wife, Jada, preparing a patatas bravas. This was Jada's kitchen, her domain, and she moved with the efficiency and poise of a professional chef utilizing utensils that seemed to be a part of her fingers. She popped open the European wood cabinetry, grabbed some potatoes, sliced them on the quartz countertop, then pulled out an egg from her high-end Viking sub-zero fridge. Catching the discussion between Anthony and his mother, Jada looked their way and said with an easy nonchalance, "Your kidney's next."

Anthony immediately felt like a piece of meat, or, more accurately, a spare body part that could be cut out and ordered into another person's body at will. Not good, even if that body belonged to a nephew.

This is what you put your head next to every night, Cyrus? My God, don't sleep too soundly, my brother, Anthony thought.

Jada turned around to flip the patatas and Anthony shot his mother a "Can you believe she just said that?" look.

His mother subtly rolled her eyes in agreement.

Anthony stood up, letting Julia slide off his lap. The little girl landed on her feet, then darted into the playroom to join her brother.

"Let's get some wine, Mom," Anthony said.

Victoria rose, then muttered under her breath, "Some people lack more than just basic social skills." Victoria moved with the grace of a dancer while holding the upright dignity of a well-to-do Brit who has flowed well into retirement. She followed Anthony into the living room.

As Anthony approached the small bar area, Cyrus popped the cork off a bottle of Mendoza then poured out three glasses. He handed one each to his mother and brother.

"Gan Bei," Anthony said, as he raised his glass in a toast.

 # CHAPTER TWENTY

IN HOLLYWOOD, THERE'S an old adage that says, "If the scene is about what the scene is about, then you're in deep shit." The point was subtext makes a scene fly off the page. The opposite was happening here. At Exegesis's main office a few miles from Brickell Bay, Cyrus and Jada had informed Anthony that his role at the company was not quite as secure as he'd once thought it was. The shares he'd taken in exchange for a greatly reduced managing director salary were only for the Macau company, not for any of the other entities popping up in Singapore or Australia as well as on the drawing board for future expansion in Asia.

Perhaps Cyrus should have named the company something other than "Exegesis Asia" to ensure there was no misunderstanding? Surely the word Asia implied the company would be working across the entire continent of Asia, i.e., the largest and most populous continent on the planet. From Cyrus's implication, Anthony was only getting twenty percent of a company confined to Macau. All the work he'd done to help build the other Exegesis companies throughout Asia would, at the very least, be worthless to him; at worst, they were direct competitors to his Macau company.

"Call me crazy, but I thought giving up my life in L.A., leaving my job, saying goodbye to friends I had known for over a decade, even breaking up with my girlfriend at the time, then moving halfway around the world to start a completely new career in what was an entirely new industry for me, would have amounted to something. Deserved some reciprocity, maybe? A touch of loyalty," Anthony said, his cheeks reddening in anger and his cadence getting a little high in the register.

"Of course, it amounts to something," Cyrus said in a deep, placating voice.

"The fact that I'm a complete natural at this job would make me think you'd want me to stick around, but apparently not."

"We do want you to stick around, but this expansion has been in the works for years. You're not part of the Indian company, did you expect shares in that?"

"I haven't done anything for the Indian company, so of course not. The Asian company had two worthless employees before I joined twelve months ago. Now it's making some real money."

"We've spent a lot of time and money getting this operation going," Cyrus said.

"Maybe so, but I'm the one who got feet on the ground and, more importantly, I'm the one who did the hard work of, you know, closing deals, deals that actually bring in some real money, to say nothing of the clean-up work I've had to do after you and your team's continual screwups."

Cyrus sighed and shook his head. "You're overvaluing your contribution."

Anthony shot Cyrus a contemptuous look. "And you're undervaluing it. Is that why you gave me shares in the company – because you thought my contributions were worthless?"

"The goal was never to have you move out there for good," Jada said.

"Really, were you planning on hiring someone else? Or was Cyrus supposed to run things from Miami, twelve thousand miles away from all the action? Because if that was your brilliant plan, it was an extremely naïve one," Anthony said, his eyes drilling holes into his brother's eyes.

Cyrus's lowered eyebrows signaled that this was exactly the idea.

"Really?" Anthony said, shaking his head. "Cyrus, what about when you need someone to take a meeting in Manila, Hong Kong, Macau, or

Singapore? Is your one kidney body going to be okay hopping on a plane, crossing continents, going here, there, and everywhere, trying to close numerous deals in multiple countries while you're also running the US company? A company that, if you opened your eyes, you'd realize was a dysfunctional mess?"

"We are hiring consultants in Asia, you know?"

"I know because I'm the one finding them. You know, these are Asian men in their late twenties and early thirties. No disrespect to them because I do have a lot of respect for what they do, but they have very limited selling skills. Jesus, some aren't even presentable. You think you can put them in front of a sixty-year-old American CIO who has three decades of experience running a casino IT department? They'd get fileted. You need people with gravitas, people with greying hair at their temples."

"People like you?" Jada chimed in.

Anthony turned to look at Jada directly. "You could do a hell of a lot worse than me. Especially for what you're paying me. And actually, I've been extraordinarily surprised by how well I've done, thank you very much."

"Sure, you've done a good job, but what I really need is someone who truly understands the technology we're selling," Cyrus said.

"I seem to know enough to make a $400,000 sale in Sydney, a $200,000 sale in Manila, to say nothing of a deal I'm about to close in Macau," Anthony said.

"With a big assist from us out there. We're the ones with the experience to deliver on these projects. You'd be nothing without us," Cyrus said.

The put down surprised Anthony. Perhaps his self-assessment of the job he'd been doing was overinflated, but deep down he knew it wasn't. A normal person walking into the job Anthony had taken would have been overwhelmed, especially since it came with such a dysfunctional main office. Anthony steeled himself, took a deep breath, and glared at his twin, deeply disappointed in him. He couldn't think of a time he was more disappointed not just in his twin but in his fellow man. He felt used and abused. He almost stood up to leave the room, but something kept him there. An understanding that he might not like how things were shaping up now, but perhaps he could prove his worth over the next few months and get Cyrus to see the necessity and value of having him lead the entire Asia operation. And agreeing to pay for that privilege in money and/or in shares of every entity Cyrus had in Asia, not just the rapidly depreciating Macau one.

Anthony rose from the table. "Cyrus, why don't you and I have a chat?" He headed to the door, adding with venom, "In private."

♦ CHAPTER TWENTY-ONE

THE TWINS JUMPED into Cyrus's 911 and headed to South Beach. They drove up Collins Avenue in silence for about ten minutes. The Fontainebleau Miami Beach passed on the left. Although it was one of the most historically and architecturally significant hotels on Miami Beach, Anthony mostly remembered it for its role in *Goldfinger*. There, Bond met the woman who would later die of skin suffocation after being painted in the film's titular color. Macau also had a connection to that movie; Ian Fleming had spent some time in Macau and heard about a man who enriched himself by trading gold at a time when it was illegal to sell the precious metal anywhere else in the world. *Another dubiously made Macau fortune*, Anthony thought, but he'd keep the story to himself, for now. This wasn't the time to discuss Bond trivia.

Anthony stared out at the passing white sand beaches in stoic silence. There was also the option of finding other work. If anything, these past twelve months had taught him the growing value of his newfound skills. Software was a thriving industry and anyone able to navigate the Asian market should be a hugely valuable resource. Cyrus and Jada might not be willing to pay Anthony what he knew he was worth, but others surely would be. "Pay people what they're worth or they'll pay themselves," was one of Anthony's favorite work related quotes. He knew he had proved his worth, even if Cyrus didn't want to recognize it. Perhaps other motivations drove Cyrus's actions? As children, Cyrus had always lived in Anthony's shadow. Maybe Anthony was encroaching too much into territory Cyrus considered his domain? Perhaps deeper psychological motivations were at play here.

Then there was the Cash issue. Packing up and leaving Macau was not the smart thing to do. Anthony had too many pokers in the fire. Too many interesting financial opportunities to pursue. To say nothing of the beautiful Vivian, whom he desperately wanted to see again, especially after this ambush, with his ego taking hits from all sides.

Cyrus turned onto Collins Avenue and pulled into the parking lot of Tequiztlan, a Mexican restaurant a block from Cyrus's old condo, the place where Anthony had lived for twelve months while helping Cyrus get through his divorce. Cyrus cut the engine. The twins climbed out of the Porsche, entered the restaurant, and grabbed two seats at the bar.

"Thanks for ambushing me back there," Anthony said, while settling onto a barstool.

Cyrus exhaled in loud, impatient annoyance. "Look, before you get all ornery on me, there are certain things I can't tell you right now, but trust me, you'll be taken care of."

"It's not *you* taking care of me I'm worried about. It's your wife screwing me out of what I believe is rightfully mine. You need to stand up to Jada and do what's best for yourself and the others who took care of you before she was around."

"You mean what's best for you?"

"This isn't solely about me. I've lived on the cheap all my life to ensure I don't get caught up in this kind of BS. And I gave up a lot to move to Asia and head up *our* company there."

"You can be a real shit, you know?"

"Yeah, when someone treats me like excrement they can flush away with the flick of a wrist, I tend to be a real shit. All other times, I'm the most loyal friend and brother and twin you could ever have. You know, you can call me up, ask me to uproot my life and move three thousand miles across country to help you get through a divorce. I believe most people would value that kind of loyalty. You, weirdly, don't. Just my luck I get an asshole not just as a brother but as a frigging twin."

Cyrus shot daggers at Anthony.

"Look, Cyrus, I just want what's best for you," Anthony said. "Remember with your mortgage company, when you refused to give me shares, and you said, and I quote, 'Do you want me to put you in my will?'"

Cyrus didn't respond, his eyes flitting about, cheeks blushing.

"How idiotic is that?" Anthony said. "You're five minutes older than me. Admittedly, your diet's a lot less healthy than mine and you'll probably die before I do, but what kind of person asks his twin brother to do work for him in this life, with the expectation of paying him off in the next one?"

"Maybe it was a mistake sending you out there," Cyrus said.

"The contracts I've closed, the consultants I've found, and the money flowing into the company coffers beg to differ. Many people would be desperate to lock me down to a long term deal. You, oddly, have me in one and want to squirrel out of it. I can't make heads or tails of this."

"What gratitude you show for all I've done for you."

"What gratitude you show for all I've done for you. You had two people working in Asia before I moved out there, one got fired because his training sucked and the other is a Chinese woman I've spoken to once, someone who's been completely useless at her job, to be quite frank."

"Look, I might be selling the company."

"What?"

"You have to trust me on this, I'll take care of you and explain everything later. Right now, I'm under a non-disclosure agreement and I can't reveal anything else. I shouldn't be letting you know about this."

"I'm a partner in the business."

"Not the U.S. one."

"When can you tell me?"

"Things are moving quickly now, maybe in a few weeks. A couple of months, tops. In the meantime, I need you to close more deals. You have to trust me on this. I'm your twin brother, I'm not going to screw you over."

Anthony looked into his brother's eyes, then glanced down at the middle finger on his right hand. When the boys were ten, Cyrus had dropped a grate on that finger, almost slicing the top off. Luckily, doctors had stitched it back on and Anthony's finger had healed back close to a normal, but Anthony had thirty other stitch marks across his body because of his twin's childhood rambunctious stupidity. Of course, Anthony forgave his twin for the scars left over from that childhood ignorance, but he wouldn't have any forgiveness if he got screwed out of what he believed was rightfully his share of the company now. "Don't let her screw me over."

"Of course, I won't. You're my twin, you know I'll take care of you. I promise," Cyrus said.

The promises were adding up, but Anthony was feeling less and less confident Cyrus would honor any of them.

♦ CHAPTER TWENTY-TWO

ANTHONY CAUGHT A flight to Los Angeles, hoping a return to home territory would prove less dramatic. However, it wasn't to be so. Staring at the faux Chinese Cultural Revolution posters dominating the wall behind his agent's long and immaculate glass desk blemished only by a stack of his unproduced scripts, he understood the symbolism.

Anthony hadn't spoken to his agent, Heidi Wu, in months. The move to Macau had happened so suddenly he'd barely had time to say goodbye. Now he sat before her, the slate of failed scripts towering over the table like a monument to his screenwriting impotence. He hoped the memories of their once torrid affair would temper any sense she had of jettisoning him. However, if separation was on the agenda, he was ready. Plan B awaited in the wings. Sun Tzu once said, "Victorious warriors win first and then go to war, while defeated warriors go to war first and then seek to win." Anthony might be a wounded soldier on a few professional fronts right now, but he had already won this upcoming battle many times in his head.

A well put together Chinese American woman in her early thirties, Heidi Wu, unlike most Asians, hadn't aged well. Dark circles under her eyes, leathery skin stretched tight across low, and hollow cheekbones gave her a sallow look. However, her striking black and white striped, three-piece power ensemble balanced everything out. She cut an imposing figure. An impatient squint filled her dark eyes as she stared at Anthony lounging in the white Barcelona chair before her.

Heidi's hand came down on the tall stack of Anthony's unproduced scripts like a judge's gavel pounding out a harsh judgment on the bench. "You write scripts that would have worked in the early 2000s, Anthony, not 2019."

"What can I say, I was ahead of my time," Anthony said, a playful smile dancing across his lips. But her criticism was spot-on and stinging, although he wasn't about to show her missives were hitting their mark.

For a few seconds, Anthony took the metaphorical slings and arrows of disparaging comments with unaccustomed unprofessionalism and quibbled on each and every salient point she made; the characters were too old, the settings too commonplace, genres too tired or even dead. Above all else, the scripts lacked a certain "Je ne sais quoi," explained Heidi in bastardized French.

"That's a wonderful term so many non-French speaking people use to add panache to a sentence when what they really mean is they have no idea what they mean," Anthony said.

Heidi shot Anthony a squint of annoyance. "Lionsgate rejected *Sunday* because the characters were too old. *Jukebox* is set in World War Two. No one does World War Two anymore."

"Clooney just did a remake of *Catch 22* for Amazon."

"Clooney makes everything hot. Attach Clooney and I'll sell any one of your scripts in a heartbeat."

Anthony nodded acceptance of Heidi's take.

"*Sunday's* too clever for today's audience. As is *Scavenger Reef*," Heidi said.

"A murder mystery without a murder, are you kidding me? That's marketing gold. Any agent worth her salt could sell that script and every one of my other scripts. What about *Machiavelli*?"

"Period pieces only work if there's a supernatural element to them, like *Game of Thrones*."

"*Gypsy Hearts*?"

"You still own the underlying rights to that book?"

"They expired last month, but no one really checks those things, do they?"

Heidi shrugged and added a contrite warning, "Knowing your luck, they would. You'd get a bite. Someone would contact the novelist; discover they could nab the book out from under you and screw you out of the deal."

"Screw *us* out of the deal," Anthony said, a slight pleading in his voice. He wanted solidarity, a verbal commitment they were still a team fighting the good fight against "the man," whoever the man happened to be in the entertainment industry these days.

Heidi remained stoically silent, noncommittal.

Anthony's eyes locked onto Heidi's. "*Us*, Heidi."

But she was unmoved.

Anthony motioned towards the ironic Commie propaganda posters on the wall above her. "Entertainers of the world, unite."

Heidi, however, avoided his probing gaze.

Uncomfortable silence passed between the two, until Heidi broke the tension with those four simple words that contain more meaning than the entire exegesis of the King James *Bible*, "We need to talk." It's a statement always received with the three-plus-one hammer blow of Beethoven's 5th Symphony. Da-da-da-Dum: We-need-to-Taaalk! The most dreaded phrase in a relationship.

For Anthony, the unmistakable meaning of those four simple words so synonymous with four other words of finality, "This. Relationship. Is. Over." He bolted out of his chair and hurried over to Heidi's desk. His brow furrowed in deep consternation; his mouth dropped open in complete surprise. The words of so many others tossed aside before him tumbled out, "You're dumping me?"

An ironic smile danced across Heidi's full lips. "Weren't you the one who told me writers were supposed to change their agents once a year?"

Her swift parry succeeded, disarming Anthony, momentarily confusing and confounding him. However, the pause was brief as the perfect riposte came to his lips, "Yeah, writers change their agents, agents don't change their writers. You see, you're supposed to need us a hell of a lot more than we need you because you don't do anything unless we do the work first. We're supposed to hold all the power in this relationship."

"I'm very well aware of the flawed impression you have of my chosen career, but sometimes, through no fault of either party, things just don't work out."

"But why?"

"What do you want me to say, your diction's too small? It's you, not me? We're just incompatible on a literary plane?'"

"This is no time for jokes. Just tell me the truth."

"I did, remember, your writing's dated. I can't sell it in today's market."

"Good stories are like well tailored suits. They transcend time."

"Not. Always. There has to be an audience for them and it's hard to crack the Marvel superhero universe these days with a story of aging pols. No one's buying intelligent stuff anymore."

"Like they ever did."

"We had a few good decades."

"Decades ago."

Heidi nodded. "Look, you've got great potential, Anthony. You're one of the best writers I rep, but office rent, food bills, and expensive vacations to Siem Reap don't get paid on potential."

"Nice to see you've got your priorities in order."

"Ever been to Siem Reap? It's really a life-changing yoga retreat."

"Heidi, I've had eight directors attached to seven different scripts."

"And not one of those scripts got made. That's a huge and telling problem."

"Can't you get me a paid gig?"

"Don't think I haven't tried. The problem is you're one of thirty writers I represent. Whenever gigs come up, producers want writers with credits, which you don't have. I can't lie about that."

"Why not? You're an agent, lying should be second nature to you."

"Be nice, Anthony, we have a long history together and, while you're the only writer I rep who's seen me naked, don't cross the line. You're in Rubicon territory."

"My bad."

"Apology accepted."

"That wasn't an apology."

"Was to me. And that's all that matters."

Anthony shrugged.

"Have you ever thought that maybe you're just not cut out for this business? No shame in that. Most fail," Heidi said, then glanced over at her assistant, a handsome young man in his early twenties, who appeared in the office doorway.

Anthony knew what this intrusion meant. Heidi had choreographed it beforehand to try to cut their meeting short. Anthony shot Heidi an irritated glare. "Really, you're giving me the harried assistant at the door sendoff routine?"

Heidi shrugged, a wry smile breaking across her lips.

Anthony waved the young assistant away. "After all we've been through, this meeting's not over yet."

Heidi nodded to the assistant to retreat. He complied. Heidi turned to Anthony, giving him an overly expressive wave of the hand to signal he had the floor.

"I come to bury the hatchet not to raise it," Anthony said.

Heidi smiled. "Speak, Mark Anthony."

"I might actually need your help negotiating a contract. Free money for you."

"More Siem Reap fun in the sun vacations for me. I like that," Heidi said, a widening grin spreading across her face.

"What would you say if I told you I've been hired to write the biography of a Macau junket operator who was just falsely accused of murder and he's willing to name the names of the CCP members who are using his casino junket room to launder millions of dollars out of China? Kind of like a Chinese version of the Panama Papers."

"I'd say you've got my full attention. Story."

"A gambler took out a loan in this guy's junket room and was accidentally tortured to death because his family refused to pay the ransom. Live on WeChat, by the way, so there's a nice social media angle for you Hollywood jackals."

"How do you know your junket operator's not guilty?"

"Two men have already confessed to the crime."

"And how do you know this guy?"

"We're implementing some facial recognition technology in his junket room."

Heidi mulled over the idea as she stared at Anthony for a few moments.

"Timely as hell with the Hong Kong protests all over the news. The *Umbrella Revolution*," Anthony said, teasing out the last two words. "As irrelevant as my other work might be, this is about as timely as it gets. CNN is camped out in Central, live streaming protestors getting their heads cracked every day. A direct line runs from these HKU students to those murdered in Tiananmen Square three decades ago."

A knowing smile cracked Heidi's lips. "This was all Kabuki theater, wasn't it?"

"What do you mean?" Anthony said in as innocent a tone as he could muster.

"You were holding back on me. You knew I'd complain about the lack of relevance in your scripts when you had a story ripped from the headlines, as they say, in your back pocket?"

"It's a common complaint you have."

"Because it's a relevant complaint."

"What do you say?"

Heidi stuck out her hand. "I'd say, congratulations, you still have representation."

"You know, shortly after the Academy Award winning screenwriter Joseph Mankiewicz arrived in L.A., he sent a telegram to a journalist friend in New York saying, 'Millions are to be made out here and your only competition is idiots. Don't let this get around.' Times haven't changed much since then, have they?"

"No, not much, not much at all."

"Present company excluded, of course."

"But, of course."

CHAPTER TWENTY-THREE

Anthony flew back to Hong Kong, then grabbed the ferry to Macau. Several days later, it was time to show Cash the A.I. work they'd done. Simon had completed the first phase of the work and was ready to reveal it.

Anthony pushed open the twelve-foot tall, wooden entrance doors, then entered Galaxy Macau's cavernous foyer, with Simon shuffling along at his side. A towering Thai lady greeted them with a warm smile and a hand-touch to the heart.

Mainland tourists filled the place, snapping pictures of a dazzling show of light, sound, and water, which included a massive diamond rising out of a cloud of smoke in the center of the lobby. Several half-filled cafés and restaurants lined the foyer. The casino floor spread out beyond, not quite stretching out as far as the eye could see, but this was the largest casino floor in the world and a wall of smoked glass separated it from the lobby to block the view. Above all else, the Asian gambler wanted privacy when betting.

An old and worn backpack hung from Simon's shoulder. It almost fell off when he subtly rubbed his crotch.

"Really? Riding bareback with a Macau hooker?" Anthony asked while shaking his head.

"It's not my fault, man. The condom broke," Simon said in his lazy, drawn-out, Southern drawl. "I gotta see a doctor ASAP."

"You didn't buy the condom here, did you?"

"Course, I did."

"Jesus, you can't do that. The XLs here are mediums in the US. Of course, it frigging broke."

Sensing someone watching him, Anthony scanned the lobby. He soon spotted Detective Fonseca sitting in a cafe across from the Hermes Junket Room. Detective Fonseca gave Anthony a curt nod and a raised espresso cup as an acknowledgment, then his eyes dropped to the newspaper spread across his table.

Anthony ignored the detective and led Simon into the Hermes Junket Room. Designed in a minimalist style, the room looked like something from the mind of Philippe Starck with a full-on Asian twist. Classy décor filled the place, a blunt contrast to the usual junket room's mishmash of nouveau-riche ostentatiousness, bold crassness, and profound obnoxiousness that would have fit right at home in the court of Louis XVI. The Hermes Junket operation wooed a more sophisticated set, aiming for high rollers who preferred their gambling in an unconventional setting that was quietly theatrical yet contained a touch of the subversive.

Two white jade horse statues guarded the entrance. Jade is the stone of luck for the Chinese, while horses are coveted symbols of faithfulness, speed, nobility, and strength; all, paradoxically, the opposite qualities typical junket operators prefer in their gamblers, but fronts and façades have their place in Macau, too. A giant aquarium filled with bright reef fish covered the back wall, its soft reflected light spilling across the plush ivory carpets, bringing calm and serenity to the room. This was exactly what Anthony needed to temper his rising anger as he strode over the room's thickly padded carpet.

"Let's get this done as quickly as possible, please," Simon said.

Anthony spotted Cash approaching and pasted on a friendly smile. "Get ready to show him what you've done."

Anthony and Cash shook hands.

"Let's go to my office," Cash said, then led the two men into a spacious back room overlooking Galaxy's skytop pool. Its white sand beach extended across the integrated resort's grounds, complete with a volley-ball court and four rows of deck chairs.

Simon whipped out his laptop, booted it up in seconds, connected it to the A/V line, and then navigated to a file containing two hundred faceprints. He pulled up the first one. The image contained the face of a young Asian man with the feminine features of a K-Pop star sitting at one of the Hermes junket room tables. Key points across the face described the picture's match accuracy, 97.8%.

"So, I've culled through your junket room video and created faceprints of your players going back the past six months, which is, of course, hundreds of players. I've compared these faceprints against your player cards and developed a decent training set."

"Those people I don't care about, we have their information already," Cash said.

"I know. So, I've compared the anonymous faceprints against Google Images to try to undercover these mystery players. And this is what I found." Simon said while clicking on a folder, which opened and revealed over a hundred faceprints. He clicked on the first file. "They're in ranking order, starting with the ones we're most confident about. Humans have a match accuracy rate of about 97.5%, so this is slightly better. Now, I don't read Chinese, so I don't know how you say his name, but do you recognize this man?"

A gratified smile broke across Cash's face. "Yes. I know him well."

"The ID set is a little thin, so I cross referenced all pictures with Google Images and a few people popped up, celebrities mostly. And this guy." Simon flipped to the second file, an image of an overweight, balding man in his sixties squashed in his seat at a baccarat table. The accuracy match, 95.5%.

"Hu Xianan, was one of my best clients," Cash said.

"Was?" Anthony asked.

"He won't be gambling much with us anymore. He was the former deputy Communist Party chief in Shenzhen, the third highest-ranking official in the city. He tried to launder $144 million out of China six months ago, offering a fifty percent cut to anyone who helped him get his money to the West. Unfortunately for him, no takers. Last month, he was arrested and charged with seriously violating party discipline, the CCP's euphemism for corruption."

Anthony shook his head. "Astonishing amount of money."

"The apartment containing his money had a view of the Hong Kong border. He was that close. Can you imagine what it must feel like to have more money than you can ever spend in your lifetime, be willing to give half of it away just to get it over a border that was a few thousand meters from where you lived? Now, he'll spend the rest of his life in jail. Maybe gamble on fighting crickets with his fellow inmates for cigarettes, if he has enough to bribe the guards?"

"Nice retirement."

"Could have been worse. Could have been executed, as many others convicted of similar crimes have been. Like the old saying goes, 'If the Party executes every official for corruption, it will overdo it a little; but if the Party executes every other official, it can't go wrong.'"

Simon's eyes flicked between the two impatiently. He jumped in, "Things get a little thin after this, you really need a better ID set." He clicked through several images without much of a pause between them.

"Where can we get that?" Anthony asked.

Simon shrugged. "In the US, you could use Clearview AI but, in China, I have no idea. Knowing China, though, there's gotta be a Clearview clone. Or you could go straight to the source, the police."

Anthony glanced at Cash. "That possible?"

"Everything's possible in China for the right price," Cash said.

For the next ten minutes, Simon squirmed in his seat as he pulled up image after image of gamblers, money launderers, and gambling fools, the matching accuracy lowering from 95.5% all the way down to 15.7% on the last frame. As Simon whipped through the last twenty images, Cash had little time to put a name to a face, but it was clear he didn't recognize anyone.

"I've uploaded a copy to the shared drive," Simon said.

"Impressive work," Cash said, beaming brightly.

Simon slapped his computer shut and packed it away in his bag. He looked between Cash and Anthony, a sheepish smile breaking across his face. "Shall we go?"

"Let's grab a coffee," Cash said.

Simon's eyes popped open wide. He shot Anthony a desperate look, begging for the offer to be rejected.

"That'd be great," Anthony said, ignoring Simon's impatient glare.

Cash led the two from his office towards the junket room.

"Trust me, you'll love this coffee," Anthony said, with an acerbic smile. "They have a Van Der Westen Speedster. It produces some of the finest coffee in the world. Civet beans that come out of the ass of civet that is indigenous to Indonesia. The civet eats the bean, digests them, and the cat's stomach acid reacts in a way that makes this some of the richest and most flavorful coffee in the world."

"That, or the cat has a very keen sense of smell and only picks the best beans," Cash said.

CHAPTER TWENTY-FOUR

Anthony stepped out of the Hermes Junket room, with Simon at his side. They made their way through the lobby, where a smattering of mainland tourists lingered under the cavernous roof.

"Couldn't give a rat's ass about what comes out of the ass of a civet," Simon said as his eyes squinted into a frown. "My crotch is on fire."

"You know, it is *your* fault the condom broke. You should have brought some from the U.S. if you were planning to screw around," Anthony said, shaking his head in annoyance. His shoulders slumped when he spotted Detective Fonseca lingering in the *Diamond Show* area waving him over. "Give me a second," he said to Simon.

"Come on, man, I'm dying here. Let a doctor put me out of my misery."

Anthony ignored Simon's pleading eyes and stepped over to Detective Fonseca, who glanced up at the five meter tall diamond in the middle of the lobby.

"You know, technically, we're standing in the biggest building in the world," Detective Fonseca said, eyes focused on the diamond.

"Bigger than the Pentagon?" Anthony asked.

"That's what they claim."

"I guess that speaks volumes about the progress of humanity."

Detective Fonseca's dark eyes turned to Anthony. "How so?"

"Biggest building in the world used to be dedicated to the destruction of large, Middle East despots and small, Southeast Asian communist countries; now it's solely dedicated to the destruction of the Chinese baccarat player's fat wallet. Progress."

"Indeed," Detective Fonseca said, putting a finger to his lips. "But don't say that too loud around here."

"And let slip the dirty little secret that Macau is the biggest money laundering operation in the history of the world?"

"Macau is very sensitive about letting people know who butters its bread. The politicians here and in China wouldn't like word to get out." Detective Fonseca said, stepping towards the casino floor. "Come."

Anthony turned to Simon, whose arms went to his side in a "What now?" gesture. Anthony ignored it and followed Detective Fonseca towards the casino entrance.

"You know he's being railroaded, detective," Anthony said.

"This isn't China, Mr. Wilson, we have to prove our case."

"To a corrupt judge?"

"Be careful, Mr. Wilson, we also have libel laws here."

"It's too bad we're not in China. Cash could just pay someone to do his time, go his merry way."

"You've been here how long? Eight months and you've already grown this cynical?"

"I'm a writer, detective, I was highly cynical before I arrived."

"I thought you Americans were such optimists."

"Haven't two men already confessed to the crime?" Anthony asked, glancing at his watch.

"The absence of evidence is not the evidence of absence. And who can trust the confession of a gangster? Candor and truthfulness, not exactly in their nature."

"I'd love to chat, detective, but I have another meeting to attend."

"You a gambling man, Mr. Wilson?"

"Aren't we all?"

Detective Fonseca passed a Nepalese guard, a muscular man in his late twenties with a dark-skinned face, standing at the entrance of the casino. The guard greeted the detective with a knowing nod. Detective Fonseca pulled out his iPhone and browsed to a video, which he played. Two hulking men beat a rail thin young man in grainy footage, seen from above, the God angle, as it's called in the business. "Evidence."

Anthony studied the video, but his anxiousness instantly disappeared. "An obvious fake, detective."

Fake versions of the "Cash murder" as it had been dubbed were popping up on WeChat, Youku, Douyin, TikTok, and other Chinese social media platforms to the consternation of the Chinese censors as well as Cash's defense team. Deepfakes were a thing these days, with AI technology getting so sophisticated it could fool even a discerning eye, as the viral videos of comedian Bill Hader seamlessly morphing into Tom Cruise and Arnold Schwarzenegger had shown. However, those fakes required sophisticated hardware and expensive software as well as deep R&D pockets, something the average TikTok influencer lacked.

"I'm surprised it fooled you," Anthony said.

"It didn't. But remember we're in Macau, fictional movies put triad bosses away all the time."

"Wasn't that just once? And, if anything, Broken Tooth deserved a long stay for that film's horrendous plot, cheesy dialogue, and wooden acting."

"You might want to be less derogatory towards a man who could have you killed. This is the first place he came to after he was released from prison, you know?"

"I heard he's now safely ensconced in Hong Kong, retired from the triad. Even had his tooth fixed."

"You heard wrong, Mr. Wilson. At least about the retirement. But do you think you can move in and out of these groups and societies without being one of them?"

"I'm not looking for saints, detective. I'm looking for clients."

"That's good because if you were looking for saints you came to the wrong place. More devils than saints to be found in Macau's thirty square kilometers of paradise," Detective Fonseca said.

"But you have so many beautiful churches here."

"No better place for the devil to hide than a church confessional."

"Detective, from one realist to another, as long as the money's not dirty, I have every right to take it, don't I?"

"You don't know how many interrogations I've had that start with a line like, 'I had no idea where the money came from.' The problem is that wonderful catch-all, conspiracy to commit. Ignorance isn't always bliss, Mr. Wilson, sometimes it's ten-to-fifteen."

"Conspiracy to commit isn't an easy thing to prove, though," Anthony said.

"Oh, you'd be surprised, what with all the secret listening devices we have these days. The Chinese have gotten extremely good at manufacturing some truly impressive surveillance equipment."

"As well as some surprisingly weak evidence."

"We shall see. How's the ICO coming along, by the way?"

"You tell me. You probably know more about it than I do."

"This is the way I see it. You will go public. Successfully. Cash will then do a runner with as much money as he can. And you'll be the chump holding the empty bag with your tiny *gweilo* dick flapping about in the cool Macau breeze," Detective Fonseca said, using his pinkie to show how lamely said dick would flap. "And then I'll be there to slap a pair of handcuffs on you, like I did with your buddy, Cash. Then Macau will kindly provide you with room and board for a forced Macau vacation that will last, oh, a decade, maybe two."

"A staycation, I think, they call it these days, but you know what, I do so much prefer getting away. International travel is so underrated. Something about vacationing in the same town you live in takes all the fun out of the concept of time off."

Detective Fonseca nodded. "Kind of like shitting where you eat. You're right. And if it was up to me, I'd be diving off the coast of Sipadan Island, not hanging out here on the dirty black sand beaches of Macau. Now, that's freedom. You ever been?"

"I don't even know where that is."

"Malaysia. One of the world's finest diving spots. You should go, you *really* should."

"I'll put it on my bucket list."

"Why wait? The sooner the better. You're no spring chicken, Mr. Wilson. What are you, forty?"

"Forty-seven."

"You look good for your age, like an Asian, but, trust me, prison ages men. I've seen arrogant boys of eighteen go in for ten years, then come out broken shells of a man looking fifty, with the assholes to prove it."

"Embellishing a little, detective?"

"You're the writer, not me."

An impatient Anthony resisted the temptation to roll his eyes. He caught sight of Simon by the entrance door frantically motioning it was time to go. "I'd love to stay and chat, detective, but I'm late for another appointment."

Detective Fonseca spotted Simon by the integrated resort's entrance, then pointed towards him. "You know, when this place opened, 15,000 people stood in line to be some of the first to get in. They believed if they were here on day one, they'd have good luck every time they came back."

"Superstition's a funny thing, detective."

"So's luck, Mr. Wilson. You just better hope yours doesn't run out before Macau says goodbye to your freedom."

"My luck ran out a long time ago, detective. My mother once said, between my twin and me, he got all the good luck and I got all the bad luck. I've resigned myself to the fates and the furies now and expect bad luck to be the only luck I get," Anthony said, then turned on his heels and marched away.

Minutes later, Anthony and Simon piled into a cab and headed to the nearest clinic.

Simon's wary eyes interrogated Anthony. "Who was that? Another client?"

"Hardly. A detective who wants to lock up our current client," Anthony said.

Simon shook his head, and his mouth turned down as a morose expression consumed his face. "Water's getting Marianas Trench deep here. Time for me to scoot on out of here, I think."

"Thought you wanted to visit China."

"How well do you know Cash?"

"Not that well."

"He's a junket operator, man, tight with the triads. Just seeing this kind of stuff puts us at risk. You know, if any private client information gets out of Macau from one of these casinos, the CTO goes to jail."

"I know."

"And maybe the person who helps him get it out, too. Like you. Or, more importantly, me."

Anthony remained silent, mulling over what he would say next, thinking a few steps ahead.

After a few moments, Simon broke the silence: "Look, I have no problem continuing the work, but in Miami, not here. The Chinese border is what, a mile from here?"

"Yeah, over there," Anthony said, motioning towards the towering and glass-encased skyscrapers of Henquin Island across the Pearl River a thousand meters away.

"Too close for my southern comfort, thank you very much. And I'd be very careful if I were you, too, and less trusting of people. There are a lot of snakes in this business."

Anthony glanced at Simon squirming in his seat, deciding to hold his sarcastic tongue.

CHAPTER TWENTY-FIVE

From his suite at the Island Shangri-La in Hong Kong's Admiralty region, Anthony peered down at the protestors swarming through the streets forty stories below. It had become a hot zone for demonstrations due to its proximity to the High Court, where questionable judgments were being meted out to the horrors of the protestors and the delight – and shame – of Beijing's autocrats, the corruption of the courts almost complete.

"*Gwōng fuhk hēung gong,* revolution of our times," Vivian said, staring out the window, her eyes watery, her mouth turned down at the sides.

Intermittent flashes flared up along the line of policemen marching through the street. Tear gas canisters arced through the air and then exploded around the protestors, who scattered away from the plumes of black smoke engulfing them.

A faint, innocent-sounding pop reached the fortieth floor, echoing across the glass skyscrapers, displaying the stark difference between the speed of light and the speed of sound; one instant, one delayed. The eye saw something happen long before the ear heard it, so the mind questioned its reality. There was no synched behavior between eye and ear like in the movies, where even bombs landing far away produced immediate theater-rocking explosions. Watching a desperate fight for democracy unfold in realtime was almost disappointing as it lacked the urgency of a TV police car chase.

Anthony turned away from the window, grabbed Vivian's hand. "We need to get out of here. Put Hong Kong and Macau far behind us, and quick."

Vivian's brow creased and her sad, dark eyes met Anthony's. She nodded.

The doorbell rang.

Anthony kissed her hand, then let it go. He walked over to the door and swung it open. A smiling, Asian waiter offered up a white box, which Anthony took, then carried over to the coffee table.

Vivian glanced at him, head tilting to one side.

Anthony lifted out a small cake shaped like a Chinese New Year red rabbit lantern. The swirling, fiery red frosting made it look as if a brilliant candle illuminated it from within.

Staring at the cake in disbelief, a smile of astonishment broke across Vivian's face.

Anthony smirked. "You never got one as a child. I know it's not a real red lantern, but I thought this would be better. We can eat it."

"You remembered?"

"Of course, I remembered. Seemed important to you."

"That's—" Vivian started but couldn't finish the sentence as words escaped her. She shook her head, placed a hand against her chest, then pulled him into a tight embrace.

"You're welcome," Anthony said, beaming brightly while wiping away the tear sliding down Vivian's cheek.

A few hours later, Leonard Cohen's "A Thousand Kisses Deep" played softly in the background. On the bed, Anthony fed Vivian the last bite of frosting. Out of the corner of his eye, he caught sight of the large TV, where a CNN correspondent wandered through the litter-filled streets surrounding Pacific Place Mall. Several firemen stomped out the dying embers of several minor fires. A scrolling chyron revealed the damage, *"Police cleared out Admiralty after a night of violence. Fifty-five arrests, three officers injured."* Anthony grabbed the remote and flipped off the TV.

Laying in the crook of Anthony's arm, a naked Vivian licked the last of the frosting off Anthony's fork. "Why'd you never marry?"

Anthony put the fork down on the bedside table, then ran his fingers across Vivian's full breasts. "'One ought to hold on to one's heart; for if one lets it go, one soon loses control of the head too,' Nietzsche."

"You have an answer for everything, don't you?"

"Or maybe my youth was too filled with Oscar Wilde, 'When one is in love, one begins by deceiving oneself and ends by deceiving others.'"

"And a quote for everything, too."

"I love quotes, they make me look smarter than I really am."

"Or so you think."

"Touché. Although to quote Jorge Luis Borges, 'Life itself is a quotation.'"

"You're reaching peak quotation."

"You want to know the real truth?"

Vivian rolled onto her stomach, eyed him with a telling smirk. "No, lie to me, like every other man does."

Anthony chuckled as his fingers swept over Vivian's naked back. "Unlucky in life, unlucky in love."

"Enough already."

"First girl I kissed, our lips barely touched, and she fell on the floor in an epileptic seizure."

Vivian chuckled. "My God."

"True story. She was writhing around. Her mother raced in, cleared the area to make sure her daughter wouldn't hit anything, then injected something in her nostrils. I didn't know what the hell was going on."

"Your kiss, not just electric, paraplegic."

"And it gets better. First woman I fell in love with was a beautiful half-Filipino-half Irish actress I met in L.A. But unfortunately, she was all born again."

"Born again?"

"Deeply religious. The no sex before marriage kind of religious."

Vivian shook her head. "In this day and age."

"I learned that, in life, love doesn't always conquer all. After that, I made a pact with myself to remain single until I got a movie made. Ah, the arrogance of youth, but you see, I know how it works. You meet a woman, you fall in love, you get married, you have kids, and, suddenly, your ambitions get squashed. Family takes precedence. Nothing wrong with that for others, just wasn't for me. Never got a movie made, so I never got married."

"Simple, inarguable logic."

"Although both my brother and sister got married early, then got divorced, so maybe I just missed out on a couple of life's stages. What about you? How have you remained single long enough to almost become a chicken leg?"

"Maybe I'm not single."

"And here comes the twist."

"I was married to a gambler who got in trouble with the triads. He took off one day and I never heard from him again."

"How long ago was that?"

"Five years. Filed for divorce a year after he disappeared."

"Time to put everything behind you. Reinvent yourself, as I did."

Vivian nodded. "Time for you to make me a star. I want to be a diva."

"Good to have realistic goals."

"Sounds like a good job, diva."

"It is if you can get it, but all joking aside, we need to get some tape on you. I spoke to a friend who's a casting director in L.A., she's willing to look at your work."

"What work?"

"We'll shoot a few scenes in and around Macau. Make you look like a famous Macau actress."

"I don't think there are any famous actresses in Macau."

Anthony took Vivian's face in his hands. "There will be now."

Vivian smiled as her eyes dropped to look at the floor. "Yes."

"You know the secret to making it in Hollywood?"

Vivian shook her head.

"Sincerity. If you can fake that, you've got it made," Anthony said.

Vivian chuckled. "Another quote?"

"But of course. You think you can fake sincerity?"

"What do you think I do all day in my current job?"

A playful smile broke across Anthony's face. "Profess your love for me."

Vivian climbed on top of Anthony, looked deep into his eyes, and confessed in a breathy whisper, "I think I'm falling in love with you, Anthony."

For a moment, Anthony's heart skipped a beat, and he was taken aback. He looked away, his tongue silenced.

Vivian smiled. "Well?"

After a few seconds, Anthony's gaze returned to Vivian. "That's good, very good. Very. Sincere."

CHAPTER TWENTY-SIX

EVEN THOUGH THE experience was not a new one, the second time on a private jet loses none of its luster. It might even get more indulgent. As the Hermes jet angled skywards, climbing through a bank of thin, wispy clouds, Anthony glanced out the window at Macau's small airport disappearing below. He could surely get used to this kind of travel. This was the second time Anthony had stepped onto a plane without a clue where it was headed. "Southeast," Cash had disclosed with an easy nonchalance as the plane rolled down the runway. Anthony questioned no further. He trusted Cash knew where they were headed, why they were going that way, and what they needed to do once they got there. Everything was firmly under control.

With his seat back, feet lounging on a footrest, the diamond-encrusted cowboy hat plopped atop his head, Cash flipped through listings of South Beach properties.

Anthony glanced over at him. "I might have an idea that can help you, both financially and maybe even legally."

"Go on," Cash said.

"Have you heard about the NBA's NFT *Top Shots*?"

Cash shook his head. "What's an NFT?"

Anthony grabbed his phone and opened a VPN app. "Before I answer that question, let me ask you something, what's the one thing besides jewelry stores, watch shops, and pawnbrokers surrounding every Macau casino?"

"Bookstands?"

"Filled with?"

"Magazines documenting the latest political scandals in China."

"Exactly. Stories about corrupt politicians, complete with pictures of caught-with-their-pants-down-men, often literally, as well as lurid tales of their lascivious exploits."

"Lascivious exploits?"

"Their sexual peccadillos, ah indiscretions. The Chinese tourists eat that shit up, right?"

"How does that fit with an NFT?"

Anthony browsed to the NBA's *Top Shot* page, which had the title 'Officially Licensed Digital Collectibles' above about thirty video game clips. "Non-Fungible Tokens, NFTs, are digital assets, either images or digital videos, stored on a Blockchain. Since they're logged on a ledger with a unique identifier, they're legitimized, at least to those who care about those kinds of things. They're one of a kind but can also become part of a series. The NBA is making a fortune selling NFTs of its game highlights. People buy five second clips of a player dunking a basketball, then trade them amongst each other like baseball cards. Some investors are getting seriously rich doing this."

"Wait, back up a second. People buy digital highlights of a basketball game?" Cash asked, brow furrowed in disbelief.

"I know unbelievable. This is probably just the latest iteration of the tulip bulb, South Seas shares, or the Beanie Babies craze, but huge fortunes can be made before bubbles go pop, especially if you're the one growing the tulips or minting the NFTs in our case."

"Go on."

"We turn your images and videos into NFTs, stick them on a Blockchain, secure them, then leverage them. Anyone comes after you, you release them to the world. These would go viral in China in a heartbeat. The bigger the politician, the higher the opening bid price. We charge according to the good old economics of supply and demand. We'll call them the *China's Most Wanted NFTs* collection. Best of all we can do this anonymously, selling them in a dark pool, so no one knows who's doing the selling."

Cash pondered the ramifications for a moment. "Many politicians would go to jail for life if these images were released."

"Even the threat of them being released could protect you."

"Some might be executed," Cash said while glancing towards the window, ruminating on the idea.

"You're the whistleblower exposing the crime. You can't control how justice is meted out. And let's be frank, these corrupt politicians have already cast their lot."

"Cast their lot?"

"Lived their corrupt lives."

"You know how to do this?"

"Yeah, not that complicated. We just need to get the people identified. And then everything has to be done anonymously. If any of these NFTs get out, the Macau gaming board will be coming after you hard."

"It's their worst nightmare."

"You won't be able to come back to Macau if these ever get released. It wouldn't be too hard to figure out this was coming from your junket room."

"They'll kick you out, too, if they find you're involved."

"I've got two passports that allow me to travel almost anywhere in the world. I think my welcome in Macau is already wearing thin."

Cash motioned the act of balancing two scales up and down. "Let me weigh my options – spend ten years in a Macau jail for a crime I didn't commit or never return to Macau again. Not a hard choice."

"I'll get the NFTs prepared and ready for sale for free, as long as I get a twenty percent cut of the sales."

"You like the idea that much?"

"I don't like the idea, I love the idea."

Cash threw out his hand. The two shook. The rabbit hole was getting deeper and deeper.

CHAPTER TWENTY-SEVEN

THE RIDE INTO Sanya revealed a modern city struggling to keep up with the pace of its development. The highway from the airport into the city had lanes for 'heavy vehicles' and 'light heavy vehicles'; more 'lost in translation' signs that brought a chuckle to Anthony's lips. Once in the city, scooters sped up the clogged street, zipping in and out of traffic, often gunning through red lights. Some even drove on the wrong side of the road. A concerto of maddening horns and shouts from frustrated drivers perfectly soundtracked a visual assault of the senses. Western music blared from packed bars and restaurants lining the street. If you sprinkled a few more western faces into the crowd, the scene would differ little from California's Manhattan Beach or Miami's Brickell Bay subdivisions.

Bright red billboards filled with 'The Core Values of Socialism' caught Anthony's attention. The twelve concepts included things one would never associate with the CCP or socialism: freedom, the rule of law, justice, equality, patriotism, and the funniest of all, democracy. Orwell's Oceania was alive and well in Sanya, China.

Anthony glanced at Cash to catch his attention, then nodded at the billboard while mouthing, "Democracy's a core value of socialism?"

Cash subtly rolled his eyes. "News to democracies everywhere, I'm sure. Propaganda gets more insidious by the day."

At CCP headquarters, Bohai and his deputies greeted Cash, Anthony, and Vivian like old friends; smiles and handshakes all around, with a hug or two mixed in. Another long night of dining and drinking followed. "The white monkey" did his thing, effortlessly spinning tales of how Bitcoin, Ethereum, and now Polkadot would make them all multi-million-aires, if only they were smart enough to sign on the dotted line.

After a dinner of local delicacies, including Hainan Chicken, which wasn't actually from Hainan, Bohai invited everyone to a night of KTV.

Ten women donning traditional Chinese blue silk dresses embroidered with golden dragons strutted into the center of the room, their firm, slender legs revealing plenty of skin peeking out from the long slits that ran up their thighs.

The Mama-San, a svelte woman in her late fifties, entered. She still carried the beauty that once turned heads from Beijing to Dongguan to Macau, and left heartbreak everywhere in between. Her look tonight was all business, as steely as a moneychanger searching for loose counterfeit bills in a handful of new hundreds.

A hush fell over the room as the men spotted the Mama-San. This meant the show was about to begin. Excited and expectant eyes turned towards the entrance as the lights dimmed.

The girls paraded in a straight line before Anthony. After a few moments, the Mama-San gave a command and the girls swiveled, showing their butts. They all struck a series of poses as if they were contestants in a voguing competition, trying to one-up each other to catch enough male attention to warrant a request for their presence.

The drinks flowed. The women strutted. As the hours slipped by, the female attire slipped off. A few half-dressed slender beauties led several of Bohai's colleagues out the door to their hotel rooms above. Several topless ladies propositioned Anthony, but he rejected their advances.

Throughout the evening, the carousel of women rotated in and out. The place was like a strip club without the seediness or the stripping, and with a vibe of celebration. Like reveling in a great moment of your life with twenty of your closest and hottest female friends. By two a.m., one of those friends might become a friend with privileges, although a price would be exacted for said privileges.

Although the atmosphere remained jovial, the soundtrack was atrocious, a horrendous mix of cheesy ballads, crossover country, and Andrew Lloyd Webber Broadway standards, neither up nor anywhere near Anthony's musical alley. He prayed "Feelings" wouldn't arise. A Mandarin version of Charlene's "I've Never Been To Me" or "*Gu Dan De Xin Tong,*" caught him off-guard. He listened closely to the chorus to figure out the English version. It wasn't too hard to place the song as it's probably one of the most recognizable ballads in the world, including, obviously, on the Mainland. Now and then, a '90s rap tune popped up. Anthony couldn't help but laugh at the sight of middle-aged Chinese men decked from head-to-toe in hip-hop attire, warbling out rap anthems like "The Humpty Dance", "Fight the Powers That Be", and The Notorious B.I.G.'s "Juicy". Even Sir Mixalot's "Baby Got Back" got play.

"Much funnier when the English lyrics are interspersed with Cantonese ones," Anthony said to Cash, who agreed with a knowing nod. They both belted out the chorus – "*Awg oi die si fut.*"

A few hours into the night, with his eyes unfocused, his hand movements exaggerated by his drunkenness, Cash lectured Anthony about England's action during the Opium War, saying it was forgivable, a sign of the times. England's actions were horrific, but so were America's during the war in the Philippines, the Portuguese's during their colonial times, the Dutch in Indonesia and Africa as well, the Germans in Europe during World War I and II, to say nothing of the Imperial Japanese. Or even the Chinese Emperors, who took their servants and guardsmen to the grave with them, killing them by starvation in an Emperor's cold grave.

"These were all different, less civilized times. Not like today," Cash slurred out.

Anthony nodded vaguely, uninterested in discussing the topic.

Cash raised his glass towards Bohai, who had a short-skirted, giggling woman on his lap. "You know, dictatorships usually last about seventy years. Guess which anniversary they just celebrated here."

"Seventieth?"

"Smart man, smart man," Cash said. He leaned in to explain Xi had been a compromise candidate. Neither side wanted him, but neither side had enough votes for their preferred choice, so they compromised into the second coming of Mao. One of China's powerful princelings, Xi chose authoritarianism over capitalism, a far cry from his father, who had worked with Deng to open up China in the '90s.

"Like I said before, talent skips a generation," Anthony said.

"Unfortunately, he might take down the positive work of two generations. You know what the vote was to change the Chinese constitution and allow someone to extend their rule beyond the normal ten year presidency?" Cash asked.

"Another time," Anthony said.

Ignoring Anthony, Cash continued, "Something like 2,030-to-2. So, two people voted against the man becoming a dictator for life. How weak is your constitution if one official can change the most important part of it? What's surprising is no one tried to do it before."

"That all-pervading Chinese philosophy of self sacrifice, I guess," Anthony said, motioning towards Vivian, who was deep in conversation with one of Bohai's security guards, a short but muscular man in his early thirties nearby.

Cash nodded. "There's no more self-serving an individual than a Chinese communist party politburo member. You don't get into a high position like that without serving yourself and getting everyone around you to serve or slave over you as well," Cash said, raising another toast in Bohai's direction.

This time, Bohai caught the gesture and raised his glass in return. A toothy smile followed, then a quick chug.

Cash slugged his beer. "What does it say about your country if you have instant messaging, social media, live-streaming apps, and you allow your people to be rounded up like Jews during the Holocaust, then put into concentration camps? What does it say about you if you allow all this while history has judged those who did similar things not just harshly but as some of the worst atrocities ever committed by man?"

Anthony raised his finger to his lips. The alcohol dulled his senses, but he was all too cognizant to know politics had no place in a KTV lounge deep in the heart of communist China, especially one being generously sponsored by the local communist party leader. Anthony tapped Cash on the leg. "Perhaps a discussion for another time, Cash?"

Vivian ventured over. She shouted a few words to the man she had been talking to in a goodbye greeting.

Cash caught the conversation and said a few words to Vivian in a language Anthony couldn't quite ascertain. It was neither Mandarin nor Cantonese, perhaps a local Hainan dialect? He was about to ask Vivian as she settled in beside him, but Cash cut in, "You know, there are villages in China where you can hire thugs to send a message to your enemies? If a business partner cheats you, hire some thug to teach him a lesson. If you want someone killed, you can even hire a hitman there. Circumvents the police, who can't always be trusted anyway. Zunyi, world-famous for its muscle and hired hitmen."

Anthony had seen maps of China broken down into its industrial sectors; need some electronics manufactured, visit Dongguan; want some motorcycles, ride on over to Bishan; feel like exploding some fireworks, visit Changsha; household appliances got your fancy, try Hefei; need some fur or leather goods, Jiaxing's got you covered; want to hire a murderer to take out a cheating business partner, Zunyi's bulletproof. China truly was the Wild, Wild East Cyrus claimed it was. Perhaps he should visit, find someone to ensure his business partner didn't screw him out of what was rightfully his?

"In America, we call that South Central," Anthony joked with a disarming smile.

Cash nodded noncommittally, then spread his hand across the group before him, "All of these people talk about the Asian Century, with China leading the way, but you know what Deng said? The man most responsible for China's rise."

An impatient Anthony shook his head and shot Vivian a warning look about Cash.

"The Asian century may never rise," Cash said.

"Another time, Cash, please," Anthony said.

"These people are too ignorant to understand what we're saying."

Anthony moved closer to Cash, then chided him, "Another. Time. Cash. Let's tally up the yuan and discuss this on safer shores."

Cash turned reflective for a few moments. Then he nodded, realizing Anthony had a good point. "You're right. Safer shores. You have a way with words, Mr. Wilson, a wonderful way with words."

"And you do not, right now," Anthony said.

"Yes, shut the hell up," Cash slurred.

But the statement was lost in a round of rowdy cheers led by Bohai. Glasses clinked in another raucous toast, spilling expensive Maotai on the carpet and table.

"*Níng wèi tàipíng quăn, bù zuò luànshì rén,*" Cash said raising his glass high. Everyone looked his way. Glasses lifted high throughout the room as everyone repeated the toast.

"Better to be a dog in times of tranquility than a human in times of chaos," Vivian translated.

Anthony nodded and clinked his glass against Vivian's.

Bohai and his entourage spent the last part of the evening holding court at an outside fire pit overlooking the calm waters of the South China Sea, which shimmered under a silvery moon. They chain-smoked and downed shots of expensive whiskey with chilled beer chasers. These men, in their forties, acted like Anthony's twenty-something fraternity brothers in the U.S., drinking up a storm with the sole goal of getting wasted, downing anything and everything that came their way, with no concern for the wicked hangover that was surely tomorrow's boozy revenge. The stark difference here was these guys were full-grown men who should know better. However, maybe this was the way they got through the day and night? Let the alcohol dull the senses, so the inherent hypocrisy and contradictions of Chinese society didn't make them want to blow their brains out.

Bohai sat down beside Anthony and offered him a cigarette. Although he didn't smoke, Vivian had warned him not to reject anything offered by a high status individual in China. It was about being a gracious guest and accepting what was offered, even if it was a stick that led to black cancerous lungs. By rejecting it, Bohai would lose face, so Anthony took it. If you want to do business in China, you adopt the local customs. You accept the cancer stick, and you enjoy it. So, Anthony took the cigarette, dipped in to take the offered light, then drew a deep breath of smoke. He exhaled it slowly into the cool night air, away from Bohai. The rush of nicotine energized him, awakening him.

Towards the end of the evening, the discussion turned to how much these local party leaders had learned from the great party secretary, Xi Jinping, and how profoundly "Xi thought" inspired their lives.

It was all rather off-putting, probably what living in North Korea was like. Each citizen desperately trying to out-fawn the other to prove their fealty to the 'Dear Leader,' a man who was great at nothing more than winning the North Korea birth sweepstakes or lasting long enough in the bloody, cutthroat musical chairs of Chinese politics to reach the top spot before the music died. These local party leaders seemed desperate to prove their fealty to the Great Leader, to be his greatest ass kisser. It was a pathetic sight to behold.

The presence of an outsider, an American at that, was an added bonus as these men were showering praise of Xi in front of a citizen from the country China considered its biggest rival and greatest threat. Anthony guessed they were putting down markers of fealty that their fellow CCP members could testify to at the next party meeting. What a terrible way to live, so foreign to anyone raised under a healthy democracy. Although calling America a "healthy democracy" right now was a bit of a stretch.

A proud Bohai spoke glowingly about China's incredible rise over the past few decades. When the conversation threatened to venture into a discussion about Taiwan, Cash could no longer hold his tongue and stepped before the group.

"As per the words of the great leader Deng Xiaoping himself," Cash said, "If one day, China should turn into a superpower and play tyrant to the world, the people of the world should identify it as social-imperialism, expose it, oppose it, and work together with the Chinese people to overthrow China."

Vivian quickly translated it for Anthony, who slapped Cash on the back and laughed heartily.

"Yes, yes. Social-imperialists," Bohai yelled, smiling in a wide toothy grin as he stepped over to Vivian and Anthony. "But, Cash, you should spend more time studying our great Xi's thoughts, not these ancient leaders."

Cash raised his glass in a toast.

Bohai said a few words in Mandarin to Vivian. Anthony caught "Pe Pe Fu." She translated the rest: "Cash sloppy drunk tonight."

'Pe Pe Fu,' perfect description, Anthony thought, then added, "Pressure of the trial is getting to him."

Vivian translated Anthony's words for Bohai.

Bohai nodded in sympathy, then replied to Vivian. She translated:

"Too bad this didn't happen in China. We could have easily made it all go away."

In some ways, the Chinese justice system did have its advantages, no doubt, thought Anthony. *As long as you're in charge of that justice system.*

"Cash say you make movies," Bohai said, struggling to come up with the right English words. He wrapped his arm around Anthony's shoulder.

Anthony nodded, a knowing smile breaking across his lips. There's just something about Hollywood that fascinates all, even corrupt politicians inside deep red China.

Bohai turned and rattled off something to Vivian in Mandarin that seemed to impress her. She explained to Anthony that Sanya had recently opened a film academy, complete with production and living facilities, training studios, international exchange centers, libraries, dormitories, student canteens, and faculty quarters. The school opened in the fall.

"Maybe you can come speak there?" Bohai said.

"Be honored to," Anthony said.

Bohai smiled.

"Maybe we can even make a movie? Maybe you can help us raise some money for it? Shoot it here, do post here, then own the IP, which we can sell in territories outside China?" Anthony said.

Vivian explained the proposal.

Bohai smiled knowingly. "We meet tomorrow. Talk details."

"Let's do lunch," Anthony said, using the ironic slang so popular in Hollywood to schedule a meeting to discuss entertainment matters, not just at lunch but at any time.

Vivian translated, but the obvious joke flew over Bohai's head.

"Once Cash sobers up," Bohai said, nodding towards Cash, who was being led out of the room by a tall, skinny Russian woman.

The idea was not a new one. Anthony had thought about it before. The only difficulty would be coming up with a storyline that could eye of the needle the Chinese censors and their ridiculous propaganda demands, not an easy feat. Or maybe shooting it in Macau was an option. They had censors there, too, but much less stringent ones. He'd have to look into more potential Macau stories.

The next morning, a ringing phone awakened Anthony. He grabbed his mobile and answered the call with a groggy "Hello."

"Pack up, we gotta get out of here ASAP," Cash said in a raspy, pained voice. "Problems in Wuhan, no time to explain. Airspace in China might be shut down in a few hours. We got to be wheels up in an hour."

"Shit," Anthony said, rolling out of bed. "What's Wuhan?"

But all he heard was the dial tone.

On the airport tarmac, Anthony watched several baggage handlers load up the Bombardier's luggage storage. An overflow of bags meant four of them had to be stowed in the cabin, which made for an interesting ride as Anthony tried to completely ignore them on the three hour flight back. Thoughts of the five-year old girl hunched over a sewing machine, stitching up fake Gucci loafers while slaving out a fourteen hour shift at some dim Dongguan factory flickered through his mind.

CHAPTER TWENTY-EIGHT

THE TRIAL STARTED with Cash's lawyers fending off an angry volley of questions from the black-robed, Chinese judge, whose deep facial lines, receding hairline, and pudgy body spoke of a man in his early fifties who had partaken in too many of the finer things in life. Judge Ho bore the countenance of an angry shop owner who had caught a thief red-handed and was about to mete out some deeply personal and extremely painful justice with a spiked baseball bat.

Ten smartly dressed male and female reporters representing the Macau and Hong Kong press filled the front row. Macau rarely made international headlines but a story combining gambling, the mysterious world of high rolling junkets operators, underworld triads, loansharking henchmen, and, ultimately, a murdered gambler ticked many of the catnip boxes driving modern journalism. The prominent social media element, the WeChat live-streaming murder, also added extra spice.

The judge's rapid fire Cantonese questions were delivered in an angry diatribe at Cash's lawyer, Justin Abrego, a stout Portuguese man who took the incoming flak with professional aplomb. He fired back at the judge in a volume similar to the verbal missives coming in, but with a tone containing considerably more respect.

Cash's usual expressiveness went into overdrive; his hands gesticulating wildly, eyebrows raising and lowering in random patterns of confusion as he repeatedly conferred with counsel. Now and then, his head shook in defiance, while his eyes stared back at the judge in deep disappointment.

During a break in the proceedings, Detective Fonseca marched into the courtroom. He slid into a seat beside Anthony.

"Why are we even here? Two people have already confessed to the crime, detective," Anthony said.

"And yet we still have a weeping mother," Detective Fonseca nodded towards Dr. Ling Ling, a teary-eyed, dignified woman in her sixties sitting alone in the front of the room. Anthony had noticed her earlier. She had similar trouble understanding the heated volleys of Cantonese invective fired to and fro in the courtroom. However, that didn't stop her from leveling Cash with a penetrating glare. Her clothes were expensive but understated. The quality high, but the labels hidden, which is the opposite of how most wealthy Chinese dress. Throughout the proceedings, she wiped tears from her cheeks with a colorful Hermes scarf.

"One can never quite fathom the pain of a parent losing a child. Reverses the natural order of things," Detective Fonseca said.

Anthony wanted to roll his eyes, but he knew how inappropriate an action like that would be in this setting. However, the detective's attempt at emotional manipulation bordered on clunky and offensive.

"And remember that wonderful catch all we so love, 'conspiracy to commit,'" Detective Fonseca said, pulling out an envelope. He offered it to Anthony. "Cash might not be who you think he is."

Anthony took the envelope and quickly pocketed it. "What's this?"

"A rap sheet and not of the musical kind."

"I used to work in film financing. That's an industry even dirtier than the casino business. I learned a thing or two about people, made me a pretty good judge of character, detective, so I rarely get in over my head."

"A lot of Chinese government officials think the same way when they come to Macau. Think they can gamble with embezzled money, double it up, then go back home, put the original money back, and keep the winnings for themselves. That none will be the wiser. Problem is they gamble the money away, then return home in shame, and try to figure out a way to steal even more money to cover their initial theft. Then enough money to cover the second theft. Then the third. And the fourth, until they get caught. Then they either lose a limb to a triad or a head to the state."

"Gambling reveals character flaws like no other vice, detective."

"I'm sure that's what Sheldon tells himself before he drifts off to sleep every night, comfy under those $1,000 Egyptian cotton sheets."

Anthony shook his head.

"Do you know what the SDN list is?" Detective Fonseca asked.

"The Specially Designated Nationals list?"

Detective smiled contritely. "That's the one. Filled with people who you, as an American, can't do business with."

"What about it?"

"Word has it Cash will be joining that illustrious list very soon. And then, since you're an employee of an American company or a Macau company owned by an American company, or even just because you were one of those lucky enough to have been born under the stars and stripes of the great United States of America, you won't be able to do business with him anymore."

"Why's he being put on that list?"

Detective Fonseca ignored the question. "My advice, get paid as soon as you can. Then skedaddle on out of here, to more hospitable shores."

"I'm touched you're concerned about my well being, detective."

"I'm not. If you've lost my card, call the station, any station, to reach me at any time. The one thing people forget about the police is we're deal-makers above all else. And sometimes we peddle in life's most precious commodity, time."

"Noted," Anthony said, using the term he had learned from Cyrus and his Filipino friends; a word that acknowledged you've heard what the other person has to say, and you have committed to do either something or, just as likely, absolutely nothing about it.

"It's later than you think, Mr. Wilson."

"That sounds like a threat."

"It is, but from above, not from below. From Buddha or whatever God you worship," Detective Fonseca said as he stepped away. After a few paces, he stopped and turned back to Anthony. "And don't kid yourself, there's no honor amongst thieves, no matter how beautifully tailored their fake designer suits are." Detective Fonseca strode up to the front of the room to give his testimony.

Cash's eyes followed him throughout. Once the detective settled on the stand, Cash's eyes swiveled back to Anthony, leveling him with a hard, questioning stare.

After the day's trial, Cash exited the law courts building surrounded by his entourage of attorneys and junket girls. They skirted the gauntlet of unruly reporters, who shouted out pointed questions about Cash's role in the murder.

A reporter from the Macau TV channel TDM shoved a microphone into Cash's face, then threw out a question in Portuguese. Cash's lawyer pushed the microphone away, then led Cash to the awaiting Hermes Bentley. Cash climbed in, followed by Anthony.

"L'Arc," Cash said to the driver, who immediately pulled away, almost driving over the feet of a journalist pressed up against the car's windows.

Cash leaned back into his seat, his eyebrows angled in concern. "What'd the detective want?"

Anthony pulled out Detective Fonseca's letter and offered it over. "To give me your rap sheet. And to let me know you are about to be placed on the Specially Designated Nationals list."

Cash pushed the letter away. "Better than being atop *The Hurun Rich List.*"

"*The Hurun Rich List?*"

"In America, you have the *Forbes Rich List*. In China, we have *The Hurun Rich List*, also known as the 'pig slaughter list' because its members are so frequently purged by the CCP. Get too big, too recognizable, speak up too much, and they'll cut you down to size. Like they're doing to Jack Ma."

"To get rich, not so glorious."

Cash nodded. "And whatever you do, don't be outspoken about your riches, because rubbing your wealth in the faces of the peasant farmers who live on a dollar a day isn't a good communistic look."

"Unlike in America, where we demand our rich shove their wealth in our faces."

"Don't worry about the SDN list. They threaten every year and never follow through."

"You weren't up for murder in any of those years."

Cash nodded as he glanced out the window at the blood red sky, with a thousand-yard stare. "Sometimes you just want to disappear. Drop off the face of the earth. Not an option with the CCP. They have spies everywhere. Name one place where there aren't at least a hundred thousand Chinese people."

"Antarctica?"

Cash smiled wryly. "Maybe, but they're all Chinese spies, owing everything to the CCP."

"Can you drop me at One Central?" Anthony asked.

"No. I have a surprise for you."

CHAPTER TWENTY-NINE

THE RESTAURANT WAS a temple to red. Bold slashes of the color were everywhere, on the walls, the tablecloths, the waitresses' dresses. Even some of the male diners had embraced the distinctly Asian color, wearing bright red shirts and Chinese style changshans. It was the color of luck after all. If we could see the diner's underwear, it'd probably be red, too.

Cyrus stood by a table in the corner, silhouetted against the beautiful red Macau skyline. A bottle of champagne iced in a bucket by his chair. As Anthony approached with Cash at his side, a huge smile broke across Cyrus's face.

"What are you doing here?" Anthony asked.

"From that astonished look on your face, Cash is great at keeping a secret," Cyrus said.

Anthony's furrowed brow and puzzled eyes questioned Cyrus, still not understanding what his presence there meant.

Cash slapped Anthony on the back. "I'm buying your company."

"You're the potential buyer?" Anthony said, eyes flitting between Cyrus and Cash.

"Me and my investors are," Cash said.

"But why?" Anthony asked.

"Like you Americans, I love my freedom," Cash said with a smile.

A troubled Anthony wanted to inform Cash he was buying into a dysfunctional company filled with inept employees overseen by a corrupt owner. A company probably worth far less than what Cyrus was asking for, but he couldn't. He either kept silent on the downright dysfunction and illegality he'd witnessed at Exegesis or speak up and short-circuit a sale that could give him at least some semblance of freedom.

A waitress stepped up behind Anthony and pulled out a seat for him. He sat. The waitress moved to Cash, but he spotted a friend nearby, excused himself, then walked over to a portly Asian man having dinner with a stunning Russian blonde in her twenties dressed to the nines.

With wide eyes and raised eyebrows, Anthony glanced at Cyrus sitting down at the table. "You look like a poker player who just won a massive pot on a lucky bluff."

"It'd be like you selling a script," Cyrus said with a mocking smirk.

"Touché."

Cyrus grabbed the bottle of champagne from the ice bucket, and removed the foil. "You're not going to ruin what might be the best night of my life."

A waitress hurried over to the table, took the champagne from Cyrus and proceeded to open it.

"Should you be traveling so soon after surgery?" Anthony asked.

"Definitely not, but I figured being here would probably help fast-track the sale."

"Meaning you're trying to close the deal before Cash realizes he's paying way too much for a highly depreciating asset?"

"Your twin spidey sense still working, I see, but you might want to bite your tongue. Your twenty percent of Exegesis Asia could amount to a few hundred grand. Not a bad payday for less than a year's worth of work."

Anthony's sarcastic tongue was silenced by the rather generous amount. After a few moments of pensive thought, he said, "Not as good as selling a script, but agreed, not bad. What's the catch?"

"No catch. You're right, it's generous. I'm taking care of you because I recognize the value you brought to the company here in Asia. You've been a great wingman to the buyer as well as helped the company project a nice multinational vibe."

"As well as cleaned up a few embarrassing messes as well."

The champagne popped. The waitress poured a glass for Cyrus, then Anthony.

"This isn't the film industry," Cyrus said. "Software's a complex business, implementations always get a little messy. The important thing is we made the sale. All of our current problems will soon be a thing of the past, meaning someone else's problems."

Anthony smirked. Cyrus was right, this meant the slate would be cleaned.

"You planning on sticking around to run the company under Cash?" Anthony asked while offering his glass up for a toast.

Cyrus clinked his glass against Anthony's. "Some details still need to be hashed out. You're welcome to stay, however; that's the deal I made with him."

"He's close to being a convicted felon, so the road might be getting a little bumpy from here on out."

"You think it's that bad?"

"If today's legal proceedings are anything to go by, it's not looking good."

"Well, good, that just means he needs to leave Macau sooner. Anyway, time to celebrate. Maybe we can use some of the sale proceeds to build a production company together?"

Anthony glanced at his twin noncommittally.

"Re-option all those novels you previously adapted. Wouldn't cost too much to acquire those rights, right?" Cyrus said.

"No. And the scripts are already written, so all the script development work is basically done."

"There you go. There's a convergence of software and entertainment happening right now, so it could be a perfect second act for us."

"But F. Scott Fitzgerald said there were no seconds acts in American lives."

"Then we'll do it in our British ones."

Cyrus was correct, the novel rights wouldn't cost too much to re-attain. This turn of events mooted the pesky questions of financing, but Anthony's experience with Exegesis Asia in Macau raised all kinds of ethical questions about Cyrus's behavior. You can't choose your family, the old saying goes, but you can choose your business partner. Anthony was feeling the need to be a little wiser on that front. Working with Cyrus had been eye-opening, something he never wanted to do again.

"Honestly, how much is he paying?" Anthony asked.

"Five million."

Anthony whistled at the high price.

"Look, he gets a fully formed company, which allows him to apply for an EB-5, 'Immigrant Investor' green card visa. Pretty smart, if you ask me?" Cyrus said.

"Not five million smart."

"Company's worth a lot more than you give it credit for."

"It's a pretty dysfunctional company from what I've seen. I gotta say, though, this is another stroke of fantastic luck for good old Cyrus Wilson.

Cyrus spotted Cash approaching. "Let's get into the nitty, gritty details later."

Anthony glanced over at Cash, then spoke out of the side of his mouth: "You remind me of that joke about vampires, 'Why are vampires massive sociopaths? Because they have zero capability of self-reflection.'"

"Ha, ha."

Anthony and Cyrus innocently smiled up at Cash, who settled into his seat as the waitress filled his glass.

CHAPTER THIRTY

A WEEK LATER, Anthony paced across the carpeted floor of Cyrus's large suite at the Venetian Macao, staring at the Cotai Strip beyond the floor to ceiling windows. It was becoming a mini-Europe, a half-scale replica of the Eiffel Tower loomed above a structure that looked like London's Westminster, which was an odd theme choice for an integrated resort; what with politics being the antithesis of entertainment for most people. The construction site for SJM's Grand Lisboa Palace, a recreation of France's Versailles Palace, was also visible. But only someone profoundly ignorant of history would think it advisable to create a casino in the likeness of something symbolizing historical grandeur, excess, greed, avarice, and over-the-top opulence. Adding an out-of-touch queen's ignorant directive would run the risk of pissing off the gambling gods by recreating it in China's gambling mecca. Building a knockoff of Versailles wasn't just an impolite poke in the gambling god's eye, it was an entire fireplace poker smashed through the retina, into the brain, and through the back of the skull. Surely the gambling gods would exact some kind of karmic retribution for this bastardization?

But thoughts of poor Feng Shui'd properties were of no importance right now as Anthony turned to Cyrus, who charted a sailing course from Macau to Cebu on a map of the South China Sea spread across the desk.

Jada fiddled with a suitcase on the bed, finally popping it open. As usual, her morose expression and sullen countenance sucked all the life out of the room.

"It's money laundering, plain and simple. We could spend a lot of time in jail for a crime like this," Anthony said, massaging his brow as if suffering from a deep migraine.

"That's not true. Not in the Philippines, where you can always buy your way out of trouble, *any* kind of trouble. At least from what I've heard," Jada said while pulling up a false bottom that revealed a space where a few kilos of cocaine could safely hide.

Cyrus looked up from his map and glowered at Anthony. "Look, it's risk-reward, Anthony, and, if I were you, someone who's taking minimal risk and potentially making a small fortune, I'd shut the hell up."

"If we get stopped, we'll bribe the customs officer," Jada said.

"And if that doesn't work, we'll bribe the judge at the hearing," Cyrus said.

Jada's hands went to her hips "And if that doesn't work, we'll bribe the judge at the trial."

"And if that doesn't work, we'll bribe the prison guard in the jail," Cyrus said.

"Nice to see you've got all the bribery angles covered," Anthony said.

Cyrus and Jada had convinced themselves that American exceptionalism trumped Third-World ignorance every time; that bribery was a way of life here to be exploited to the max; that slipping a couple of crisp Benjamins into a corrupt official's sweaty palm solved every imaginable problem. This was true to a certain extent, but the Quezon City jail contained more than a few Westerners who thought similarly, and realized too late that a misplaced bribe as easily bought extra prison time as it did vaunted freedom.

Anthony pointed at Jada. "Be careful standing arms akimbo like that. In the Philippines and Malaysia, it's seen as a strong message of outrage. You might find yourself in a fight you didn't expect."

Jada's brow furrowed in disbelief. "Really? Where'd you learn that?"

"In my travels around the Philippines and Malaysia these past few years. Surprised you didn't know it. You seem so well versed in the local culture."

Cyrus shot Anthony a glowering look. "Cut the attitude, man. We're freaked out enough already."

What they were doing was unquestionably illegal and nerves were frayed. It was a moment when Cyrus let his guard down, asking for a truce so everyone could focus on the task at hand. Jada was cool and calm, while Cyrus's eyes darted about the room like a spooked gazelle sniffing the odor of an approaching lion, but unsure which way the scent blew in from.

Anthony raised his arms in a "My bad" gesture.

"Look, Cash is already working his angle with his junket buddies over there," Cyrus said. "They know the system. They know the right people to bribe. Plus, the Philippines' coastline is like a sieve. The Chinese are smuggling hundreds of people in a week to work in the junket-owned casinos and sportsbooks there. We'll be fine. We're just a couple of Western tourists out for a little fun in the Philippine sun."

"Why isn't he doing this?"

"This is the deal we made, we help him get everything out of China and we get a little extra on top, which isn't actually that little," Cyrus said.

"You trust him?" Anthony asked.

"Of course not, that's why I don't sign off on anything until the money is safe and sound in our bank account in Cebu."

"Well, don't expect me to be sailing across the South China Sea with you."

"We're not asking you to sail with us. That's why Jada's here. She's an accomplished sailor in her own right. It's only about five hundred nautical miles, a four day trip, tops."

"Then what exactly do you need from me?" Anthony asked.

Jada folded her arms across her chest and glanced at Cyrus impatiently. "Great question."

"There's a regatta sailing out of Zhuhai next weekend, we'll load up the night before, then sail out under the cover of the race, head north to do some sailing amidst the beautiful and world-famous Philippine islands, maybe look for some of that Marcos gold along the way," said Cyrus, smiling brightly.

"You're not worried about pirates?" Anthony asked.

Cyrus turned back to his map. "More concerned about crazed Chinese fisherman, to be honest."

Jada dismissively waved her hand. "There aren't pirates in waters this far north."

"It's a pretty crowded waterway these days, with American warships hovering about because of China's Nine-Dash Line bullshit," Cyrus said.

"What happens when you get into Philippine waters?" Anthony asked.

"That's where you come in. No one's going to think anything of a couple of day-trippers coming out of Hong Kong. You're our insurance policy, brother. Anything goes awry, you're going to be on the ground there to help us. Got it?"

Anthony nodded and smiled contritely at Cyrus. "Two hundred thousand reasons for me to be there, right?" He headed towards the door.

Cyrus shot Anthony an impatient, cutting look. "Hey, Cash said you were getting friendly with a cop here."

"Calling it friendly would be a stretch. The detective was sniffing around the ICO and wanted help putting Cash away. I was throwing him off the scent."

Cyrus shot Anthony a warning look. "Nothing gets in the way of this sale. *Nothing*, you hear me?"

"Like you said in Manila – smash and grab," Anthony said.

"That's right, smash and grab. And only communicate on Signal going forward."

"Signal?"

"The app."

Anthony nodded.

Cyrus turned back to his map. "And don't worry so much. We've got this in the bag. It's fate. We've got Cash covering the Zhuhai angle, you covering Cebu. Jada and I are great sailors. And, as you said, I'm fortune's favorite son."

Anthony's mother had once joked about the odd luck of the twins. As with most jokes, there was an element of truth to it, but Anthony put his tough times down to his crazy career choice. The entertainment business was one of the most difficult businesses to attain success in. The old joke about overnight success taking ten years to accomplish was true for the ones who made it, but there were hundreds of thousands of others who, even after years of back breaking dedication had slipped into quiet and ignoble obscurity; their hopeful Hollywood dreams crushed on the harsh rocks of entertainment biz reality. But if Cyrus's luck got them through this, Anthony wouldn't ask Hermes, the god of gambling, for anything ever again.

Anthony returned to his apartment, where he booted up his computer and logged into the cloud server that was running the facial recognition match for the *China's Most Wanted NFT* set. The system had discovered another 220 faces with a match accuracy level high enough for a prosecutor to be confident of conviction in an American court.

China's Most Wanted NFTs were turning into a rogues gallery of high-ranking, Communist party members, several famous Chinese celebrities, a few well-known Canto-pop musicians, some eminent industrialists, as well as a lot of low ranking CCP members who appeared in several local slow news day stories. Many articles quoted these party hypocrites, who spoke glowingly about the party's ongoing fight against poverty when it was clear the only poverty alleviation they had interest in were the ones alleviating their own personal poverty.

Some of these politicians had already been put away for corruption as Xi's campaign against his enemies, both perceived and real, had netted thousands of individuals who were probably guilty of nothing more than following the party line and practicing the standard, and even expected, forms of political bribery in China. The deeper Anthony delved into this work, the more he realized the inherent truth in Cash's earlier quip, "If the Party executes every official for corruption, it will overdo it a little; but if the Party executes every other official, it can't go wrong."

CHAPTER THIRTY-ONE

SITTING IN THE cockpit of *The Gambler*, a beautiful forty-foot Pretorien yacht, Anthony glanced down at the official Exegesis Asia company tax documents spread out on the small table before him. His eyes squinted displeasure, then he looked up and surveyed the desolate Zhuhai marina. Three a.m. Not a soul around, the water gently lapping against the boat's hull was the only sound. He exhaled a deep breath of condensation in the cold, dry air. An ominous feeling crept over him, concerns not just about signing off on fake numbers Cyrus had pulled out thin air but rather about the profound illegality of their actions.

Wrapped up in a stylish, Burberry puffer jacket, Jada lingered by Cyrus. She shot Anthony an impatient look. "Don't take so long. Doesn't mean anything anyway." As usual, she spoke the quiet part out loud.

Anthony signed the documents. He could always fall back on the position he was the innocent victim of a deceitful businessman's scam. That he was an in-over-his-head writer set up by a Machiavellian twin who had tricked him with phony numbers, false hopes, and the exaggerated promise of untold riches. A lot of which, like all good lies, contained more than a few elements of truth.

Cyrus and Jada countersigned the documents. She then took them and descended into the cabin.

Anthony stared hard at Cyrus. "You don't realize what's going on here, do you? Jada's playing you like a fiddle."

"You don't know what you're talking about," Cyrus said.

"This sale was your idea?"

"Yeah, I've wanted to sell out for years now."

"Really? You seemed to love your work."

"Time to move on. The salad days of making easy money in software are long gone."

"Why'd you offer me shares in the company if you were planning to sell?"

"I didn't know I was going to sell until now. An opportunity I couldn't refuse came along. Events moved in a direction I liked, so I pushed them where I could, but don't envision me as some kind of malevolent Rasputin pulling all the strings behind the scenes."

"Trust me, I don't. The Rasputina role belongs to Jada."

Cyrus shot Anthony a scowling look. "Underestimate me at your own peril."

"Permission to come aboard, captain," Cash shouted from below. His voice echoed across the marina, startling the brothers.

Cyrus and Anthony peered down at Cash, who lugged a duffle bag up the gangplank towards the ship's stern.

"Permission granted," Cyrus said, a nervous smile playing across his lips as his eyes swept the deserted pier. "Although it's your boat, so I'm hardly captain."

"Change of plans, I decided gold would be quicker," Cash said as he lugged the bag onto the deck. "Things are getting a little hairy here."

Cyrus grabbed the duffle bag from Cash, then placed it by the cabin door.

Cyrus, Cash, and Anthony stepped off the boat and strode towards Cash's Mercedes Benz Sprinter van parked nearby.

"They say life begins at forty," Cyrus said, running his hand across *The Gambler's* smooth fiberglass hull. "Nice boat. Always loved the Pretorien. Beautiful construction."

"And more secret compartments than an Egyptian pyramid," Cash said with a smile.

Cyrus laughed.

"Get everything safe and sound into your Cebu bank account, sign the company over to me, and she's yours. My closing deal gift to you," Cash said, coughing several times.

"Let's worry about gifts once everything's safe and sound in my Cebu bank account. We'll call that my superstition. Great name, though," Cyrus said.

"Kenny Rodgers," Cash said as an explanation, but it got lost in a rough bout of dry hacking.

"You okay?" Cyrus asked.

"Just picked up a bug in Dongguan. A good night's rest should be enough to sleep it off," Cash said between another round of coughing.

"Take a seat on the boat. We've got it from here. Jada can make you some tea," Cyrus said.

Cash clicked the Mercedes FOB. The trunk slowly rose as Cash shuffled away. A huge smile broke across Cyrus's face at the sight of several luxury luggage bags lined up in the trunk.

"You look like you just won the lottery," Anthony said.

Cash grabbed a small bag. "I think I have. Now, we just have to make sure we don't lose the ticket before we cash it in." Cash headed to the boat.

Anthony grabbed a bag and followed his twin. "Why are you doing this? Taking all these risks? I thought you had plenty of money."

"I'm an American, I've been living on credit for twenty-five years. We were doing okay, but then Brandon came along. You have any idea how much his medical bills are?"

"You can't pay them if you're in jail."

"You worry too much. Look the Philippines' coastline is like a sieve, we'll be fine."

As he loaded up the bags, a rush of excitement consumed Anthony. Like watching the ending of a horse race that was about to make him Pick 6 rich, Anthony couldn't help but smile, realizing this could be the biggest score of his life. He hoped that Philippine coastline was as porous as everyone claimed, or any officials getting in the way of their trip as easily bribed as Jada and Cyrus believed.

An hour later, five suitcases stuffed with Chinese yuan, several bags of miscellaneous uncut jewels, and gold bars worth about a million bucks were stowed inside the cabin. The gold and jewels were hidden under the bunk and the suitcases looked like nothing more than what a couple might take on a holiday trip, especially a rich American couple.

As Anthony closed the Mercedes's trunk, Cyrus approached and handed him a walkie-talkie. "That's an ArgoTrak. It'll give you our location at all times." Cyrus then offered a small purple velvet bag to Anthony. "And take this too. Put them in the safety deposit box at BCM. And don't worry, they're uncut, so they'll be under the legal limit if you get stopped at the border. Worth ten or twenty percent of cut ones. Meet us in Cebu on Friday. There's a burner SIM in there as well as our satellite phone number. I'll let you know if we deviate from our charted course. But we won't."

Anthony took the bag and pocketed it. There was that generosity again, Cyrus tossing something much more valuable than scraps at subordinates. A bag of precious stones he probably hadn't quantified. Perhaps it was more of a bribe to keep Anthony in line than anything else? Anthony couldn't tell which one it was, but he didn't care. He just wanted to survive this ordeal without seeing the inside of a jail cell or the dirt-filled bottom of a shallow grave.

Cyrus stepped towards the boat. "Let's grab a good luck drink with Cash."

"I think it's time for me to go. I'm exhausted."

"Gotta have a drink for good luck. You know how important luck is to the Chinese."

"Chinese aren't the ones needing it, the Americans are. And you've got fortune to spare, or so you say." Anthony turned and walked away. He tossed the velvet bag into the air, then caught it, yelling out, "See you in Cebu."

An hour later, to his great relief, Anthony crossed into Macau without a hitch. He used his UK passport, the expendable one that could easily be ditched if he needed to hide a trail. He knew the Wan Chai border gate would be the safest place to cross because it was the smallest and oldest crossing to Macau in China. While waiting for the ferry, Anthony examined the washed-out black and white photos on the wall taken in the '70s or '80s. Vast tracts of farmland surrounded a one story border gate harkening back to a quieter, simpler time in China, a starvation cannibalism time, a time when parents swapped kids, so they didn't have to eat their own.

Once he got home, Anthony poured the rough stones into his palm. He studied them carefully. He knew nothing about diamonds, especially uncut ones. They were rocks that someone somewhere deemed valuable, and that made them precious. An act of brilliant marketing more than anything else. Yes, they took millions of years to form and could be cut and polished in ways that made them glitter and sparkle as if their light projected from a thousand suns, but their value was still man-made. Nothing more. Nothing less.

As Anthony cradled the raw jewels in his palm, he felt their heaviness while thinking of the advice given to screenwriters who had act three trouble, *You don't have a third act problem, you have a first act problem you never solved.* The advice worked for relationships, too. Cyrus and Jada revealed an astonishing level of entitlement in the past, entitlement Anthony had blindly ignored to his huge detriment now. The couple's generosity had always hidden a cruel streak; every "gift" cataloged, only to be remembered and brought up down the line, when things were demanded in exponential return. Here, have a free coffee on me now, but I expect a Kobe beef dinner in return. Here, I've got this round of shots covered. Now, about that pound of kidney flesh...

Anthony checked the safe, noticing something odd, the starting number wasn't forty-four, the Chinese bad luck number he always placed it on. Maybe it was time to change maids? He'd worry about that later. He spun the knob, unlocked the safe, and placed the jewels inside. He shut the safe and then returned the knob's starting position back to forty-four.

Anthony crashed on his bed. He couldn't figure out how this was all going to end, but he feared he might be the sacrificial lamb being set up for the slaughter, something he'd felt the first time Cash handed him a small fortune in yuan after their trip to Zhuhai. Everything seemed too easy, too convenient. As sleep consumed him, Anthony dreamt of a TV documentary he'd seen about the sardine run off the coast of Southern Africa, which took place every year from May through July. Dubbed the "Greatest Shoal on Earth," billions of sardines spawned in the cool waters of the Agulhas Bank, then moved north. Concentrated near the surface, the sardines were quickly spotted by schools of marauding predators. Copper sharks, blacktip sharks, and spinner sharks attacked from above; gamefish, cape fur seals, and dolphins torpedoed in from below; gannets, cormorants, and gulls divebombed from the heavens. Ignoring each other, the naturally antagonistic predators focused purely on the shimmering mass of sardines that undulated around them. When the predators struck, the prey split into a thousand pieces, darting away, desperate to avoid the razor sharp teeth and arrowlike beaks of their hunters. After each attack, the sardines shapeshifted back into an orb that offered little protection.

CHAPTER THIRTY-TWO

THE ECONOMIC AND political miracle that is Hong Kong was due in large part to the perfect union between a tireless Chinese work ethic and the strict moral, legal, and ethical framework laid down by the Brits over a century-and-a-half ago. It also had a lot to do with the ease of getting incorporated. You could set up a company in less than a day, if not within hours.

A visit to the aptly named 'Companies Registry,' where the filling out of a few simple forms, and the payment of a small fee were the only requirements needed to create an official Hong Kong company. Anthony completed the registration forms, paid the fee, and handed over his UK passport for inspection. Within an hour, he was the proud owner of Hong Kong's newest company, Exegesis Asia Limited, a company whose name was strikingly similar to the one he worked for in Macau. And that was the whole point.

This gave Anthony the chance to play his own shell game with what would be, for now, a shell company. Anthony would pull a clever sleight-of-hand and get the clients he had helped bring to the table for the Macau company to his similarly named one in Hong Kong. Once he convinced those clients to sign contracts with his Hong Kong entity, he'd rename the company to whatever he wanted and then go about his merry and twinless way. Anthony knew just the incentives to offer – tax breaks. Juicy, juicy Hong Kong tax breaks because there were no taxes on services in the Hong Kong S.A.R.

When Anthony finished the company paperwork, he strode out of the air-conditioned Pacific Place Mall smack dab into the middle of a demonstration, a massing throng of agitated protesters girding for a fight along Queensway Boulevard. Traffic standstilled. A concerto of horns rang out from the annoyed drivers, while a cantata of voices crying out last minute instructions circled the anxious crowd. A percussion of stomping feet rumbled across the boulevard, heightening the tension to a fever pitch.

Perfect setting for a movie, Anthony thought, then chided himself for assuming everything in life should be viewed as a movie stripped down to its most basic dramatic tension. These were real people, with real lives being stripped bare of the very essence of life, freedom. Being half-American, he remembered the year the Berlin Wall came down; "The End of History," as one political scientist put it. Unfortunately, history never ends; authoritarians rise and fall and rise again.

Black-clad protestors prepared for an impending police attack, fear etched on their grave faces, their eyes flitting about like soldiers in a foxhole trying to figure out from which direction the enemy would come. Umbrellas in a rainbow of colors popped open. N95 masks slipped over anxious faces. Thick, choking clouds of tear gas were on the way. Everyone knew the drill.

As sweat beaded across his brow, Anthony recognized two things; a protest against Beijing's draconian new security law pushed by Hong Kong's idiot Chief Executive Carrie Lam was about to explode, and it was time to split. Any way he could. These protests were crippling the city, turning a ten minute ride into a two hour, slow moving nightmare slog of a commute.

Cars would be stuck in bumper-to-bumper traffic for hours, trapped by the troubles and Hong Kong Island's uniquely slender geography, which provided few escape routes for adventurous drivers. The nostalgic two decker tram line was out. Even though it had its own lane, it'd be stuck behind the swarming protestors for hours. The subway was useless because this was the protestor's preferred route to appear and disappear. The government had caught on to their antics, forcing the trains to ride right through any station where protestors congregated.

But Anthony couldn't leave. He'd often wondered what it'd be like to stand in the presence of history. This was his opportunity to do just that. He was struck by how young the kids appeared, many in their early to mid-teens, who sang "Hong Kong independence, only way" in unison.

On the edge of the crowd, in their own self-contained pen, journalists from the world's media gawked as excitedly as gamblers who'd just bet on the "Meron" at a Pasay cockfight and were waiting for the bird handlers to drop the cocks into the blood-stained pit. They'd be documenting history, with live updates beamed from the rubble filled streets, showing some cops cracking heads, clouds of teargas engulfing the street, and then maybe some blood curdling down the gutter to demarcate the end of the show.

Drawn towards the periphery of the crowd, Anthony's senses heightened. He knew it was time to leave, but the writer in him demanded he soak up as much of the scene as possible. His head swiveled to and fro, documenting as many details as he could; a sea of people in black T-shirts, wearing white and yellow hardhats, and surgical masks to hide their facial features. A man wearing a balaclava under a black hoodie raced forward and tossed a Molotov cocktail at the police line. Was this an undercover cop trying to make the protestors look like the aggressors? Many suspected such underhanded police tactics.

Protesters celebrating the eighty-eighth anniversary of the Japanese invasion of China had popped up throughout the city. "People fighting for democracy glorifying second world war atrocities," the CCP shills lamented. "What's the difference if your oppressor is Chinese or Japanese, you're still being oppressed," countered the democracy supporters.

Anthony wouldn't put it past Beijing's disinformation agents to scrawl pro-Japanese imperialist graffiti and blame it on the protestors.

Tear gas canisters arced high into the sky and then descended with a whistling, demonic cry. One smashed onto the pavement near Anthony. Plumes of grey smoke exploded into the air, then crept along the ground towards him. Protestors scattered, coughing violently. Perhaps this was too much reality?

Anthony cried out as the mace burned his throat. Tears streamed from his eyes as his nose filled with an acidic, vinegary smell. He felt an intense tightness in his chest. Struggling to breathe, he turned tail and ran, joining a wave of protestors sprinting across Queensway Boulevard, away from the police line, away from the tear gas. He tried to hold his breath for as long as he could to avoid breathing in the mace, but he couldn't for long.

He knew the geography well and headed towards Harcourt Road. The way out of here was over the water: the Jesus way. But on a ferry, not walking across it. Anthony headed towards the Wan Chai Ferry Pier, a little-known route across Hong Kong's world-renowned harbor. This would get him to TST, where he could grab a ferry back to Macau.

Even with the annoyance of the demonstrations, Anthony held no contempt for these fighters of freedom, truth, and democracy. He empathized with their plight, but Anthony had his own battles to fight right now. *Hong Kong was going to have to fend for itself*, he thought, as he bound onto the Star Ferry. He wiped away the beads of sweat streaming down his face and sucked oxygen deep into his lungs. Happy to have avoided arrest, he made a mental note to watch the news later to see how many heads had been cracked, how many canisters of tear gas arced across Hong Kong's beautiful skyline, and how many unfortunate Hongkies had been arrested and were about to be deported to a cold cell in a Chinese prison, the tragic end all these protestors fought so hard to avoid. Life is cruel, especially when born under what the locals dub the 'Exhaust Fan,' Hong Kong's red and white flag that contains an image of the Bauhinia blakeana, a Hong Kong orchid. Every known Bauhinia blakeana is believed to be a clone descended from a single, sterile specimen first discovered around 1880. How symbolically appropriate. The CCP would love nothing more than the Hongkies to be sterile clones who demanded nothing from their leaders and believed in absolute servitude.

CHAPTER THIRTY-THREE

AT JUSTIN'S OFFICE in the Bank of America building in Central, Hong Kong, Anthony rolled a handful of precious stones onto the lawyer's glass-topped coffee table. Anthony had carried the rough stones to Hong Kong a few days after the protests in Admirality. In Tsim Sha Tsui's rabbit warren of streets, he found a jeweler interested in the cutting work. A day after dropping them off, he picked up the stones, then went to see Cash's lawyer to make a deal.

Justin picked up the stones, eyed them while holding them up in the late afternoon sun. "There's a twenty percent tax."

"Twelve. It's not too hard to find a corrupt banker in Hong Kong these days," Anthony countered, with a firm smile.

"Getting harder."

"Corrupt bankers are about as common as street protestors around here."

Justin squinted one eye to get a closer look at the stone. "Fifteen sounds fair."

"My jeweler appraised them at a hundred and five thousand U.S., so let's say ninety-K in White Tiger coins. And this is all under attorney-client privileges, of course."

Justin stuck out his hand. "*Para bom entendedor, meia palavra basta –* to a good understander, half a word is enough, as we say in Portuguese."

The two shook hands.

"So how exactly do these White Tiger coins work?" Anthony asked.

Justin tumbled into a detailed explanation about web3 wallets,

MetaMask browser extensions, and seed phrases that went over Anthony's head. Handing over a hundred and five thousand dollars in jewels to someone who was almost a stranger might be dumb in normal circumstances, but these were anything but normal circumstances. Shady goings on in high rises was how the rich expanded their wealth. Ten thousand dollar suits often hid ten cent souls, but a handshake on a financial deal with one of Cash's associates was about as solid as one gets in crypto.

"This is all Shanghainese to me," Anthony said, even though it wasn't completely.

"I'll send you details on how to open your Coinbase and Metamask accounts. It's pretty simple once you get the hang of it."

"So's brain surgery after you've done it five hundred times. More importantly, you think this a good investment?"

"It'll be mooning in a week."

"Mooning?"

"Rising sharply in value."

"Every new technology needs a colorful lexicon to go with it, huh?"

Justin nodded while lining up the diamonds in neat rows. "Hyperbole sells like nothing else in this business. Trading's all about supply and demand, right? As insiders, we get to see the demand side of the equation and that's looking really good. I've been involved in seven other ICOs and this is looking like the most oversubscribed ever."

"You putting in any personal money?"

"Yeah, at least a hundred grand."

"That's a lot of faith."

"Not my first rodeo with these guys. Talking about cowboys, when was the last time you saw Cash?"

Ignoring the late night, money running rendezvous in Zhuhai, Anthony scanned his memory for the meeting before that. "Haven't seen him since the trip to Sanya last week. Haven't spoken to him since then, either. I've been rather busy with my own work." Too much information. Anthony remembered people with guilty consciences often offered up too many details about an event in an attempt to cloud suspicion. However, those additional particulars often did the exact opposite, giving trustworthy people reason to suspect something was amiss.

"We have contingency plans for unforeseen situations like this. In case of the death or the disappearance of a principal, God forbid. Cash's work is done at this point, except for a few AMAs," Justin said.

"AMAs?"

"Ask me Anything Q-and-As. But we can handle them, we'll just say he's out sick. Seems like something's broken out in China, actually. Hopefully not another SARS-like virus. Last time we had one here I was stuck in a hotel for a week."

Anthony nodded while glancing at the sparkling diamonds on Justin's desk. He picked one up. "Make it $85,000, I might need this one for something."

Justin nodded. "Eighty-five, it is. As long as my jeweler confirms their value."

🎲 CHAPTER THIRTY-FOUR

March 24th, 2019

WITH HIS HANDS scaling along the boom to keep his balance, Anthony hurried across the deck of *The Gambler*, eyes scanning for any sign of life or indication of threat. When Anthony reached the cabin, he took a deep breath and steeled himself. He inched open the door. The stench of urine hit him like a punch in the face. A dim blue light flickered somewhere inside the cabin. He unzipped his backpack, slipped his hand inside, released the gun's safety, then slid his finger onto the cool metal trigger.

As Anthony descended into the cabin, he coughed a few times. His eyes adjusted to the darkness. A disheveled mess came into view. Sprawled against the hull, Cyrus shivered uncontrollably. On a bed in the bow, a thick duvet covered Jada's sweaty body, her breathing sounding labored and wheezy.

Anthony removed his shirt and wrapped it over his face. If he shot Cyrus and Jada now, all this money and gold would be his. And his alone. The seductive tunnel-vision of greed consumed him. Anthony had never felt a desire so raw before. It sure was alluring. His mind raced through plans and stratagems to get the loot to Cebu. Could he trust the fishermen to help him out? Would they get nosy? Demand to see inside the suitcases?

Cyrus's eyes flickered open, staring out uncomprehendingly.

Anthony tucked the gun into the small of his back and grabbed water from the fridge.

Cyrus's eyes locked onto Anthony's. He took the offered water bottle, drank a few sips, then exhaled in a gasping breath.

Anthony needed to remain calm, and refrain from breathing too much. This place was probably a virus incubator.

Cyrus gazed up at Anthony with cogent eyes, his expression reminiscent of an Alzheimer's patient experiencing a flickering moment of lucidity. "We're sick, you need to get us help."

"What happened here?" Anthony asked.

Cyrus rolled onto his back. "Get help." He groaned, then crawled towards Jada. With fingers wrapped around the galley table's leg, he pulled himself across the floor but was too weak to make it and fell against a board, gasping for breath, trying to suck air deep into his lungs.

The old fisherman appeared in the doorway, his emerald eyes flashing bright in the midday sun. "Everything okay in there? Storm's com–" The words started out of his mouth but were cut short at the sight of the gun stuck in the small of Anthony's back.

Anthony glanced at the cabin door, but only caught sight of the fisherman's disappearing figure. "Wait! Wait! It's for pirates!" Anthony jumped up and hurried out of the cabin.

The frightened captain stumbled across the slippery deck, then jumped aboard the Bangka. "Gun! Gun! Gun!"

On the Bangka, the fishermen scrambled for cover, all flailing arms and stumbling limbs. Eyes flitting about in jittery fear begged Anthony not to shoot. The captain throttled the engine. The boat chugged away, belching thick clouds of black smoke in its wake.

"Shit," Anthony said, placing the gun on the deck. He glanced at the desolate shore a mile away, then at the cabin. Cyrus and Jada were as good as dead if he left them there. The money was his if he could somehow get it to shore. Easier said than done though when you're stuck on a boat in the middle of nowhere, and you don't know how to sail, plus two family members are dying of some unknown disease in a cabin not far below. The one thing Anthony knew for certain – he wasn't a killer. He wasn't a sociopath. Leaving Cyrus and Jada here wasn't an option.

He jumped from the boat feet first. Water shot into his nostrils, a painful rush that Anthony welcomed as it might wash away the deadly virus.

For a moment, Anthony was the thirteen-year-old boy back at boarding school, comforting his twin, whose sobs of disappointment brought salty tears to his eyes. On that fateful day more than thirty years ago, Anthony had been called into the headmaster's office to be informed that he had passed the entrance exam to his new school and his time at Hurstpierpoint College was coming to an end. After hearing the news, Anthony rushed out of the office, ready to scream to the heavens in excitement, but he held his tongue, anxiously waiting for his twin to receive similarly good news. The fact the two had been separated because the news was different for each twin hadn't crossed his mind.

Within a few minutes, Cyrus shuffled out, eyes downtrodden, mouth turned down, tears streaming over his reddening cheeks. "I failed."

"What?!!" Anthony said, eyes searching his twin's reddening ones.

"I failed. I failed. I failed," Cyrus repeated as if the words were a mantra that might bring some solace to the situation. "I'm not going with you. I have to stay here. Repeat the year." It was the first time the twins had been separated in their lives.

Back in the cool, calm waters of the Visayan Sea, Anthony swallowed a mouthful of seawater and swilled it about as he swam toward the sun in swift, powerful strokes. Once he broke the surface, he spat out the water. He climbed aboard the boat, grabbed the VHF radio, flipped it on, then pushed the distress button.

Within moments, the radio crackled to life, "What's your emergency?"

Anthony brought the microphone to his lips. "Mayday, Mayday, Mayday. This is *The Gambler*. I have two people who need immediate medical assistance aboard ship. Repeat, I have two people who need immediate medical assistance aboard ship."

Once Anthony hung up, he grabbed the Prada duffle bag from the cabin, then dragged it to the edge of the aft. He made several trips into the cabin, his mouth covered with a T-shirt, his breath held as he collected the gold.

Slumped beside Jada, Cyrus faded in and out of consciousness. His chest rose and fell in fast labored breaths as if oxygen wasn't getting into his lungs. Jada's cadaverous, blue-tinged face looked like she might be close to death.

Anthony ignored them both. He had little time to at least salvage some of their riches. The seductive pangs of greed returned, filling his mind with the idea of running away and keeping everything for himself. But how? His plan made no logical sense, so he pushed it aside, and focused on the task at hand. The more gold he dropped into the ocean, the more money he could return to at a later, safer date.

With sweat streaming down his face, Anthony grabbed two gold 1KG bars from the duffle bag, wrapped them in a towel, and shoved them into his backpack. He added the rest of the gold to the duffle bag, then zipped it shut. With a strong push, he tipped it over the boat's edge. It plummeted into the watery depths.

Anthony took a six inch stack of yuans from one of the suitcases. Who knew if they'd be there when he returned? He was sure all the valuables would be confiscated if discovered. Maybe he could return later to collect the gold if he could bullshit his way out of this situation? He wasn't a great bullshitter, and this required Madoff-level bullshitting, but he had to try.

Who knew what the coast guard was going to do once they arrived?

Or what they would confiscate? He might be able to bribe his way out of an ugly situation if it arose, although he remembered Cash's quip about the bribes in China versus the bribes in the Philippines. Hopefully, Cash, a man who had been right about so much, was dead wrong about this.

Two hours later, the waters around *The Gambler* teemed with activity. Three Philippine Coast Guard cruisers surrounded the boat, bobbing in the rising swells. Several men in hazmat suits lowered an epiguard with Jada in it onto one of the cruisers. Sweat streamed down her ghostly white face. The medics glanced her over with troubled eyes. Cyrus wasn't in much better shape when he was lifted off *The Gambler* minutes later.

Anthony was the last to board the cruiser. A chubby, middle-aged Filipino medic, whose cherubic face was squashed into an ill-fitting PPE face covering, grilled him about the situation; why was he there and how did he get onto a boat in the middle of Kinatarkan Reef with two people needing serious medical attention? Anthony's vague answers offered little; his twin brother was an avid sailor, and always wanted to cruise the Philippine islands; a history buff, he wanted to dive the Japanese warplane wrecks that littered the Mactan coastline; he wasn't at the Cebu rendezvous point so Anthony hired some local fisherman to look for them. They had split the minute it became clear there was a problem. No, Anthony couldn't describe them well except for the captain's mouth of missing teeth, dark eyes, and plain looks.

When the medic pointed at the stern of the boat, Anthony followed the directions and asked, "Where are you taking me?"

"Where we take all quarantined people, Big Foot Studios," the medic said.

"Big Foot Studios?" Anthony said. He had heard of the place and even sent a pitch to the company years before, but this made absolutely no sense.

"You're going to be living on a movie set, Mr. Anthony," the medic said. "At least for the next couple of weeks."

A few hours later, the cruiser pulled into the Aduana Coast Guard Sub-Station, where Anthony was hustled into a hospital van that took him to Big Foot Studios. Four sandy brown buildings filled a four-hectare lot on the island of Mactan, a few lights lit up the offices but no movies were being made now. Hazmat-suited doctors and nurses processed Anthony as if he were a prisoner entering detention.

He was led to the quarantine center, which looked like a dorm room in an airplane hangar, complete with 100 beds spread across the clean concrete floor. A nurse pointed at an empty bed in the corner. It'd be Anthony's home for two weeks at least. He hadn't lived like this since his boarding school days in England decades earlier. The sinking feeling in his stomach reminded him of the one he'd had while watching his father's rental car disappear up the boarding school's gravel driveway and seeing his mother's slow, sad wave saying goodbye.

CHAPTER THIRTY-FIVE

"He who has a why to live for can bear almost any how." The quote from the crazy German philosopher Friedrich Nietzsche spoke to Anthony. His life had not been easy, but he'd never once thought it unbearable. There had always been a "why." He always believed his talent would take him places, but a sound stage on the edge of the Cebu Strait in the middle of a typhoon with a pandemic raging around the world was too crazy a thought, even for his highly active imagination.

However, there might be no better place to write the "Great Macau Novel" as Anthony dubbed it, tongue firmly planted in cheek, than the shadowy confines and desolate corners of an empty sound stage rattling from a once in a decade storm. The place brought him back to the Hollywood sets where he had whiled away countless hours while earning little more than a hundred bucks for a fourteen hour shift. But at least that fed him during those starving screenwriter days. Those wasted hours of waiting around for the director to shout "Action" had been the perfect time to research whatever script he had been working on at the time. How far he'd come, in so many ways, good and bad.

With the typhoon shaking everything not bolted down outside, a virus raging around the world, his fellow quarantined companions breaking into mumbled prayers and desperate "Our Fathers" every time the roof threatened to rip off its moorings, the place had an ominous end of times vibe to it. The perfect setting to write a tale about money laundering junket operators, corrupt CCP officials, *Keystone Cop* hitmen, cryptocurrency scam artists, and, above all else, a twin brother's heartless betrayal.

The irony of being stuck on a movie set at a time like this was not lost on Anthony. It was as if his old career had snatched him back and imprisoned him just to remind him he'd given up on his writerly ambitions way too soon.

The whole scene had a *Key Largo* feel to it. All it needed was the ghosts of Humphrey Bogart and Lauren Bacall sauntering into frame, or the apparition of Edward G. Robinson yelling at Claire Trevor to "Go ahead and sing," then denying her the whiskey reward she so desperately wanted because, as Robinson snidely put it, her singing was "rotten."

The words tumbled out in a torrential flood of creativity. His story turned out to be the picaresque tale of a benevolent Macau junket operator's desperate attempt to flee his country while pulling one last scam, it's always one last scam, isn't it? Colorful characters weaved in and out of a mesmerizing tale seen through the eyes of a fish-out-of-water, naive *gweilo* software salesman, whose former career as a wannabe Hollywood screenwriter gave him a unique perspective on Macau's dysfunctional lunacy. The ending of the book, however, proved problematic. Should the traitorous twin live or die, Anthony knew not. Perhaps he was taking too much from real life and needed to let the story lead him? Become a pantser, like Stephen King, recommended.

This was the kind of creativity he'd longed for his entire life. He succumbed to the force, typing away in a fury. He had read about artists going on benders, stepping out of the bullshit travails of life, zoning into a creativity that silenced the world and all its inhabitants around them. It brought not just art but genius. Now that the fates were with him, he wasn't going to let them go until he sucked every last drop of creativity out of them.

Every few hours, Anthony rang Cash's phone, but the call always clicked into voicemail. Was Cash in real trouble? Had he pulled a runner, as Detective Fonseca had warned, and Sam Slater speculated on CNBC's

   Andrew W. Pearson

YouTube channel?

"Had the man who knew how to make an impressive entrance, and an even more dramatic exit, pulled a Houdini and vanished into thin air?" Sam asked with grave seriousness in her latest videos.

Her other video featuring the discussion with Cash at the Macau Bitcoin conference had gone viral. She was milking the story as best she could, no matter what grave she pirouetted over in the process. A journalist through and through.

But if Cash had disappeared, what was the point? No money was missing, at least according to Justin. But maybe Justin was in on the scam and would disappear off the map soon enough, too? And maybe the family pictures on Justin's desk were merely a clever front to make investors think he was a family man whose life was deeply rooted in Hong Kong? Seeing conspiracies everywhere never boded well for the psyche though. "Just because you're paranoid doesn't mean they're not out to get you," is a clever saying, but better to be tripped up every now and then by a well crafted scam than envision conspiracies and plots around every innocently turned corner.

Perhaps Cash had contracted COVID and was recuperating in a hospital somewhere in China? He had carried the symptoms and had traveled to Wuhan a week before the Zhuhai meeting, so he had the opportunity to catch the virus. Perhaps he gave it to Cyrus and Jada? Maybe he had succumbed to the gruesome death? Maybe his body had been burned like so many other COVID victims in China? So many questions, so few answers, such high stakes.

The viral videos escaping China's great firewall proved disturbing; a nurse squeezing three dead infants into a body bag to save on the hospital's dwindling supplies of cadaver bags; corpses discarded from windows into parking lots filled with portable incinerators, which torched the infected day and night; satellite images showing high levels of sulfur dioxide above Wuhan that proved mass cremations were underway, at least according to the conspiracy theorists.

Forty thousand urns were distributed in Wuhan, but family members of the dead couldn't pick up the ashes of their loved ones alone. They had to come with a work associate or a friend, not a family member, to ensure the grieving didn't get out of hand and the fingers didn't point too firmly at the CCP. It was another tactic straight out of the authoritarian's playbook, make the populace think spies were everywhere, so they fear speaking openly, even about the crushing death of a parent or a wife. The CCP knew if you kowtowed after one of life's deepest losses, a death your government was probably culpable for, the captives would capitulate forever.

The mystery of Cash's disappearance proved good news for the ICO, making it even more desirable. Rumors on Telegram and Twitter speculated that Cash had betrayed one of the Macau junket operators and was now styling a new pair of concrete shoes somewhere in the Pearl River Delta off the Taipa coast. Or he had executed a "rug pull," a new term that referred to a cryptocurrency owner abandoning a project after stealing all of the investors' money, like what happened in Macau.

The White Tiger core team did little to tamper down the speculation. Any press was good press to the ICO and any press that had to do with triad suspicions of foul play added a sexiness to the cryptocoin that could hyperdrive sales. And they were right. The conspiracy angle didn't hurt one bit. Quite the opposite, demand shot through the roof.

Anthony called Vivian every day of his quarantine, letting her know how much he missed her. On a Facetime call, he asked her advice on how to set up his Coinbase account. She proved more than adept at this crypto world, and he was impressed by how quickly she immersed herself in it. She, too, had no idea where Cash was, but feared he was preparing for an "Exit scam" as she called it.

"You think there's any chance Cash would be involved in something like that?" Anthony asked.

"I don't know. There are no red flags here; the team's credible; the return projections are realistic, and it's based on a pretty successful business model. Yes, it's being heavily promoted, but what do you expect? It's a business centered around gaming, which is always going to be newsworthy, right?" Vivian said.

"Listen to you, becoming a right crypto expert now, aren't you?"

"You thought about what you're going to do once you get the coins?"

"Not really. One thing at a time with crypto."

"You should think about staking."

"What's that?"

"Like putting money into a high-yielding savings account. You lock up your coins to let them participate in running the blockchain and maintaining its security, also providing liquidity for the exchanges. You earn rewards calculated in percentage yields, usually much more than you'd get from a savings account."

"How do you know so much about this?"

"Have you seen my day job?"

Anthony nodded. "You'll never get rich working for other people."

"This could be our way out."

Anthony smiled at her use of "our." "You're right, it could be *our* way out."

On token generation day, the ICO rocketed five-fold, proving, once again, that all press is good press. That day, a Telegram message came in from Cash, asking for a quick Bitcoin loan to make a last minute coin purchase. However, word immediately spread within the White Tiger Telegram community that several fake accounts claiming to be Cash had popped up and should be ignored. Cash was still missing. Anyone giving cryptocoins to the fake Cashes would be kissing their hard earned cash or cryptocoins goodbye. Forever. Donating everything to some crypto scammer's e-wallet.

Half the work that day was uncovering cheats hoping to make a quick buck by tricking the gullible into buying bogus coins on fake platforms. Detective Fonseca had been right, the crypto world teemed with scammers of all kinds, not just the questionable promoters, but also the cockroaches who came out of the blockchain woodwork hoping to get digital wallet addresses from naïve, unsuspecting fools. A fake website popped up and emails to the hosting site warning of fraud quickly shut it down, but it was like playing whack-a-mole with swindlers; shut down one site here, see a fake Telegram group pop up there; report a bogus Twitter account here, spot a phony Discord thread spreading false info there.

By the end of the day, the coin was trading at fifteen cents, a five-fold increase from the price of Anthony's preopening coins. Anthony calculated the value of his holdings at $450,000, not bad for the limited amount of work he'd done on the project and the modest investment he'd made with Justin. Anthony logged into his MetaMask account and sold off his stash, converting it to Bitcoin, not exactly the stablist of investments but way more secure than the alternative.

Anthony held back a scream of excitement but did a little jig of celebration in the small confines of his room. However, it also wasn't lost on him that, although he had finally attained some semblance of financial freedom, he couldn't spend a dime of it. Quarantined on a soundstage in the middle of Cebu during a raging pandemic, Anthony wasn't even sure how to access the money even if he had something to spend it on. Like *Key Largo's* Claire Trevor, who was so desperate for the whiskey denied her by Edward G. Robinson, Anthony feared he might never be able to use any of the profits from his crypto sale.

Since his youth, he'd always felt destined for professional success and the riches that came with it, but his fear had always been that once he attained it, the grim reaper would sickle everything away. Seeing how things were playing out now, that dark storyline didn't seem too far-fetched, and it reminded him about the Chinese hitmen on his tail. Anthony jumped on Google and searched for any news of the story in Macau but found nothing. Perhaps Detective Fonseca was keeping it under wraps to help smoke out the conspirators or maybe the detective lied about a hitman being on his tail? His methods and intentions had been questionable at best, but making up a tale like this was too much, even for a corrupt Macau cop.

On the seventh day of quarantine, a young Filipino nurse decked out in PPE came to administer a nucleic acid COVID test. Anthony came up negative and the nurse walked him through the studio's front entrance, then pointed at an idling hospital van.

An orderly, wearing a hazmat suit and a protective N-95 mask, climbed out of the van and pulled open the side door, then pointed a silent order for Anthony to get in, no explanation offered.

"What's going on?" Anthony asked.

The orderly repeated the mimed direction, this time with squinting eyes and a frown that revealed impatience.

With a shaking head, Anthony climbed into the van.

"Where you taking me, sir?" Anthony asked as he peered at the orderly climbing into the driver's seat. He glanced into the orderly's bored eyes in the rearview. The orderly handed him a N-95 mask, then turned around and cranked up the ignition. The van pulled out of the Big Foot Studios parking lot and headed towards Quezon National Highway.

CHAPTER THIRTY-SIX

THE HOSPITAL VAN pulled into the entrance of Cebu's Chong Hua Hospital. The hazmat-suited orderly jumped out and led Anthony through a warren of hallways, up to the office of Doctor Satya Rah.

An Indian man in his early forties, Dr. Rah exuded Bollywood star charisma and had the casual countenance of someone whose life has been easy. He pointed at a chair spaced six feet from his desk. "You are Anthony Wilson, Cyrus Wilson's brother, correct?"

Anthony eased into the chair. "Twin, actually."

"Even better. Identical?"

"Fraternal. Why?"

"He donated one of his kidneys recently."

"Yes. His son was born with defective ones."

"Ah, very noble," Dr. Rah said, head bobbing, an easy, carefree smile breaking across his lips. "But unfortunately, he's only got one kidney left and that one's being ravaged by this horrendous virus. His blood type is O-negative, not too common around here. We don't have a lot of donors in normal times, and we're faced with this COVID crisis that seems to be getting worse by the day. Your kidney would, I believe, be a perfect match."

And, for Cyrus, the pendulum of luck snapped forcefully back.

"Of course, I can help," Anthony said. And, at that moment, he would do anything to help his twin, an instinctive response.

A bright, relieved smile broke across the doctor's face and his hands rose to the sky in a motion Anthony thought a little overdone. "Cyrus might only have a week or two to live if we don't get him another kidney ASAP."

"You can operate that quickly?"

"We have to."

As the doctor explained the procedure, Anthony zoned out, glancing at the window, where a plane drifted down from the sky, heading toward Mactan International Airport.

"I assume you are free for all of these tests?" Dr. Rah asked.

Anthony snapped out of his reverie. "Anything for Cyrus," escaped his lips.

"Nice to see nobility runs in the family."

CHAPTER THIRTY-SEVEN

AFTER A STANDARD battery of tests, Anthony returned to Big Foot Studios in another hospital van. On the ride back, he called Cash. Again, no answer. Voicemail full. Then he rang Detective Fonseca.

"Glad to hear you're still amongst the living, Mr. Wilson," Detective Fonseca said, his tone veering into at least somewhat pleasant territory. "I was worried about you there."

"I wanted to propose a truce," Anthony said.

"Didn't know we were at war."

"You're a detective, aren't you at war with everybody?"

Detective Fonseca grunted a chuckle.

"Has the Chinese water torture yielded anything yet?" Anthony asked.

"Mr. Wilson, we're much more civilized than that now. We still use the water, but with a board, not the dripping. Thanks to your CIA, who made it fashionable again in Iraq."

"From the Inquisition to Macau, by way of Iraq – humanity progresses."

Detective Fonseca grunted another chuckle.

Through the van's windows, Anthony watched the world pass by, everything seemed normal; Jeepneys crammed with commuters spewed thick clouds of black exhaust smoke into the street while a few brave souls hung off the back, their hair flying about in the wind, their wide smiles revealing not a care in the world even though that world was racing by them at forty miles an hour. A tuk-tuk stacked to the brim with vegetables edged its way forward while motorcycles and scooters zipped around it. Street urchin kids in threadbare clothes lined the side of the road, waiting for the traffic lights to turn red, at which time they could wander amongst the stopped cars begging for money from the bored drivers, who mostly ignored them or tapped on the window to ask them to go away.

"All jokes aside, any breaks in the investigation?" Anthony asked.

"My colleagues are still trying to retrace the first killer's steps and track down some footage of the meeting, but nothing concrete to report as of yet. As you can probably imagine, working with the Chinese police is no walk in the park."

"I might know who's involved."

"Cash?"

"Once again, detective, confirmation bias. You really should be careful your biases don't cloud your professional judgment. Make you miss important clues that point to other, more guilty parties."

"Like who?"

"I'll send you some images of them."

"*Them*? Nice, we have a conspiracy. How many enemies have you made while you've been working these black sand beach shores, Mr. Wilson?" Detective Fonseca said, his words dripping with sarcasm.

While ignoring the question, Anthony fired off several pictures of Cyrus and Jada via WhatsApp.

"This man looks mighty familiar, like you but handsome. Sure there are a few extra pounds, but sometimes that adds gravitas."

"He's my evil twin."

"That would make you the good one, which I highly doubt."

"Let's just call me the better one. Bar's pretty low with Cyrus. And 'had' might be the more optimum word as he's fighting for his life in a Cebu hospital, suffering from COVID as we speak."

"Sorry to hear that, I guess, but why would they want you dead?"

"The usual reason – greed."

"One of those seven deadlies the Christians so love. But do you have anything more concrete than a hunch about a family squabble?"

"Just a hunch, for now, that's why I'm calling you."

"Why do you suspect them?"

"For now, I'll plead the fifth."

"We don't recognize that in Macau, which makes it easier to beat out confessions."

"Studies have shown that coerced confessions can't be trusted, detective."

"And life has shown that people who start sentences with 'Studies have shown' don't know very much about life and should stay in their ivory tower think tanks and bother no one, especially busy Macau detectives."

"Anyway, no comment for now. Maybe somewhere, sometime, after all this is over, I'll share the gory familial details with you."

"Who's the woman?"

"My sister-in-law, who's the majority shareholder of the company."

"I always thought working with family was a mistake, then I became a detective and saw how horrific people behaved towards each other, *especially* when it's family."

"Working with family's fine. It's working with sociopaths that's the problem. But she's suffering from COVID, too, so maybe both my problems will work themselves out without me having to lift a finger."

"Sorry to hear that."

"Anyway, nice chatting…"

"Before you go. I probably shouldn't be telling you this, but your forthrightness deserves some reward."

"Pray do tell."

"Cash's ex-wife reported him missing yesterday. She hasn't seen him in ten days, but I'm sure she's just covering his dirty tracks."

"How can you be so sure?"

"Call it a detective's intuition."

"Not a detective's confirmation bias?"

"Maybe, but *you* could also be the one suffering from confirmation bias, you know? When did you last see Cash?"

"Maybe ten days ago. On a trip to Sanya." This time Anthony didn't hesitate. The lying was getting easier.

"Sounds like he's pulling a Le Minh Tam."

"A what?

"Not a what, a who. Le Minh Tam, CEO of Sky Mining, disappeared from Vietnam last year with $35 million of investor money, including lots of sweet, little old ladies' life savings."

"But no White Tiger money is missing, the coin went public this week and its price has skyrocketed."

"No money's missing now, but just you wait."

"Cash can't steal anything as he's locked out of the company's bank accounts."

"He'll find a way to squirrel in, as he always does. Or maybe his coin allotment was enough for him to live on? I'm sure he took care of himself very generously."

"All I know is he hasn't been in touch with anyone at the ICO in a week."

"I'd sell out as quickly as I can if I were you."

"I've sold the ones I can, but there's a lock-up period for pre-ICO coin investors."

"Don't think, just do. Don't get greedy."

"Pigs get slaughtered, I know. Although I'm not sure that idiom has any relevance today. Seems as though the greedy aren't getting slaughtered. Quite the opposite. They're the ones buying the hundred million dollar yachts while the rest of us eat slop out of long communal troughs."

"Nice visual."

"For some reason your hostility towards cryptocoins makes me think you once got burned by them."

"This isn't about me, Mr. Wilson, this is about that tiny *gweilo* dick of yours flapping about in the cool Macau breeze and me slapping a pair of handcuffs on you, remember?"

"And I thought we'd become friends."

"Detectives don't have friends, they just have pre-arrested acquaintances."

"I'll have to remember that once I return to Macau."

"As for Cash, remember, none of us are whom we seem."

"Trust me, when someone puts a hit on you, you look at everyone in your life differently."

"Ninety percent of the time, the victim knows their murderer personally. I'd advise you to go through your Rolodex and, besides each name, place a number, one through a hundred of the likelihood they are the person who wants you dead. Also place a value, one through a hundred again of what your death would mean to them financially. Net negative or net positive. It could prove highly revealing. Maybe even save your life. At this point, it'd be foolish to trust anyone."

"Thanks for the heart-warming advice."

"Please do stay safe, Mr. Wilson. It's much easier closing a case with a live witness than a dead victim."

"I'll keep that in mind while I try to stay alive."

"But, if you do plan to die, do me a favor, do it in the Philippines, not Macau. Keep my paperwork to the minimum."

"Wouldn't want to put you out, detective," Anthony said, then hung up.

CHAPTER THIRTY-EIGHT

A CHEAP SOUND system blasted a tinny version of Diana Ross's "I'm Coming Out" to the delight of a cheering section of doctors and nurses filling a small stand near a disinfectant tent. Anthony smiled, recognizing its gay anthem quality, then closed his eyes as a nurse sprayed disinfectant over him. It was "graduation day" and one negative nucleic acid test stood between another two weeks of quarantine and coveted freedom.

What freedom there was in a COVID-infected country like the Philippines was uncertain, but at least Anthony could make plans to retrieve the small fortune of gold sitting at the bottom of Kinatarkan Reef. Anthony collected the certificate verifying him COVID-free, slung his backpack over his shoulder, waved to the doctors and nurses, then joined the group of Pinoys exiting the main gate. Freedom.

Two hours later, Anthony stared in silence at the destruction of *The Gambler's* living quarters; upturned shelves, bunk askew, the kitchen table ripped off its foundation, a splintered pole in its place. Tools, papers, and discarded food littered the floor.

"COVID-19 is a virulent virus. The decontamination team had a lot of work to do," said the masked coast guard officer without a hint of irony.

Anthony had bribed the strapping and handsome officer to get aboard, but he now realized he could have walked right into a trap. The officer's countenance was that of someone who took orders seriously, except, of course when "consideration" was involved.

"But there were several suitcases on board," Anthony said. Sweat dotted his brow from the humidity made worse in the cramped quarters of the ship.

"Funny thing that, we didn't find any suitcases, Mr. Anthony," said the officer, examining Anthony's face for a reaction; eyes direct and challenging, muscles tightening under his starched white shirt.

"There were five suitcases, at least that's what my brother said. He asked me to pick some things up because he's in the hospital with COVID."

"This a vacation trip for your brother and his wife?"

"With some business thrown in."

"What kind of business, sir?"

"We work with casinos. IT consulting."

"Ah, I see."

Anthony recognized an air of contempt appearing on the officer's face; the mouth curved into a slight sneer. Because the Philippines was a Catholic country, the casino industry was seen as a sin industry and workers in the business were often looked down upon. "Were they taken somewhere else during the cleaning?" Anthony asked.

"We didn't find any suitcases. Or any stacks of money in those suitcases," the officer said, staring hard at Anthony.

"Stacks of money?"

A haughty smile appeared on the officer's face; it said he was in on the pantomime. "Exactly, Mr. Wilson, what stacks of money?"

Anthony stared at the officer for a few seconds, unsure how this was going to end. With his hand, he wiped the sweat from his brow.

"Nothing is missing, Mr. Wilson," the officer said.

The money had disappeared into the widows and orphans fund of the Philippine Coast Guard. Anthony glanced at the officer, instinctively knowing he could be in real trouble if he didn't play this scene to perfection. The officer had moved to block the one escape route.

The smile and cheery countenance returned to the officer's face. "You a good dancer, Mr. Wilson?"

Anthony's brow furrowed. "A-a-a good dancer?"

"Cebu is famous for three things, Mr. Wilson, its beautiful beaches, its beautiful women, and its dancing inmates. I don't know if you've seen the *Thriller* video that went viral in the early days of YouTube. Two hundred inmates from the Cebu Provincial Detention Center dancing in unison to Michael Jackson's most famous song."

Anthony remembered it well. Men in orange jumpsuits gyrating to the hit song as a transvestite playing the role of Ola Ray cowered in mock fear while trying to evade his or her fellow 'zombie' inmates.

Anthony smirked. "I've seen it, officer."

"Looks like fun, doesn't it? But, trust me, the Cebu Provincial Detention Center is no place for foreigners. The Philippines is famous for its hospitality. Our people are always smiling, they say. Well, I don't think you'd like the kind of Philippine hospitality the CPDC offers. They still do it, to this day. It's a tourist attraction, although the playlist has changed. More Lady Gaga now. But you will have plenty of time to work on your cha-cha-cha if you're interested in pursuing lost suitcases."

"Never been a fan of Michael Jackson or Lady Gaga for that matter," Anthony said, eyeing the officer cautiously. "Thank you for your time, officer."

The officer stepped aside, offering Anthony a way out. "Nothing's missing, Mr. Wilson, you sure?"

"You know what I love about dealing with the Pinoys?"

"What's that, sir?"

"Your English is so good, we understand each other on a subtextual level," Anthony said as he stepped past the officer.

It was a statement that seemed to go right over the officer's head, which turned to the side.

"For a writer that's important," Anthony added, almost to himself.

"You have the title for the boat, Mr. Wilson?"

"My office is trying to dig it up," Anthony said. A blatant lie. He was the office.

"Maybe we can overlook that fact if you can get the boat out of here right away. If you can provide some consideration," the officer said.

Good God, these people have no shame, Anthony thought, digging into his pocket for the last of his cash. "If you help me get the engine started."

Thirty minutes later, Anthony navigated the boat out of the marina, under the watchful eye of the Philippines Coast Guard officer, whose salute contained the profound respect normally reserved for an admiral.

"Glad we could be of assistance, Mr. Wilson. You have the look of a fine sailor, but don't get caught between the devil and the deep blue sea now," the officer said.

Anthony ignored the comment, his attention consumed by his latest task, steering a forty foot yacht out of the marina. He piloted the boat into the Cebu Strait, then headed for the commercial marina, where a slip had been rented. He still had the bars of gold on him, and it was time to cash them in, then figure out a way to collect the rest of the loot from the bottom of Kinatarkan Reef. *Not everything was lost.*

♦ CHAPTER THIRTY-NINE

THE BRIGHT RED and green LED light of a pawn broker's sign, three spheres suspended from a bar, glowed on the wall of a small strip mall next to a pet store. Jewelry, accessories, gadgets, game consoles, laptops, and tablets filled the glass front shop window.

Inside the store, the owner, a scrawny Filipino man in his sixties, with a double-eyed loupe atop his bald head, and his chubby face carrying a half-amused, half-accusatory smile playing across his peeling lips, looked over Anthony's gold bar. "Sorry to tell you this, boss, but 'dis ain't real gold."

Anthony's shoulders slumped and his eyes squinted in displeasure. *Everything was lost.*

The pawnbroker pulled out a knife, and scratched the bar's surface, leafing away gold flakes. "Not even a good fake. This is supposed to be a Perth mint gold bar, but it shouldn't be this shiny. Should be more matted, more muted. Color's all wrong, too."

"Are you kidding me?"

The pawnbroker slid the bar back to Anthony. "No, unfortunately, I'm not. You got taken. This is a worthless chunk of tungsten."

"Shit."

"Where'd you get it?"

Anthony picked up the gold bar and dumped it into his backpack. "China."

The pawnbroker chuckled. "Made in China. Figures. I see many of them these days. People need to be more careful. How much you pay?"

"I don't know. It's a friend's."

The pawnbroker shot Anthony a 'sure-it-is' look, then added, "Well, tell your friend, he's a sucker who got robbed."

"I'll be sure to let him know," Anthony said, slinging his backpack over his shoulder. He exited the store, barely holding back his desire to slam the front door. This meant the entire stash of gold sitting on the bottom of Kinatarkan Reef was probably as worthless as the sand drifting around it in the languid tide too. Would Cash have known the gold was fake? That made no sense. Although maybe it did if he thought Cyrus wouldn't check it before stashing it in Cebu. How ironic the bag containing the 'gold' was probably far more valuable than the 'gold' itself, if the bag wasn't counterfeit too. The odds of that were probably fifty-fifty.

Anthony returned to *The Gambler*, his home until the operation. He had prepaid the marina for a couple of months of slip fees. The hope that the virus would be quickly contained had proved to be wishful thinking. Hotspots were exploding across the globe. The virus was ripping through the elderly community in Italy, filling up hospitals with the dying, mortuaries with the dead, and cruelly separating loved ones without even a kiss or a hug goodbye.

As Anthony swept up the debris littering the cabin floor, he noticed a sealed envelope addressed to Cyrus in the trash. He tore it open and pulled out a letter. It was an official-looking letter all in Chinese, with Cash's signature scrawled in red ink. Anthony pulled out his phone, tapped on the Google translate app, then scanned the letter. It was the boat's title with Cash's signature relinquishing ownership; the section for the new owner was left blank. Anyone could add their name and take full ownership of the boat. A smile broke across Anthony's face. *Maybe not everything was lost, after all?*

CHAPTER FORTY

On *The Gambler*, Anthony watched another mystical hour come to a close as a charcoal black sky consumed the sun's dying cadmium red rays. He slugged his coffee, then got back to work on the novel. The tale about a young gangster in the tiny enclave of Macau came into view, replete with machine gun assassinations once orchestrated by colorfully named gang leaders like Fatti Pui, and Broken Tooth but now by a gangster modeled after Cash Cheang. As he wrote with a fury he'd never experienced before, he was reminded of a line from one of his favorite novels that captured Macau's essence so well, "Neither fiction nor nonfiction, but a flickering between them."

Anthony's mobile phone rang. It was a WhatsApp call from Detective Fonseca. Anthony answered with a curt "Hello."

"I'm sending you some photos," Detective Fonseca said.

Several images popped into Anthony's phone. He clicked on them. Grainy shots of what looked like two people sitting in a fancy café that could have been in Paris, but for the large Chinese characters displayed on the wall art behind them.

"That's the first hitman and the person who wants you dead. Recognize him?" Detective Fonseca asked.

"This the best you can do?"

"For now."

"This evidence might work in a Chinese kangaroo court, but it'd be inadmissible in any American one. A brown check scarf and a cap are about all I can make out," Anthony said.

"I know but give them some time. They're pulling footage from other shops cattycorner to the restaurant."

"They've interviewed the restaurant's workers?"

"Yes."

"No one recognized a *gweilo* entering around that time. Our kind do tend to stand out, you know?"

"No."

"These images taken from video?"

"Yeah."

"You know you can identify people by the way they walk these days, gait recognition. It's more accurate than fingerprinting."

"Really?"

"Apparently, a walk says a lot about a person. Ted Bundy could tell a victim by the way she walked down the street."

"Who's Ted Bundy?"

"One of America's most notorious serial killers."

"Ah, we don't follow those in Macau."

"For an example closer to home, police in China are nabbing jaywalkers with gait recognition as well as setting boundaries in Xinjiang to spot Uighurs leaving set areas."

"You a biometrics expert now?

"Yeah, as a matter of fact, I am. It's part of my job. Casinos want to recognize their high rollers once they walk in the door. Macau banned facial recognition technology for anything other than security purposes a year ago, so we had to find a workaround."

"Did *we* now? I'm sure the gaming board would love to hear about those workarounds."

"I'm sure you have much more important things to do than file reports about speculative technology with the DCIJ, detective."

"Doesn't sound so speculative to me, at least not from the way you're

     Andrew W. Pearson

describing it."

"I'm a salesman, detective. Hype is my default tone. As Cyrus once said, half the shit we pitch can't be done, but if we told our customers which half, they wouldn't buy any of the software we're trying to sell them. Any news on Cash?"

"Not a peep. I'm sure he's holed up in some presidential suite somewhere overlooking a beach while sipping champagne and watching naked hookers tally up his ill-gotten gains."

"That's quite the visual you have there, detective, I'll have to put it in one my books."

"Your life's a life, Mr. Wilson, not an allegory."

"If you're a writer, your life better be an allegory," Anthony said, then hung up.

CHAPTER FORTY-ONE

Cebu Pacific flight 362 touched down in Macau at 10:35 p.m., just about on time for its customary one hour lateness. Anthony streamed through immigration, then customs. He showed his COVID-free nucleic acid test to a pair of hazmat-suited nurses, then walked out of baggage claim, straight into Vivian's awaiting arms.

Beaming brightly, she smothered his face with kisses. "I missed you so much."

An hour later, Vivian sat before a mirror in Anthony's bedroom, applying perfume to her slender neck while reading Maggie's famous three minute monologue from a dog-eared copy of Tennessee Williams' *Cat on a Hot Tin Roof*, ending with, "That's the truth, Brick." She glanced expectantly at Anthony, whose eyes took in her beauty. Her little black dress delicately silhouetted her slim figure, revealing long, toned legs.

"You look glorious," Anthony said.

She playfully smacked his arm with the book. "And. The. Performance?"

"Let's get out of Macau. Let's go to Cebu. Live on a boat. Learn to fish and sail. Learn how to survive on the water. Hunt for sunken Japanese treasure all day, make love all night, when we're not watching movies. I'll teach you all I know about acting, which isn't much, I'll admit, but you'll be safe out there on the water, away from all this COVID craziness."

Vivian's eyes widened in excitement. "Let's."

Anthony took her in his arms and kissed her neck, one finger slipping under her dress strap.

They moved to the bed, where she unzipped his fly, smiled seductively, "I like a man with a large appendix."

Anthony chuckled. "I think you mean a large appendage. Although 'I like a man with a large appendix' does make an interesting start to a vampire flick." Baring his teeth, he played the role of the innocent soon-to-be male victim in a vampire movie, "I think you mean a large appendix, honey."

Vivian giggled.

Anthony feigned the role of a female vampire speaking in a heavy female Eastern European accent, "No, I like a man with a large appendix. More to digest." Then he dove into her neck, nipping at her tender flesh as she playfully giggled away.

Several hours later, with Vivian lying across his chest, Anthony stared out the window deep in thought, but then prodded her awake. "So how does that liquidity mining work?"

Vivian rolled over, on the edge of sleep, and explained, "Mining's not buying and selling, you're loaning your coins to the cryptocurrency exchange."

"Like margining a stock?"

"In a way, I guess. It's safe because the funds are in your account. All you need to do is buy a mining certificate, which costs nothing, a hundred MOP."

"You doing it?"

"I've sold all the White Tiger coins I'm allowed to, moved that money into Ethereum, which I'm mining now."

"Give me the details tomorrow."

Through sleepy eyes, Vivian nodded, then rolled over.

CHAPTER FORTY-TWO

A POUNDING ON the door woke Anthony. He rolled out of bed, slipped into some pants, grabbed a shirt, then headed to the living room.

"Immigration!" Detective Fonseca shouted from the other side of the door.

Anthony pulled open the front door, revealing Detective Fonseca lingering in the doorway.

"Why didn't you tell me you were returning home? Embarrassing for me to find out from immigration," Detective Fonseca said.

"I've had psycho girlfriends who weren't as interested in my whereabouts as you, detective," Anthony said.

"Surprised you felt safe enough to come back, actually."

"Maybe I was getting as far away as possible from the two people I thought most likely to be involved in this. You know how much murder goes for in Cebu these days?"

"With Duerte's war on drug pushers and drug users, probably about twenty bucks."

"Exactly. Can't outsource it at that price."

Detective Fonseca pulled out his iPhone and offered it up. "Does this walk look familiar to you?"

Anthony took the phone and looked down at the video playing on the screen. "Can't say that it does, but I've never really focused on the way people walk."

Detective Fonseca sauntered in. "Good to know. I guess that means you're not a serial killer."

Anthony smirked.

"I'll send you a link to the video, you can review it in detail later. See if it triggers anything from your seedy and shady past." Detective Fonseca said.

Anthony handed the iPhone back to Detective Fonseca.

"Come, let me buy you some Stone Soup," Detective Fonseca said.

Anthony glanced back into the bedroom.

Detective Fonseca's eyes followed Anthony's gaze. "Oh, sorry, did I disturb you?"

"No."

"Taking advantage of our fair maidens again?"

"I'll be right with you detective, let me get a jacket," Anthony said, stepping into the bedroom.

In the shadow of the 17th-century fort that kept Macau safe from marauding pirates and overly ambitious colonialists for five centuries, one of its best-kept culinary secrets, Mariazinha, hid on a quiet cobblestone side street. The restaurant was known only to a select group of diners who frequented it more than they probably should, but did so to ensure the place stayed in business and seats were always available to those in the know.

Detective Fonseca strutted in the door, Anthony at his side. The waitresses, bartenders, and restaurant manager greeted Detective Fonseca with bright smiles, warm hugs, and hearty Portuguese salutations. Anthony's eyebrow flash expressed his surprise at the camaraderie. He didn't know how to feel about this softer, more humane side of Detective Fonseca, who introduced him simply as Anthony, but with a warm slap on the shoulder that seemed to imply close friendship.

The manager led Detective Fonseca and Anthony to a table by a hearth containing the dying embers of a small fire. Detective Fonseca lowered himself into a seat while the manager tossed another log onto the fire.

"Best Portuguese restaurant in town," Detective Fonseca said.

"I think I've read about it," Anthony said.

Detective Fonseca studied Anthony. "Have you ever tried Stone Soup?"

Anthony settled into a seat across from Detective Fonseca, eyeing him warily. "Never even heard of it."

With two fingers raised in somewhat of a loose peace sign, Detective Fonseca motioned his order to the dark-skinned, Portuguese waitress standing by the table. "*Duas sopas de pedra.*"

The waitress nodded, then glided away in a motion as smooth and practiced as a Russian virtuoso ballerina exiting the Bolshoi stage.

Detective Fonseca's eyes returned to Anthony. "Beware of monks seeking stones."

"Meaning?"

"There's a story they tell in Portugal about a monk who visits a small town in the hills above Porto. The monk innocently asks a villager for a stone because he wants to make some soup. The villager, thinking it's just a stone, gladly complies, and hands over a few worthless rocks. The monk places them on the ground, then asks for some twigs for a fire. The villager thinks, it's just some sticks, and complies. Then the monk asks to borrow a pot. It's just a short-term loan, thinks the villager, so he provides a pot. Then the monk needs some water, for what good is a fire laid out on a bed of stones and a pot without something to boil in it? The villager complies. The monk looks at the boiling water and says he needs some vegetables. The villager agrees and hands over some carrots, celery, potatoes, and other vegetables. By the end of the story, the monk has a hearty stew filled with vegetables, meat, and local herbs. Then he very innocently asks for some bread, for, as we all know a soup isn't really a soup without some good old crusty bread to go with it."

A growing smile of realization crossed Anthony's face. "And the villager complies."

"And the villager complies."

"We call that the foot in the door technique, but I like your folk-lore take on it, much more colorful. And more realistic with those sneaky monks and all."

"You seem like a good man, Mr. Wilson. But one who's in way over his head."

"We're probably all in way over our heads, detective. It's called living life."

Detective Fonseca pulled out an envelope and handed it to Anthony. "A good prosecutor will tell you, you don't catch the geniuses."

"What's this?"

"*Your* criminal record. A rather comical one at that – drunk and disorderly at Disneyland. What were you thinking?"

"This vodka tastes good," Anthony joked, a disarming smile playing across his lips. He opened the envelope, and pulled out the letter, seeing the FBI seal atop it. "A misdemeanor, detective. Years ago. An indiscretion of youth."

"This would all be under the bridge stuff, but Macau is particularly uptight about who it allows in these days as well as who it wants expunged. We're aiming for Olympic medalists and Nobel prize winners, not criminal convicts."

"Good luck with that. But so typically Macau, a country that has no Olympic team wants to recruit Olympic medalists to move here? Who they going to train?" Anthony said, shaking his head.

"Self-awareness is not one of the SAR's strong points, I'll give you that."

"Look, detective, I spent a few hours in an Anaheim holding cell, sobering up. I'm hardly a hardened felon."

"Perhaps, but this is something you failed to mention on your blue card application."

Anthony held his tongue, maybe the detective would make something out of this? Anthony knew, in negotiations, letting an opponent speak first, and having them lay out their demands, was usually the best move.

"You used your British passport on your blue card application. Very clever. Keeps the U.S. criminal slate hidden," Detective Fonseca said.

"Seemed like that indiscretion of youth was best left buried. Not really indicative of someone who otherwise kept his nose clean for over two decades. I'm surprised that blemish was still on my record, actually. Even more surprised you dug it up."

"We're not as backward as we appear to be in Macau."

"You might be the exception to the rule, detective."

"Backhanded compliments aren't always compliments, Mr. Wilson. You're lucky I'm not Chinese, I might take that as an attack on my face."

"And serve me cat or dog?"

"You've heard the stories?"

Anthony nodded. "And probably unknowingly eaten cat or dog once or twice."

Detective Fonseca laughed. "And I'm sure you would have deserved it."

Anthony pushed the letter across the table. "You going to make a stink out of this to immigration?"

Detective Fonseca took the letter, returned it to the envelope, and pocketed it. "I'll just keep it safe and sound, for now, should I need it for a rainy day."

"Well, you might not need it at all, detective. I'm here to pack up my things. I'll be leaving Macau for good by the end of the week."

"Something we can both celebrate," Detective Fonseca said with a tight smile.

"In the meantime, in our more important storyline, any news on

Cash?"

"Not a peep. It's like he's orchestrated the perfect exit scam."

"Without taking any money? Not much of an exit scam. White Tiger's now a legit coin, trading on legit exchanges."

"Nothing about that coin is legit, but Cash has vanished off the face of the earth, probably something he was planning to do all along. Was he acting suspiciously the last time you saw him?"

"Define suspicious, detective. Everything going on around here seems suspicious to me."

"Was he preparing to disappear? Laundering more money than usual?"

"That's not the kind of work I did for him."

"Of course, it wasn't," Detective Fonseca said with the flash of a condescending smile. "And Macau's jails are only filled with wrongfully convicted, innocent men."

"That joke's getting a little stale, detective."

"I can offer you immunity."

"From what? Making a few hundred grand on a legal cryptocoin? Detective, I don't know anything. I didn't see anything suspicious in Cash's behavior the last few times I saw him. I'm as much in the dark about his disappearance as you are. My company was just building some facial recognition technology for his junket room, nothing more, nothing less."

"If that's so, you're not as good of a salesman as you claim to be."

"True that, detective. And I'm thinking of bringing my not-so-stellar sales career to a quick end."

"A man must know his limitations."

"No surprise you can quote *Dirty Harry*."

The waitress stepped up to the table, placed the bowls of Stone Soup and some bread before the men.

"Please, eat," Detective Fonseca said in a tone that sounded like a directive.

Anthony took a spoonful of the soup, blew on it to cool it down, then ate it. He smiled at the tangy flavor, a mixture of beef, hearty vegetables, and herbs he couldn't quite place. He put his spoon down. "I assume you are also a Bond fan."

"The Daniel Craig ones aren't unwatchable."

"Did you know Ian Fleming spent some time here in Macau and *Goldfinger* is based on a man who resided here, someone who got exceedingly rich trading gold at a time when it was illegal to trade that commodity on the open market? He even has a street named after him just a few blocks from here. Another dubiously made fortune, something that seems commonplace in Macau."

"You a Macau historian now?"

"More of a film lover. There's a wonderful line in that movie when Bond is being tortured by Goldfinger. Bond looks down at the laser slowing burning its way towards his crotch. Goldfinger tells Bond to choose his witticism wisely. Trying not to show any fear, Bond says, 'You expect me to talk?' To which, Goldfinger laughs and replies, 'No, Mr. Bond, I expect you to die.' It's short, sweet, and straight to the laser point."

"And your point is?"

"Detective, I came to Macau to get rich and I did, legally. Now, it's time for me to go. I don't think I'll be sticking around to let any other potential murderer take a pot shot at me or give a specific Macau detective the chance to throw me in jail. When I was in that Anaheim holding cell, sobering up, I had plenty of time to think. I remember that time as if it was yesterday. I had one thought and only one thought on my mind – how much I loved freedom. And, in that cell, I made a vow that I would never again let anyone take away my freedom," Anthony said, rising from the table. "Thank you for the soup, detective. You're right, it is delicious, but I have more important things to do now."

"Like screw our Macau whores?"

Anthony clenched his teeth, ignoring the insult. "Don't be offended or take this the wrong way, but, hopefully, I will never see you again."

A teasing smile broke across Detective Fonseca's face. "And I thought we had reached a certain level of trust and understanding."

"Trust. That's a funny word. Used by the people who, more often than not, deserve it the least."

"You always cheat the ones closest to you, as the old Chinese saying goes."

"How do I even know you're telling me the truth about these hitmen?"

An opaque smile broke across Detective Fonseca's lips. "If you're interested, Mr. Wilson, I can give you an opportunity very few people in this world ever get."

"What's that, detective?"

"A chance to look into the eyes of the man who wants you dead."

CHAPTER FORTY-THREE

Anthony sank into the leather passenger seat of Detective Fonseca's immaculately clean, ten-year-old Audi Quattro. On the ride to the station, he stared out at the mostly empty Macau streets in steely silence. A foreboding sense of doom swept over him, but he knew this was another opportunity he couldn't pass up. The experience would be incalculable for his writing. What malevolence would he see in the eyes of someone hired to kill him?

Detective Fonseca called the station, spoke for about thirty seconds in Cantonese, then explained to Anthony the suspect would be brought in for a line-up.

"A line-up? But I've never seen him before," Anthony said, his tone filled with skepticism and doubt.

Detective Fonseca smirked. "Don't you have to see the guy first to know you've never seen him before?"

Although Anthony wanted to shake his head at the tautological absurdity of Detective Fonseca's statement, he had to agree the detective was epistemologically correct. How do you know you don't know someone until you've physically seen them?

Minutes later, Detective Fonseca pulled into the Departamento Policial de Macau. Anthony remembered the four story beige building from Cash's arraignment. Detective Fonseca parked in his assigned spot, then led Anthony into an official police entrance.

While walking through the station, Anthony recognized he was getting way too familiar with the inner workings of law enforcement. He'd once been on the receiving end of a misdemeanor, so seeing policing's inner workings from a safe and nonconfrontational distance was a pleasant change, but, still, this was way too close. However, he mentally logged every detail about the place for his story.

Detective Fonseca led Anthony through a winding hallway filled with plaques and photographs of the police commissioner smiling amongst a bank of officers standing with the city leaders at one event after another.

"We use the 'PEACE' interrogation method here," Detective Fonseca said.

"There's an oxymoron," Anthony said.

"PEACE, as in preparation and planning, engage and explain, account, closure, and evaluate. The non-confrontational approach the British prefer."

"Aren't acronyms great?" Anthony said in a sarcastic tone, a salty smile breaking across his lips.

Detective Fonseca nodded. "I've been pushing for the more confrontational Reid Technique you Americans prefer, and I think I've finally found a sympathetic ear—Beijing's."

"I bet. They're no slouches when it comes to Catherine Wheel torture techniques."

"Could teach the Japanese Imperialists a thing or two."

Detective Fonseca led Anthony into a small room lined with floor-to-ceiling, sound-reducing padding, and a one-way window that looked into a darkened room. A young officer and a middle-aged, Chinese detective bookended the window. The Chinese detective had an official-looking document attached to a clipboard.

"The person who committed the crime may or may not be one of the people you are about to view," the Chinese detective said. "You should remember, it's just as important to clear an innocent person as it is to lock up a guilty one."

Detective Fonseca grabbed the clipboard and handed it to Anthony. "Please look at them all. Make a decision about each person before moving on to the next. And sign this."

Anthony complied and returned the clipboard to the second detective, who left the room to start proceedings.

The light in the opposite room flickered on. The lineup, which wasn't really a lineup, but more like a parade, began. The first suspect, a Chinese man in his forties, walked in while holding a handwritten sign with "Number 1" over his chest.

"Do you recognize this man, Mr. Wilson?" Detective Fonseca asked while shaking his head. "It's never the first, by the way."

Anthony shook his head while the suspect turned to the side. Standing in the presence of someone who wanted you dead should be a chilling experience, but having to figure out which exact suspect it was mitigated some of the fear. Confusion filled Anthony's mind more than anything.

Suspect number one turned to the side, remained still for a moment, turned 180 degrees, and then walked out. The second suspect looked similar to the first, carrying a stuntman's resemblance to an actor he stands in for. The suspect mechanically stepped through the three positions. The third and fourth suspects followed.

"Take your time. No need to rush," Detective Fonseca said.

The faces blurred one into one another until Detective Fonseca gave Anthony a subtle nod about suspect five; this was the one. Anthony stepped closer to the window, stared at the man who might have sent him to a cold grave but for a touch of worldly greed.

"Do you recognize *this* man, Mr. Wilson?" Detective Fonseca asked.

The resemblance was slight, but Anthony had the sinking feeling he'd seen the man before and recently. He just couldn't quite place him. In Asia, he'd often been caught in situations where strangers broke into wide smiles of recognition at him when he had no clue who they were. Often, they had met, but Anthony didn't know from where. Being white in a sea of Asian faces made him stand out, so it wasn't surprising he got noticed. He'd always considered himself good with faces, but maybe his memory was failing him at this most important time. A recollection now could potentially save his life, but he came up empty.

"Do you recognize this man, Mr. Wilson?" Detective Fonseca repeated.

Anthony shook his head. "No, detective, I've never seen him before."

Detective Fonseca studied Anthony carefully, his eyes squinting in suspicion.

As the suspect stepped out of the opposite room, Anthony bolted for the door. He yanked it open, then grabbed the suspects by the collar. "Who hired you?"

The suspect's eyes popped open wide, his pupils darting about in fear. Anthony grabbed him by the shoulders and shook him. The suspect's mouth dropped open. A garbled string of unknown Mandarin words gurgled out.

"Who hired you?!!" Anthony shouted while shaking the man violently.

The suspect cowered in fear, hands shooting up to his head for protection.

"Do you recognize me?" Anthony said.

Detective Fonseca barreled out of the witness room, and jumped into the fray, wrestling Anthony off the suspect. "Settle down, Mr. Wilson, Settle down. He doesn't understand you."

Two policemen grabbed the suspect, yanked him to his feet, then pulled him away.

On the drive back to One Central, Detective Fonseca side-eyed Anthony. "So, you obviously prefer the fist interrogation method."

Anthony turned to Detective Fonseca but said nothing. Ashamed by his earlier actions, he stewed in silence.

"We often use it, too. More and more often these days, actually," Detective Fonseca said, his eyes returning to the road. "I don't blame you. I really don't. I'm kind of glad you did it."

"That why you tipped me off?" Anthony asked.

"Your actions say a lot about you. And his actions say a lot about him; he didn't recognize you. That means he's probably never seen you or, more importantly, your twin before. That's extremely helpful information. Narrows the list of potential suspects."

"Glad I could be of assistance, detective," Anthony said in a deep tone of sarcasm.

Detective Fonseca turned and looked directly into Anthony's eyes, interrogating him. "But you recognized him, didn't you?"

Anthony shook his head. "I thought I did, but I was wrong."

"I don't believe you."

"I read somewhere that ten percent of the Chinese Han population descended from one man, Ghenghis Khan. It's no surprise so many of them look alike."

Detective Fonseca studied Anthony carefully, eyes squinting in suspicion, not believing Anthony's words. His attention turned back to the road.

"Which one was he? Hitman one, two, three, or four?" Anthony asked.

"One. He got word the fourth confessed to the Zhuhai police, so he headed to Macau, figured he could hide out here for a while, or, if he did get caught, he'd do his time here rather than on the mainland. He never factored in death by crazed twin, though," Detective Fonseca said with a side glance and a disarming smile.

"What'll happen to him?"

Detective Fonseca shrugged. "An old man of sixty-five strangled his wife last year, not but a mile from here. He confessed and got a ten year sentence. Your guy wanted to, but didn't go through with killing you, so he'll probably get a lesser sentence."

"Surprised you don't have more crime with pathetically short sentences like that. Although I never bought into the theory that harsh penalties reduced crime."

"Even now?"

Anthony's right eyebrow rose. "Let's just say, the lock 'em up and throw away the key side of the argument gets more seductive with each hitman hired."

Detective Fonseca chuckled knowingly. "In law enforcement, we call that incarceration bias."

CHAPTER FORTY-FOUR

THE NEXT MORNING, after breakfast in bed, Anthony pulled out his Nikon F5 camera and showed it off to Vivian. "Time to make you a star."

Vivian clapped her hands like an excited child. "I'm ready for my close-up. And long-shot. And two-shot. Is that how you say it?"

"Yes," Anthony said while surreptitiously pocketing the diamond ring he'd planned to offer her later that day. The two shot in multiple locations around Macau, recreating famous film and theater scenes in ironically juxtaposed settings. Behind a Roman-inspired colosseum at Fisherman's Wharf, Vivian played the role of Blanch DuBois, reciting *A Streetcar Named Desire's* famous, "He was a boy, just a boy" monologue. On Legend Boulevard, next to an Art Deco building that would fit in perfect Art Deco harmony alongside Miami Beach's Collins Avenue, Vivian performed the "It does not say RSVP on the Statue of Liberty" speech from *Clueless*, with just the right amount of spritely energy the role required.

Wandering through the winding and uneven cobblestone streets of Old Town Taipa, Vivian gave a heartfelt rendition of Jo March's words from *Little Women*, "Women have minds and souls as well as hearts, ambition, and talent as well as beauty and I'm sick of being told that love is all a woman is fit for."

Sitting in Saint Augustine Square a few hours later, Vivian's eyebrows shot up in excitement at Rosamund Pike's *Gone Girl's* monologue, "I am so much happier now that I'm dead." Anthony felt the lines seemed to strike a chord deep within her. Maybe she had seen the movie and something about her first marriage resonated in that dark soliloquy?

In the last scene of the day, Vivian played the role of Marquise de Merteuil from *Dangerous Liaisons*, perfectly capturing the character's cunning and deceitful heart. The line about women needing to be far more skillful than men as they can have their lives and reputations ruined with a few well-chosen words came out deftly. Her dark eyes homed in on Anthony on the other side of the camera, giving him chills.

Back at the apartment, Anthony uploaded the footage to his laptop and opened the editing software.

"So, what happens next? You introduce me to your casting director friends?" Vivian asked.

"That's the easy part. Let's get this in the can then plan a trip to L.A. I can introduce you around then," Anthony said.

He spent the next few hours crafting the clips into an impressive showreel, marveling at how editing technology had radically improved since the last time he'd clipped together some corporate videos on an early version of Apple's *Final Cut*. After piecing together a five-minute reel, he showed Vivian an early cut. Her bright beaming smile approved. It was a smile Anthony knew others would fall in love with as well.

"I'm going to be a star," Vivian said, her tone filled with ironic playfulness.

"You know what Marilyn Monroe once said about Hollywood?" Anthony asked.

Vivian shook her head.

"It's a place where they'll pay you a thousand dollars for a kiss and fifty cents for your soul."

"Well, too late, my soul's already taken," Vivian said, then kissed Anthony softly on the lips.

Around five p.m., when the late after sun filtered across the room, Anthony popped open a bottle of Bordeaux. He poured two glasses and handed one to Vivian. They clinked their glasses together, then drank.

"By the way, you started the liquidity mining yet?" Vivian asked.

"No," Anthony said.

"I've been making three percent a month on my Ethereum balance."

"Show me how," Anthony said, sitting down on the couch. He grabbed his computer, booted it up, then pulled up his Coinbase account.

Vivian grabbed her purse, took out a sheet of paper, and handed it to Anthony. "This is the address you need to get the mining certificate."

Anthony typed the website's address into his browser as he took a swig of wine.

"And don't worry, you always have access to your funds if you need them later on. Trust me, it's easy money," Vivian said.

"Okay. Here goes nothing," Anthony said while entering his account number into the website.

Vivian rose, kissed him on the cheek, then pointed to his wine glass. "More?"

Anthony nodded.

Vivian grabbed the bottle from the counter as well as her purse.

"Let the liquidity mining begin," Anthony said as his finger hovered above the keyboard. But something held him back. He couldn't hit the enter key to set the crypto mining process in motion. Something deep inside prevented him. He thought back on his conversation the previous day with Detective Fonseca – You always cheat the ones closest to you, the old Chinese saying goes.

Vivian returned with the bottle of Bordeaux and her purse, which she placed on the edge of the couch. She refilled Anthony's glass, brow wrinkling, eyes probing with questions. "Something the matter?"

Anthony shook his head.

"You have more questions?" Vivian asked.

"Just a little cautious when it comes to sending money to unknown websites, especially when they lack FDIC insurance."

"FDIC insurance?"

"Something we have in America. Insurance that ensures corrupt banking execs doesn't steal your money. Not that comfortable with crypto, to be honest."

"Even now?"

"Even now."

"You're making five per cent a month. It's risk-reward. Live a little, Anthony. I thought you were a man willing to take risks."

"I am, of course."

"Just start small, add more later."

Vivian picked up her wine glass, drank a sip, then reached for her purse.

"Yeah," Anthony said. But before he knew what had happened, he caught the flash of sunlight glinting off something metallic. The sharp point of a push dagger's blade dug into his neck. A pinprick cut drew blood.

"What the hell?" Anthony shouted, his tone filled with confusion and dread.

"Don't. Move!" Vivian said, a strident command without a hint of empathy.

Anthony stared into Vivian's dead and emotionless eyes. The cold eyes of a calculating killer. *You*, he thought, but he couldn't quite grasp why this woman he loved wanted to do him harm.

"Just keep doing what you're doing, and it will all be over soon," Vivian said while digging the knife deep into Anthony's neck. Blood oozed across the blade. "Put in your password."

Anthony leaned slightly forward, fingers hovering above the computer keys. He typed in a password, but when he hit enter the website rejected it.

"Stop stalling," Vivian said, digging the dagger deeper into his stubbly chin. "You've been fun, Anthony, but it's time to pay up."

The words annoyed him. His hands hovered over the keyboard, but then he pushed the laptop into her ribs and tumbled off the couch, crashing to the floor. He looked up to see Vivian climb off the couch, then correct the grip of her push dagger's T-shaped handle. It fit perfectly, as if it were part of her palm. A troubling thought. Push daggers might be the smallest daggers in the world, but they were also some of the most deadly.

With widening eyes, Vivian jumped towards Anthony. The dagger slashed through the air, heading for his throat. He rolled aside.

The dagger's point stuck into the wooden floorboards beside his head. Anthony scrambled to his feet. Vivian yanked the dagger from the floor, jumped up, then eased into a fighting stance. She charged Anthony, dagger first.

Anthony retreated towards the kitchen. "What the hell are you doing?!!"

Vivian's intense eyes, raised eyebrows, and flared nostrils spoke of a fearless woman ready for battle. Her goal: complete the mission, a mission that might not end well for Anthony, but she didn't seem to care.

His mind centered, quickly overriding his initial confusion. Trying to make sense of an insane situation was a waste of time. He immediately recognized the mortal threat she posed. His body defaulted to "fight or flight" mode. His heart rate quickened, his breath shortened, and his eyes darted about, trying to find anything that could be used for protection. The world seemed to move in slow motion. He focused on the blade slicing through the air so intently everything else was out of focus. Every now and then, he studied Vivian's hips to see which way she might lunge next. An odd thought crossed his mind – at least this fight or flight mode would be useful, unlike the one on his recent flight to Manila. This moment, like that time on the flight was no time for laughter either. If he didn't handle this situation right, he might never laugh again. Staring into Vivian's eyes, he saw no mercy. She frowned at him, revealing annoyance. A chilling thought crossed his mind – her face held no fear, just steadfast determination. How she had fooled him.

The dagger slashed at him again, slicing through the air with threatening swishes. The blade got closer. And closer.

Anthony backed up, dodging each swipe.

Vivian adjusted, crouching in an offensive stance, and jabbing at him. One thrust hit, slicing a two-inch gash above his knee. He cried out as a sharp pain shot through his leg. He crumbled to the floor. Blood spewed from the wound, splattering over his jeans.

Screaming like a deranged woman, Vivian jumped atop Anthony. The dagger raised for one last thrust.

Anthony grabbed a large, framed photograph leaning up against the wall. He fumbled with it but held it up against the dagger crashing down on him. The glass shattered. Vivian squealed as shards of broken glass sliced through her hands and forearms, cutting an artery. Blood spewed across the floor.

Anthony pushed away Vivian's flailing arms, then head locked her. His muscles bulged as he squeezed tight. It was kill or be killed.

Vivian's eyes bugged out as she struggled for air. Her legs kicked about under her, desperately trying to gain traction on the floor, but her feet slipped in the pooling blood.

Anthony squeezed the choke hold hard. Vivian's eyes, so full of hate and rage moments before now held fear as she looked down at the blood quirting from her arm. She struggled for freedom, gasped for air. Anthony squeezed harder until she passed out. He let out a deep sigh of relief while letting her body go. He tested for a pulse and found one, then jumped to his feet, kicked the dagger out of her hand, and grabbed his phone to dial the police.

CHAPTER FORTY-FIVE

THE FRENCH HAVE a unique way of describing a youthful woman who sparks their imagination, *la beauté du diable*, the beauty of the devil. Something seductive, thrilling, dangerous, covetous. Something beyond comprehension. Vivian's beauty had hustled Anthony's heart the moment he had laid eyes on her, but her exquisiteness obscured a nature as devilish as they come.

While gingerly climbing the worn and chipped steps leading up to Vivian's second floor apartment, Anthony reflected on the French term he'd read about in some novel. Bandages covered his neck and his knee. He spotted Detective Fonseca at the end of the hall, then stepped up warily. Anthony caught sight of Macau's version of CSI systematically tearing apart Vivian's condo with clinical Chinese efficiency in search of murderous intent.

"I should have warned you about our Macau hookers. They have hearts of lead," Detective Fonseca said.

"She wasn't a hooker," Anthony said, his tone defensive.

"She was a casino hostess. Sorry to inform you, but prostitution comes with the job."

Anthony shook his head slowly as his eyes took in the entire scene.

Detective Fonseca offered up a bag containing a brown checked scarf and a cap Vivian had used to hide her long, flowing tresses. "Looks like she was the one, and, by 'the one' I don't mean the romantic one."

Anthony took the bag. His eyes reviewed the contents but registered nothing.

"I'll be interrogating her shortly. Then I'll need a statement from you," Detective Fonseca said.

Anthony nodded in vague agreement.

Detective Fonseca pointed at two bags of luggage sitting by the door. "Looks like she was planning a quick getaway."

A severe-looking, chubby Chinese man in his thirties, offered a plastic evidence bag to Detective Fonseca. It contained a piece of paper that had 'ANTHONY A. WILSON' monogrammed atop it, with some pencil sketchings across it.

Detective Fonseca held it up for Anthony to review. "A page out of the Wilson playbook? Looks like she was copying your credit cards numbers."

"That's not a credit card number, detective, that's something far more valuable, my private crypto key. With it and my MetaMask key, she gains access to my Coinbase account and all of my crypto coins."

"Where's that key?"

"In my safe," Anthony said. With downcast eyes, he slowly shook his head. "I proposed to her. I wanted to spend the rest of my life with her."

"Well, if you had married her, it would have been a short marriage. Your fighting spirit could have saved your life."

Anthony stared hard at the ground, shaking his head morosely, the numbness consuming him.

"You were never suspicious? Never once thought this woman was out of my league?" Detective Fonseca asked.

"Love makes fools of us all, detective. A woman's love never deceived you?"

Detective Fonseca chuckled and smiled knowingly. "Once, twice, a hundred times."

Anthony recognized there was a story there, but the detective's fleeting smile passed. "Might be a good time to show some empathy, detective."

"They beat that emotion out of us in detective school. Only the most cold-hearted and insensitive make detective. And, maybe you should look on the bright side, Mr. Wilson. You lost a love, not a life, so you did well."

"'Today was a good day,' as Ice Cube says."

Detective Fonseca smiled. "You know, you have an inherent excuse for making a mistake when choosing a twin, not a wife."

Anthony glanced out the window at the dragon boats sculling across San Vai Lake in the distance. "'Fate brings people together from far apart,' she said on our first date."

"Luckily for you, fate's not quite done with you yet."

CHAPTER FORTY-SIX

As Peter Gabriel's "Here Comes The Flood" played softly in the background, Anthony surveyed his kitchen's high-end appliances, sipping the last drop of his morning coffee. He picked up the *Macau Daily* newspaper from the counter. The cover photo of Vivian in the cat-ear hood brought a deep pang to his heart.

Unlucky in love, unlucky in life? Can you say that if you've still got a life? Still got a chance in this rat race? Anthony thought as he picked up his phone to scan the article. Using Google translate, he read it in English: "When the accused told victims to buy a 'mining certificate,' she was actually having them execute a smart contract that gave her access to the victim's crypto wallet. This is a new spin on the old honey pot scam. This one dubbed the 'pig-butchering' scam because the accused got victims to fatten up their wallets before they were slaughtered."

It never felt good to be the victim, especially when the heart was so involved.

The doorbell rang, snapping Anthony out of his reverie. He walked into the living room and pulled open the front door, revealing Detective Fonseca lingering in the hallway.

"You got your wish, detective, I'm leaving Macau. Packing up my things right now, never to be seen on these black sand beach shores again," Anthony said.

Detective Fonseca meandered in. "These are crazy times, Mr. Wilson. Go find a quiet island in the Philippines or visit Sipadan Island in Malaysia, like I recommended, to wait out this killer virus."

"Actually, I'm headed to the Philippines after I pack everything up. Now, I have a twin brother to save."

"Oh?"

"Donating my kidney as COVID's ruining his remaining one."

"Well, you're one of the lucky ones then. You're leaving with at least what you came here with and, more importantly, with a soul intact."

"I'm not sure about that, detective."

"Many leave Macau with just the clothes on their backs, so you've done well."

"Yeah, that's my motto, 'Doing weller than most.'"

"Don't knock it. We can't all be *New York Times* bestsellers, now, can we?"

"How do you walk out of a casino with a small fortune? Walk in with a big one, right?" Anthony joked, then added, "How do you walk out of Macau with a soul intact? You never enter."

A smile broke across Detective Fonseca's hardened face.

"I'd love to chat, but I have to pack," Anthony said.

Detective Fonseca dug into his pocket and pulled out an official-looking piece of paper complete with simplified Chinese lettering and the two red thumbprints that officially authorize a document in China. "Sad to say, I'm here on official business. I came to let you know we just received Cash's death certificate from the Zhuhai People's Hospital."

The smile vanished from Anthony's face and his mouth turned down. "My God. How did it happen?"

"Not a lot of details beyond a reason, COVID-19."

The news hit Anthony like a bullet straight to the heart. He had grown fond of Cash and the quirky junket operator who had shown him how to live life to the fullest. A man generous in both money and spirit. So many people had made Anthony so many false promises he'd grown cynical and skeptical of humanity. But Cash was a rare breed, far different from anyone he had ever known, a man who hadn't a financial care in the world and wanted to help others in any way possible.

"Where's the body?" Anthony asked.

"Incinerated, no doubt. It's what they do with all COVID victims in China."

"Why'd it take so long to get the news?"

"When you're torching bodies twenty-four seven, you worry about the paperwork later."

Anthony nodded. "What happened to the ashes?"

"Who knows? This virus is a thousand times worse than SARS. They're throwing bodies out of windows into mobile incinerators all over China. And they don't respect the dead the way you do in the West."

"I've seen the images on Twitter, YouTube, Weibo, and Telegram, it's like a bio attack. Horrendous."

"He was your friend, I know, and I'm sorry for your loss."

"'If you can walk with the crowd and keep your virtue or walk with Kings, nor lose the common touch,'" Anthony said, reflecting on Cash's life as he glanced out the window, where a thickening fog shrouded the skeletal high rises towering over Henquin Island. The quote meant a lot to Anthony. The ability to dine with kings and walk with paupers was a trait rare in man. Cash had been an inimitable friend who treated everyone with respect. He never talked down to or abused the lowest of the low or fawned at the feet of the richest of the rich, who were far more abundant and unnecessary than they imagined.

"Shakespeare?" Detective Fonseca asked.

Anthony shook his head. "The great imperialist writer Rudyard Kipling. A perfect description of Cash, I think."

Detective Fonseca shrugged.

"So, what does this mean for you, detective?" Anthony asked.

"We close the case. Another guilty man goes free."

Anthony turned back to Detective Fonseca. "I'd hardly say he's going free."

"Then you are definitely not a religious man. Through good actions, Buddhists hope to either gain enlightenment or ensure a better future for themselves. Good actions result in a better rebirth. Bad actions don't. I somehow doubt Cash's work on this planet helped him reach enlightenment. He'll be free to pursue the life of some other animal, something far beneath a human being, I'm sure. Maybe a rat?"

"Sometimes you must walk with sinners to truly understand sin, detective."

"Either way, an opportunity lost."

"For you or for him?"

Detective Fonseca reflected on Anthony's question for a moment, then demurred, "Both."

"You still have two triad members making sausages in his stead. Perhaps souls to be converted?"

"I'm happy to report they are making progress."

"You missed your calling in life, detective, you should have been a priest."

"In some ways I am. The interrogation room is my confessional."

Anthony nodded and laughed. "And what are your long-term plans, detective? Going to stick around while the CCP rounds up the protestors in Hong Kong and locks them up in China? Then moves on to Macau and takes more control over here?"

"They can't take any more control than they already have. They've infiltrated every important government body or association and now they're rolling out the motherland propaganda. We're being given lectures on how important it is to be loyal to the party. No wavering permitted. Macau will soon be a nest of vipers, all ratting each other out to the party in Beijing. Not my kind of place. I have twelve months left before I get my full pension, thirty years of service."

"To subdue the enemy without fighting, now that's a skill, said Sun Tzu."

Detective Fonseca stepped toward the door. "Never forget, the greatest trick God ever pulled was convincing the world he existed. And now I will pull a trick God performs so well, I will disappear. I highly advise you do the same, at least from Macau." Detective Fonseca opened the door, then turned to Anthony. "By the way, you know anything about these things called NFTs? Nonfungible tokens, is that what they call them?"

"Vaguely, some digital artists are selling art that looks like bad seventies album covers or bored apes for obscene amounts of money because they put them on a blockchain, giving them a unique identifier."

"That's the one. Well, someone hacked into Galaxy Macau, stole some video footage from a junket room, and turned it into an NFT collection, which is now being sold off on a site called OpenSea. You wouldn't know anything about that, would you?"

"Not my thing, detective."

"All that facial recognition work you did for Cash. Seems like this is right up your alley."

"Speeding's about as high as I go on the rungs of criminality these days."

"It's causing quite a stir in China."

"Some corrupt officials are being made to sweat a little, is that really a bad thing? You have sympathy for dirty politicians who steal millions of yuan from their constituents?"

"I have no sympathy for any politician," Detective Fonseca said, a crooked smile breaking across his lips. "You're a fabulous liar, Mr. Wilson."

"No, I'm a fabulous fabulist, detective. There's a difference."

Detective Fonseca's brow furrowed in confusion.

Anthony threw out his hand. "A storyteller. It's another word for storyteller."

"Well, maybe they'll make a movie about you one day. Cryptofinger."

Anthony laughed. The two shook hands. Two nemeses recognizing the fight was over, and it was time to move onto other journeys, other fights, and other conquests. The difference, for Detective Fonseca, other crimes, other seedy criminals, other broken hearts, and a few untimely deaths.

"As I said before, a good prosecutor will always tell you, 'You don't catch the geniuses,' but don't let that go to your head," Detective Fonseca said, then disappeared out the door.

Although the banter was light, the news was crushing. Of all the people Anthony had known in his life, Cash seemed clever enough to avoid catching a deadly virus or recovering from one if infected. But Anthony guessed Cash was in the wrong place at the wrong time, like so many others in Wuhan and other cities around the world that were being ravaged by the once-in-a-century pandemic. Just another man chasing a dream of riches that proved fatal in the end because of something far beyond his control: fate.

Anthony took the elevator down to the lobby, then walked through the casino. Cascading melodies in the key of C Major weaved together in a sonic landscape that competed for supremacy over the loud beeps, ringing chimes, and trilling bells of false hope. Now and then, a groan punctuated the air as reality muscled in. Another gambler's dream dashed upon the harsh shores of betting reality; the house always wins.

Anthony put on a pair of headphones and strolled through the dark street as fog crept around his ankles. He pulled out his phone, then clicked on The Pogues' song "The Fairytale of New York," a profound, mood-setting song if ever there was one. Around him, neon lights haloed in the mist, projecting a ghostly, otherworldly glow.

Perfect lighting for the end of a movie. All it needed was some rain, but that wasn't coming. Anthony glanced up at the clear, star-studded sky. The gods or a mere mortal transportation department wasn't around to create a somber mood so popular at the end of movies.

Anthony ambled through the deserted streets on his ten minute walk to the A-Ma temple. Every time the Pogues song ended, he replayed it. Once at the temple, he purchased some joss paper and an effigy of a Ferrari. Why not send Cash a sportscar he could show off with pride to his newfound friends in Nirvana? *He'll drive a little classier in heaven,* Anthony thought.

Everything burned in plumes of pencil-thin white smoke, fusing into the fog in ways that made heaven and earth indecipherable, entwining together in honor of the memory of one unique soul. Although an atheist, Anthony made a prayer for his departed friend. Deeply moved by his loss, a lump appeared in his throat. A tear was quickly wiped away before it slid down his cheek.

CHAPTER FORTY-SEVEN

Detective Fonseca had once warned Anthony there was no honor amongst thieves, but Anthony had to counter that honor was about as rare as astatine, the rarest substance on earth. Loyalty was a trait seriously lacking amongst the living, whether between children and parents, brothers and sisters, spouses and lovers, or even amongst what should be the closest of all human beings, twins. Those matching souls supposedly connected by an unbreakable bond forged in the moment of mirrored creation. Everyone seemed so interested in playing a zero-sum game of life, even when it so often left both players with nothing to show for their time on earth but deep wakes of burning heartbreak, loves lost, and greedy hearts forever unfulfilled.

As a young male Filipino orderly wheeled him down a long hospital corridor, Anthony reflected on the idea of honor. His twin might have played fast and loose with the truth, he might have dabbled in the dark arts, but that didn't mean Anthony had to wallow with him in those base and bleak depths.

"You're doing a great thing," the orderly said while pushing Anthony's gurney through the doors of the operating room, which was abuzz with nurses prepping stations and doctors examining X-rays and snapping on rubber gloves. The orderly gave Anthony a proud smile. Anthony's point-of-view was like a dolly shot moving in for a close-up, but this time not to a face but to an upturned body teetering on the edge of life. Already under anesthesia, a calm, steady raising and lowering of the back revealed the breath of life still remained within Cyrus.

As expected, Anthony was the perfect donor. The night before the operation, Doctor Rah had informed him that, although a touch old for a donor, a healthy lifestyle had kept his organs young for their age. Perhaps the poverty keeping him from living a decadent life had some side benefits after all?

"Your brother will be so proud," the orderly said as he lifted Anthony onto the operating table with the help of three other nurses.

Beggars can't be choosers. Especially when it comes to human organs and you're not even cognizant enough to beg, Anthony thought, but he kept the salty retort to himself. *There's still time to back out,* he thought. But there wasn't. The Rubicon had been crossed, the die cast, an irrevocable choice had been made, as all those clichés go. He made a quick prayer to Hermes, the god of gamblers, for some luck. There are no atheists in foxholes, as the saying goes, and there probably shouldn't be too many on operating tables either.

The anesthesiologist, a fatherly figure with a cherubic face framed by a mop of curly, grey hair behind full PPE, stepped up to Anthony and looked down at him with calm blue eyes. "Count backward from ten," the doctor said in a deep soothing voice as he covered Anthony's nose and mouth with an anesthesia mask.

Anthony ignored the doctor's request. He closed his eyes to the blaring white surgical light trained on him by Dr. Rah. Then darkness and back to the cool waters of the Agulhas Bank in a dream of frenzied sardines darting back and forth in waters churning with greedy predators.

CHAPTER FORTY-EIGHT

AT 7:15 P.M., two weeks after the operation, Anthony sat by the window of Cyrus's hospital room, typing on his laptop when he heard bedsprings squeak behind him. He turned around and saw Cyrus's eyelids flicker open. Lifeless pupils gazed out in groggy confusion.

Anthony stood up and approached Cyrus's bed while removing his mask. "You're alive."

Cyrus wheezed out a cough as his questioning eyes cased the room.

Anthony lifted his robe to reveal healing stitch marks across his lower back. "Not quite a pound of flesh there, my brother, but not far off, that kidney of mine, which is in you now."

"Jesus," Cyrus said groggily. "What the hell happened?" He rose, but winced in pain, groaned, then eased back down.

"That list they put you on in the U.S. when you donated to Brandon, that doesn't work in the Philippines, so I had to fill in."

Cyrus shook his head, eyes darting about in confusion.

"You're in a hospital in Cebu. You caught COVID, which damaged your kidney, so they had to give you a new one. And you're looking at the donor. You're welcome, by the way. And, I agree, calling it minimally invasive surgery isn't accurate, it's quite invasive."

"Jesus."

Anthony pulled out a counterfeit gold bar and placed it on Cyrus's bed. "And it gets better. Sorry to tell you this but that gold you sailed a thousand miles to smuggle into Cebu was fake. Worthless tungsten."

"What?" Cyrus said, flipping on the bedside light. He picked up the bar, and inspected it with a squinting eye, scrutinizing both sides.

"Not even a good fake, apparently."

With a shaking head, Cyrus glanced over at Anthony. "Why do you have it?"

"I took it off the boat before the coast guard arrived."

"The coast guard? Jesus Christ."

"They're the ones who saved your life."

"Where's the money?"

"Donated to the widows and orphans fund of the Philippine Coast Guard."

Cyrus's eyes homed in on Anthony. His brow furrowed in anger.

Anthony threw up his hands. "Hey, don't blame me. You made it to Cebu, but the hard way. With the help of the best and brightest of the Philippine Navy."

"Shit. We under arrest?"

"You see any cops?"

"May as well be dead. We've probably got prices on our heads now that we've lost all this money," Cyrus said as he exhaled deeply and fought eyelids that fluttered with sleep and exhaustion.

"I don't know about that. Cash is dead as well."

Cyrus's eyelids popped open. "He is?"

"Of COVID. He's probably the one who gave it to you and Jada."

"Where the hell does this leave us?"

"The several million dollar question, literally. Maybe back at square one. The company's still yours, right? You didn't sign it over to Cash?"

"Planned to do that once I got the money safe and sound into our bank account here."

"If he's dead, maybe the trail to us and the trail to all that fake gold and stolen coast guard loot – goes cold with him?"

"And so it should. He's to blame for all of this. We don't get sick, we make it to Cebu, and it's clear sailing from there."

"Exactly."

"A lot has happened since you fell into a coma," Anthony said as he placed the *Macao Daily* newspaper on the bedside table. He translated it for Cyrus, who listened intently. "I have to say, my top suspect was your wife. Just cause it wasn't Jada doesn't mean she doesn't have it in her."

"Tell me about it. She's soon to be an ex-wife now. We're divorcing."

"I'd say, I'm surprised, but nothing surprises me anymore."

Cyrus opened his arms to the room around him. "Welcome to this ugly reality we all call life."

"What happened?"

"The usual irreconcilable differences. She says I was being unfaithful."

Anthony's raised eyebrow and smirk said, 'Well, you were."

"Who isn't in this day and age? And don't get all puritanical on me. Pretty sure she wasn't completely faithful either," Cyrus said, then turned reflective and stared at the sea beyond the windows. "We were putting on a show for you, thought it'd be the best way to get the deal done as quickly as possible."

"My twin spidey sense is obviously getting a little rusty."

"Mine conked out decades ago."

"Maybe when we got separated at boarding school?"

The twins shared a moment of uncomfortable silence, then Anthony broke in, "What happened, you seemed like such a loving couple?"

Cyrus smirked. "Sarcasm, the lowest form of wit."

"Not always. And what is it with you and money-grubbing wives?"

"My fatal flaw. This entire sale was about getting enough money to pay her off and take care of Brandon."

"I'm sure you were setting aside something for yourself as well."

Cyrus ignored the snide remark. "More importantly, what about our money from the jewels and the bank account in Macau?"

"I got the jewels cut and polished in Hong Kong, then I traded them

     Andrew W. Pearson

in for some White Tiger pre-ICO coins."

"Jesus," Cyrus said in a tone charged with annoyance.

"Which quadrupled in value, by the way. I sold them. We're now the proud owner of 10.56 Bitcoins. You do the math."

Cyrus's frown dropped, instantly replaced by a fawning smile. "Five hundred thousand. Jesus, well done. I've always said, you were one of the smartest people I knew."

"Never said the same about you."

"Screw you. Where's the money now?"

"Safe and sound in a Hong Kong bank account with *my* name on it. After I take my fifty-percent cut, I'll wire your share to a bank of your choice."

"Fifty percent? There's three of us."

Anthony shot Cyrus a look of bored contempt. "I'll gladly give you the hundred and twenty thousand I borrowed, with five percent interest."

Beaming brightly, Cyrus raised his hand in a surrender motion. "Fair enough."

"Fair, it's not. Extremely generous is what it is."

"So, that pretty much means we're back to square one."

"How do you figure that?"

"Company still needs a managing director in Asia."

Anthony smiled the smile of a gambler who knew his all-in bet was looking golden after the river card flushed him royal. "You asked me to give up everything I loved to help you build a business in Macau, a company you destroyed when you incorporated a direct competitor fifteen hundred miles away in Singapore. Cyrus, you're a pathological liar. I'd be a fool to ever trust you or work with you again."

At a loss for words, Cyrus's eyes flitted about while his brow creased defensively.

"And what you don't understand is my offer comes with a condition,"

Anthony said.

"Which is?"

"You go your way; I go mine."

"What does that mean?"

"We never see each other again. I take the clients I brought to the table in Asia. You, of course, keep your U.S. ones, but I don't want you ever contacting me again."

"Aren't you being a little rash? What about our production company?"

"I was putting on a show for you, thought it'd be the best way to get the Exegesis deal done."

Cyrus opened his mouth and was about to speak, but Anthony cut him off: "Take it or leave it. Those are your two options."

Cyrus's jaw tightened while he eyed Anthony for a few long moments. Finally, he nodded acceptance at the terms.

Anthony stepped toward the door. "You know what's funny about you is you think you're Michael but you're squirrely, back-stabbing Fredo. You don't cheat family. Ever."

For Anthony, like the Duval sisters, or the "silent twins" as they became known, one had to die for the other to go free. Anthony wasn't literally killing Cyrus, but he'd be as good as dead as far as Anthony was concerned.

CHAPTER FORTY-NINE

STANDING ON THE edge of Moalboal's White Beach, twenty-four months after learning about Cash's death, Anthony smiled the smile of the fulfilled. He had hit the creative and financial trifecta of film; screenwriting, novelist that the script was based upon, and executive producer of the film that the book was based on. Plenty of novelist fees, screenwriter fees, producer fees, as well as an orgy of net profits to go around.

May you live in interesting times indeed, Anthony thought, but sometimes you just don't get to choose those times. A long and torturous road had brought him to the edge of the whitest sand beach he'd ever seen, a far cry from the black sand beaches of the tiny enclave that had seeded his story. Today, a new road might be opening up, but a heated exchange snapped him out of his thoughtful reverie.

The *Cash is King* set was a madhouse. The director of photography screamed at the gaffer. The first assistant director admonished his second assistant director. The stand-ins for Vivian and Anthony loitered about like lovers who had just been unceremoniously dumped. A makeup artist mopped up the sweat from the lead actress's face because the mascara threatened to run all over the place. *Blade Runner*, one of Anthony's favorite films, had been a set from hell so maybe there was hope for his film?

The harried director, a middle-aged, overweight man, surveyed the madness. "We're a week behind schedule already, and we've got a typhoon coming! Come on, everyone, we need to get this shot in the can in ten," the director said, his English accent charming, calming, and ceaselessly demanding. He shot a forced and impatient smile at Anthony, then hurried towards his director of photography, who was finalizing the placement of a fill light.

Anthony no longer felt like one of those sardines darting about the cool waters of the Agulhas Bank, flitting back and forth in their desperate pursuit of life. Today, he felt more like one of those dolphins. Not quite the shark, an apex predator he would never be. He had more in common with the graceful and intelligent dolphin, a creature who seemed to have an odd understanding of its place in the universe, much like he did in his own life.

"Mr. Wilson, Mr. Wilson," came a melodic voice from behind.

Anthony turned. A short, muscular Chinese man hurried over. The voice, a weird amalgamation of warm southern hospitality and cool Chinglish, sounded oddly familiar, but Anthony couldn't quite place it.

"I follow your YouTube channel," said the man, referencing the channel Anthony had created to document his exploits on *The Gambler* while avoiding COVID in an eighteen-month sail around the Philippine Islands.

Seeing the gait, the cool, confident swagger of a honey badger on the hunt for a late afternoon snack of king cobra, Anthony knew exactly who it was. That could only be one person. But a rather troubling thought followed the flash of recognition: *Isn't he dead?*

The face was younger than Anthony remembered it; the nose, straighter; the cheekbones, higher, more prominent; the jawline, more defined. Other less flattering features had been softened, too. The overall look was one of improvement, for sure, but subtle enough for the brain to recognize something was amiss while not clearly understanding what exactly made it look so off. Anthony couldn't make sense of the dichotomy between the visual and the auditory. It was like seeing a ghost, but a ghost with a newly sculpted face. It was one of the oddest feelings he'd ever had. One part of his brain struggled to sync the voice, the face, and the gait as one. Another part said the man standing before him was, without a doubt, Cash. Alive and in the flesh, but a different, more improved flesh, which was weird because aging worked the exact opposite way.

Cash's style had morphed into a more sophisticated look as well. He wore a black leather calfskin coat, sans fringes, but still plenty stylish. A flashy belt buckle topped a pair of inexpensive 501s. The brown cowboy boots were the only referential hat tip to Cash's distinct country music persona of old. In one hand, he carried a copy of Anthony's hardback book.

"He looks nothing like me," Cash said, nodding to the Asian actor sitting in a director's chair stenciled with a red '$' across its back.

Shaking his head in disbelief, Anthony's tongue could no longer hold back his desperate question: "Cash, is that you?"

The man ignored Anthony's question. "Reviewers are calling it 'The Great Macau' novel. Might be the only time 'Great' and 'Macau' belong in the same sentence in a non-ironic way, right?"

It was him all right; the sarcastic sense of humor settled it. Anthony broke into a wide grin. He wanted to hug Cash but resisted the temptation, still slightly confused by the scene, the setting, and this odd "stranger" appearing out of nowhere.

"You deserve it. That's one helluva book. I'm sure the film is going to be just as good. Much better than the biography we were going to write, right?" Cash said with a wink.

A heavily tattooed female assistant director raced up and reached out to grab Cash's arm. "Sir, you're not allowed on the set."

Anthony stopped the assistant director's arm in mid-air. "It's fine, Julie, he's a friend. A dear, dear friend."

The assistant director's hands flew up in apology. "Sorry. We roll in five."

"I know. I've been waiting for this moment for well over twenty-five years."

The assistant director nodded and trudged off across the sand.

Anthony focused on Cash. "What the hell happened to you? I thought you were dead."

"I took Sun Tzu's advice, 'Of the thirty-six stratagems, running away is the best.'"

"I'm not sure Sun Tzu said that, but, honestly, what happened?" Anthony laughed.

"Funny story. Maybe you can write a sequel?"

"Go on."

"After I dumped the cash with you and Cyrus in the marina, I got sick and had to rest up in Zhuhai. I thought I could sleep it off that night, then get over to Dongguan the next day, but I must have caught COVID in Wuhan. The hotel found out and called an ambulance. I was taken to a ward full of the dying. And you'll never guess who my doctor was," Cash said, pausing for effect.

"Who?"

"Remember Heng, the gambler who died on the live stream?"

Anthony nodded.

"I was in a room with three other patients, all much older than me, all on death's door. Two were on their last leg and died shortly after I got wheeled in. The other, a frail woman in her seventies, was struggling to breathe, so was I. We both desperately needed a ventilator to survive, but only one ventilator remained."

"Like musical chairs for life, Jesus."

"Exactly. The nurses were rushing around, asking the doctor, 'Who gets the ventilator?', 'Who gets the ventilator?' I'm looking at all the other patients, thinking my odds are pretty good, but Doctor Ling Ling, Heng's mother, grabbed my chart and instantly recognized my name. She flinched, repulsed by me."

"No way."

"Now coronavirus isn't like any other virus you can get. It messes with your head and gives you hallucinations. I'm going in and out of consciousness with a high fever thrown in for good measure. Don't know if I'm alive, watching a movie, or in heaven. Through the doctor's PPE, I see calculation in her eyes, 'Do I revenge my son's death, or do I give the ventilator to the person most likely to survive?' The nurse looked at her, and asked, 'Do you know this man?' The doctor shook her head while trying to hide her contempt. She had the coldest eyes I've ever seen. The eyes of an executioner. I still get chills thinking about those eyes." To prove it, Cash shakes his body.

"Jesus Christ."

"The dead patients were wheeled out. Doctor Ling Ling takes my temperature, my heartbeat, then leans in and says, 'This is for my son'. Behind her, the nurse is yelling, 'Who gets the ventilator?' The doctor looks at me, then at the old woman, then at me. I can see tears welling in her eyes. Nurse is yelling, 'Which one? Which one?' Inside, I'm screaming, 'Me, me, me.'"

"Holy shit."

"The doctor points at the old lady. The confused nurse says, 'Really?' My heart sank. I thought I was a goner."

"Oh my God."

"After that experience, I know how a condemned man feels. A dead man walking, as you say in America. For about forty-five seconds, I see the doctor grappling with her decision as the nurse prepped the old lady for the ventilator. I'm pleading with my eyes. She knew she was sentencing me to death. Odds aren't great with a ventilator, they're non-existent without one."

"But why are you still here?"

"She couldn't do it. She looked at me, struggling to hold back tears, then approached my bed."

"The *Hippocratic Oath* won out."

"Thank God for Hippocrates."

"So, she ordered the nurse to stop prepping the old lady, that I should get the ventilator."

"Unbelievable. Amazing story. A scene for the sequel," Anthony said, shaking his head in disbelief.

"Don't, you'll blow my cover," Cash said with a wink and a cheeky smile.

"Trust me, no one would believe it."

If Anthony decided to write a sequel to *Cash is King*, this was the one coincidence he'd keep because it had everything, life-and-death decision-making pivoting on revenge, a mother's bond to a dead son, and, ultimately, a doctor's inability to commit murder. Perhaps, in the end, some redemption for both Cash and Dr. Ling Ling?

"When I got better, she came to see me. I thanked her for saving my life. Explained to her the difference between individual triad business and triad society business, which she didn't understand," Cash said, chuckling.

Anthony nodded towards the set. "I wrote a book about it, adapted that book into a script, found some financiers to make it into a movie, and I still don't get it."

"I told her I was setting up a fund in Heng's name to help problem gamblers like him kick their destructive habit. And I was getting out of the casino business for good. She was very moved. COVID changes you. You realize what matters in life. Makes you want to become a better man, both for yourself and for those around you."

"You were always a great man, Cash."

Ignoring the compliment, Cash said, "As I lay dying, I realized I should be dead."

"You should have *been* dead."

"No, I should be dead. That was the answer. Death was the solution to all my problems. That way I clean the slate. No problems anywhere. So, I paid someone in the hospital morgue to file a fake death certificate."

"They agreed?"

"For a brand-new Lamborghini, they did."

Anthony smirked. "I might too for that kind of reward, even one in such a God-awful lime green color."

"Macau and its corrupt judges closed the book on me. China and its immoral leaders closed the book on me, even America and its omnipotent IRS closed the book on me. And I get what I've always wanted, freedom. Everybody wins."

"Except Detective Fonseca."

"Him, I'm happy to disappoint."

"He thinks you've reincarnated as a rat."

"Projection."

Anthony chuckled, then remembered the Ferrari he'd burned for Cash in Macau. "Oh, I sent you a Ferrari, by the way. You think they'll hold it for you until you get up there?"

"I doubt it. The Chinese ghosts will figure out a way to steal it. Plus, it'll be rusted out by the time I get up there. I plan to live a long, healthy and anonymous life. What happened to the money on the boat, by the way?"

"Forced donation to the widows and orphans fund of the Philippine Coast Guard when Jada and Cyrus came down with COVID. And you know the gold was fake?"

Cash nodded. "We weren't the only ones cheated by Kingold fakes. I think eighty tons of their gold was counterfeit. Luckily the ICO worked out then."

"'You only need one,' as Cyrus always liked to say."

"Yep. You did okay with that one?"

"Still doing okay with that one and those NFTs. You were the one releasing them, right?"

Cash nodded. "Revenge is a dish best served on the Blockchain."

Anthony laughed, then nodded towards the set, "Neither was as good as this one though."

"Sometimes ambitions do come true."

Anthony pointed at Cash's face. "What's with the new look?"

"After all the madness in Macau and China, I thought it might be a good idea to add a new look and a new persona. Plus, I got the nose, cheeks, and chin I've always wanted."

"I like the new understated style as well."

"An octopus can change his spots, after all."

"Oh, and I know what my Chinese name is, *Hung Won.*"

"The lucky one. It fits. You found the luck you deserved."

"Finally."

Cash offered his hand. "Like we Chinese say, 'How can you tell if you're lucky if you don't gamble?'"

Anthony pushed aside the hand and pulled Cash into a warm embrace.

Cash broke the hug, "I'll be in touch if I come across any more interesting investment ideas."

"I'll be the first to invest. And I think I still owe you a book."

"No, you don't. In my mind, we're even. Like I said so long ago at the Macau Roosevelt Hotel, stick with me and we'll be hitting longshots forever."

Anthony smiled, pumping Cash's hand one last time. Cash then trudged away, breaking into a cheery rendition of the final verse of Tim McGraw's "Live Like You Were Dying," ending it with the laconically brilliant, "or dead."

In the movie *The Lemon Drop Kid*, Bob Hope pulled one of the cleverest, and maybe one of the easiest, racetrack scams around. By pretending to be the brother of one of the jockeys to one young couple, a friend of a horse owner to another, a relation to the track vet to a third, and so on, and so on, he chummed up to eight different couples during the race's walking parade. He offered "Insider tips" to each naïve couple. By covering the entire field, Hope guaranteed himself a win as long as the winning couple agreed to share a percentage of their profits for what was really a worthless tip.

Perhaps Cash had played a similar scam in Macau, buying up a wheel of exotics that was a guaranteed winner? If so, Anthony had to tip his hat to the wily junket operator. The man had gone to a great deal of trouble, and no small expense, to trick Anthony into writing his biography. But thank God he did it for what a story it became.

Anthony watched the director step towards the tent set up for the above-the-line talent on the edge of the set. The director took his chair, gave Anthony a curt nod, then stared into the scene monitor. The camera rolled, the speed sounded, and the director started the proceedings with the film world's customary call to "Action!"

Instantly, the set sprang to life; background actors snapped out of their mannequin stances and strode across their marks with impeccable professionalism; a camera glided along the ground as if floating on air while a boom mic followed the perfectly beautiful lead actors beautifully emoting Anthony's scintillatingly witty lines. Behind the camera, crew members stood transfixed while holding their collective breaths, hoping the camera captured the remarkable illusion universally recognized as cinematic magic.

"There's an old adage about biographies and autobiographies," Anthony once told Cash. "Everyone has a book in them, but for most people, that's where it should stay." Unlike most biographies however, Cash's story needed to be told because it was a universal tale of us all. A tale of betraying twins lost, other brothers found, of fools falling for love, artists discovering their voice, and leopards changing their spots; a story of hookers with hearts of lead, incorruptible detectives pushing the boundaries of justice, crooked politicians meeting their grim but well-deserved fates, and shady mobsters who lived by a code of honor that would make Socrates proud. It was the story of fool's gold lost and crypto fortunes found. Above all else, it was the tale of a man seeking and, finally, finding freedom. A tale told not by an idiot but certainly a fool. Cash lived his life on the roll of a dice, the cut of a card, the nose of a horse, and, ultimately, the vicissitudes of fate and almost died in the process. "Write what you know" is great advice if you can just live long enough to tell the tale.

FIN

為自由鋪平道路的人，不要讓他們在荊棘叢中掙扎

"For those who pave the road to freedom, do not leave them struggling with thistles and thorns."

– Chinese proverb

 Andrew W. Pearson

ACKNOWLEDGEMENTS

My sister, Anna, a great artist in her own right. Thanks for looking over me when I was out in the wilderness finding my voice.

My fellow critique circlers, especially Sandra Bustos, Ron Crichton, Jenny Torniainen, Webb Johnson, and Gary Seigel. Your advice was instrumental in helping me polish this diamond-in-the-rough into something others might actually want to read.

Thanks also to Vinzenz Rosa de Pauli and Lukas Beck, who kept me in strong coffee and great conversation. They helped me slay any writer's block threatening to derail my work.

My publisher, Melissa Carrigee, for helping me fulfill this, my greatest ambition.

ABOUT THE AUTHOR

Andrew Pearson runs a software consulting business in Macau, China. He is a screenwriter, novelist, and noted columnist for several peer-reviewed journals. He has written several books and articles on topics like analytics, AI, marketing, Chinese tech, and social media. An avid traveler, Pearson is a sought-after speaker, lecturing on such disparate topics as AI and machine learning, digital marketing, and social media. If he's not gracing the conference stage in some exotic locale, he's probably pounding the pavements of Hollywood trying to get a script made or meandering through the labyrinthine streets of Hong Kong's Lang Kwai Fong, or tearing up useless betting slips at Happy Valley (perhaps the most perfectly named racecourse in the world (for some)), or dining at a hawker center in Singapore, or grabbing some lechon at a bustling outdoor food market in Manila, or doubling down at the gaming tables in Macau. Basically, Pearson's trying to find the next great story that the world doesn't yet know that it desperately wants to see...